MANY THE MILES

ANNIE HOLDER

With sincere apologies to all Americans for the liberties I have taken with your language…

www.annieholder.com

BEHIND YOU

Mal would kill her if he knew what she was doing, but he'd demanded proof, and she was determined to get it. *The* political scoop of the decade, *if* she could obtain watertight evidence…and for that, she literally had to catch him in the act. Nothing else would do.

At ground level was a small, square window. No lights showed at the rear of the house. She could squat here all night waiting for something to happen, or she could investigate what she'd been told about the basement.

Sprinting across the well-lit garden, dropping to her stomach and wriggling sideways under cover of the nearest shrubs, she caught her breath, watched the house, and waited.

Nothing happened.

No one appeared. Was she alone here?

She scooped a small handful of gravel and threw with little accuracy in the direction of the window. Still nothing. No light within. No discernible movement.

She scooped and threw another handful, liberally spattering the window. This time, there *was* something; a writhing, squirming stripe of white like a worm crawling behind the glass. Then another. Rolling awkwardly onto one hip, she fumbled with her cellphone in its waterproof pouch. She snapped a series of pictures, zooming in on the last. Despite the camera lens having to focus through the plastic pocket, she could easily identify that the worm was a *finger*!

As she scrabbled from her hiding place, the pouch slid into the freshly dug earth. Scuttling across the lawn and crouching at the window, she tapped cautiously. More fingers, different shades of skin, hooked over the boards she now realised covered the window on the inside. Female fingers. Slim, with delicate nails. Some bitten, some with coloured varnish chipped and flaking, more and more different digits poking through. Pressing against the glass, cupping her hands around her face to block out the garden lights, she could see the glint and moisture of eyes peering back at her. The swoop of long lashes. The curve of a female cheek. Movement behind the planks of wood. A change of observer. Different skin. An earring. The collar of an animal-print blouse. Rocking back onto her heels, she felt frantically around the window for a gap where she could slide something under the frame to prise it open. Perhaps it would be better to find a stone to smash the glass? Utterly absorbed in casting about the immediate vicinity on hands and knees for a suitably heavy rock, the crunch of shoe on gravel made her start and whirl around. She saw legs in dark suit trousers, creases pressed to sharp points, and was about to dart crablike towards the cover of the hedge when something heavy struck repeatedly above her left ear, making her pitch forward, burning, throbbing agony spreading outward from the impact point. In the close and muggy night air, she registered the surprising cold of the watered lawn against her cheek, and sensed looming shadows suddenly blocking the light.

****

The sound shifted. The rumble that had been building behind him like approaching truck tyres on a deserted highway fell silent for so short a time he was barely aware of its absence, but when it guttered and roared anew, he subconsciously understood it was closer now, louder, and something more. Something worse.

Reassured that the flat slab of heat had remained unwaveringly at his back as he'd tugged at the stable doors and hauled open the gates, suddenly his left eye was prickling and blinking involuntarily, and was it his imagination or did his back feel cooler, as if he'd been snoozing in the summer grass and unwelcome clouds had momentarily covered the sun? The left side of his face felt scorched, and his ear throbbed uncomfortably. He brought up a distracted palm to cup it protectively. The released horses turned as one, like a shoal of fish reacting to danger. Ears up, eyes bulging, nostrils flaring, they surged past him directly towards where he believed the threat still was. Why would they run straight into trouble?

He swung in the opposite direction to the fleeing animals, terror tightening within him. Sure enough, the wildfire had done what they said it wouldn't. When he'd left the house, the flames were still at a distance, doing what the experts had predicted, their travel slowing as the wind dropped. Time enough to get down to the stables, turn the precious horses loose, and get back to the house for Joelle and the baby. He could carry both recovering wife and newborn son to the truck, throw in the bags they'd already packed, and hightail it into town like everyone else.

The birth had been premature, complicated, gruelling, and Jo had needed a caesarean. Days later, and she was already up and about, but sore, slow, moving with the ginger care of unpredictable pain, and unable to manage stairs or baby without assistance.

Even as he began the pelt back up the stony track from stables to farmhouse, he already comprehended the change in wind direction was not the forecasted slackening in intensity, but simply the demon casting about for fresh morsels to satisfy its voracious hunger. Now, he could see the flames shooting upward forty feet or more behind the sloping tin roof of the farmhouse, moving closer with unbelievable speed. Each heavy-bass *whump* as the next huge, tinder-dry fir tree ignited like a struck match sent a vibration through the ground under his feet. The pines glowed white-hot as they were consumed by the bright orange fire. The dense forest petered out ten yards from the rear of the house. It wasn't enough. As a kid, he'd seen wildfires leap the wide, flat lanes of empty highway in the time it took a dumbstruck boy to draw sharp breath. The sun-bleached lawn would prove a woefully insufficient firebreak. He tried to run faster. The shiny soles of his boots slipped in the stony dust and several times he nearly went over, throwing out a frantic palm to steady himself. Chest heaving in the searing, smoke-filled air, he gasped aloud with every agonising breath, each exhalation a shout of hopeless pain, burning from the inside out.

The fire roared louder the closer he got, the air around him thick with falling ash and glowing embers. Every tree that tumbled sent a shower of sparks shooting upward in a vertical column like a ghoulish firework. He could smell something that reminded him of branding – burnt fur and blistering skin – and realised it must be *him*, the hair on his exposed arms and bare head singeing with the indescribable heat. His eyes were so sore and pouring with tears he couldn't make the house out properly, an indistinct black silhouette against an inferno so bright it hurt to look at it. He was close enough to hear the screaming now. He pictured what he could not see – Joelle clutching the wailing baby to her breast, a prisoner in the upstairs of the already-burning house, leaning as far out of the window as she could get, yelling for rescue. Could she see him, illuminated as he must be by the brightness of the flames, ineffectually stumbling and staggering, getting slower and weaker with every step?

That was when the flames hit the propane tanks, punching out a fireball like a bomb blast, and silencing everything but the scream inside his soul.

****

She was able to discern only daylight or darkness through minute cracks in the corrugated metal walls of her prison.

She was glad of her wetsuit, as the floor was permanently saturated, and it at least meant she could retain some body heat despite the moisture seeping into the neoprene. It was hard to change position. She wasn't restrained, but the slightest attempt at movement made her feel dizzy, nauseous, and produced such sharp, stabbing pains across the crown of her head that it felt as if she was a plushie in an arcade game, slowly borne aloft and dangled by a gripping claw around her skull.

In the morning, a blinding shaft of white light sliced through the dimness directly in front of her, touching first her kayak shoes, then the grubby skin of her shin, sliding up her thigh, rippling across the wrinkles of wetsuit and rash vest, and finally shining straight into her squinting left eye, making black dots pulse disconcertingly before her swimming vision. The sunlight moved to her right throughout the day, stabbing harshly through screw holes and mismatched panels. Motes of dust revolved slowly in its piercing beam, like ballerinas pirouetting in a stage spotlight. Although the travelling sun marked the passage of time, the pain and disorientation made her drift, leaving her unsure whether the light waking her in the morning and the cold rousing her to shuddering consciousness at night were hours or days apart.

There was a metal bucket beside her. She didn't know how it had got there – whether it or she had arrived first – only that it had water in it. Uncertain whether it was suitable to drink, she tentatively tested it whenever she was thirsty, passing cautious drops from fingertips to tongue. She used it sparingly, as she had no idea if the bucket would be refilled once it was empty. There was no food...or perhaps there had been and she just didn't remember it? She felt too sick to eat anyway.

She knew there was a reason for her being here but couldn't recall what it was. She had no idea who her anonymous captors were. Square jaws and neat haircuts, cufflinks and tiepins, gun holsters showing when their jackets swung open. She supposed she was meant to be frightened, but was too far-gone to care about anything but the longing for gentle hands to lift her out of the cold and wet, support her pounding head, lay her tenderly on a dry mattress, and cover her chilled body with a soft blanket.

She opened a swollen eye and observed the first blade of light carving through the darkness, illuminating one neoprene-shod foot. Sun-up. Contemplating reaching for a scoop of water from the bucket, she found she lacked the energy to lift her arm. She licked her dry lips, and drifted again…

****

Awakening. The sun had moved. Full daylight now. The prison was already hot and close. Crickets called unceasingly until her ears rang. Barely able to open her heavy eyes, peering from under her lashes, she was startled to focus on the gleam of an unusual belt buckle in a shaft of sunlight, shiny shoes squelching footprints in the slimy dirt of the damp floor. Alarmingly close voices murmured right above her, but she couldn't look up at the faces without tilting her head, and moving was simply not an option if she didn't want to pass out again. Were they discussing her? Her fuddled brain struggled to make sense of it.

"Any idea yet?"

"None."

"Definitely no ID?"

"Nothin'…"

"And she was where?"

"On the fucking grass, man! Trying to prise the basement window open!"

"Shit…"

"One of the ones that got away, do you think?"

"Dressed like that? Anyway, if you got away, would you come back?"

"I guess not."

"So, what's your explanation, she just kayaked past in the dark?"

"I don't know…"

"That's the end of the canal! One way in, one way out. You've got to *mean* it to go right up there! What was in the kayak?"

"A map of that spit of land and the channels around it."

"Nothing else?"

"No sir, Mr Logan, we've had it apart. You think she's a cop?"

"With no back-up, no radio, no gun? She's no cop…but she had to have a reason to be there. And she hasn't said a thing?"

"Floyd hit her a coupla times…probably a bit hard. He panicked! We both did!"

"What'd he hit her with?"

"Butt of his gun. She hasn't moved. Got a pulse, but it's weak. I ain't sure she's really conscious any more."

"Jesus… This is a big fucking problem! I hope Floyd knows that."

"Yeah, he does."

"Look…here's the deal. Whoever she is, just get rid of her."

"What – "

"Wait until it gets dark, chuck her in the trunk, drive her somewhere, and dump her."

"Where?"

"I couldn't give a shit. Far away from here. You and Floyd created this goddam problem, you can fix it. I want her gone, tonight…okay?"

"Yeah, okay."

"Good. And we won't speak about this again."

"Sure thing, Mr Logan."

"Oh, and Tyler?"

"Yessir?"

"Coveralls and gloves, yeah? Burn them when you're through…and *not* near the body, right?"

"Understood."

"Just get it *done*. No fuck-ups, and no one need ever know."

****

Her body lifted, torso flopping heavily down a wide back, hard swell of a shoulder digging uncomfortably against her pelvis, pressure in her hanging head pulsing and building agonisingly. A swinging trail of glutinous, acidic vomit escaped one corner of her mouth as she tried to beg to be righted before her brain exploded. Carried swiftly from her prison, she could feel a breeze on her exposed skin, and hear the unmistakeable rustling of dry leaves in what must be tree canopy above. Behind her, she heard the clatter of the bucket being lifted and the gush of the water emptying out, washing away any evidence of her presence there. The blood flow returning to her bruised and numb buttocks made them burn and itch like chilblains, nerve endings leaping. She tried to speak again, but all that escaped her lips was another bubble of sticky saliva.

When she next awoke, it was to perceive movement. The rocking motion of vehicular travel along an uneven road surface induced the uncontrollable urge to vomit once more. One monumental effort to roll onto her side lest she choke resulted in further loss of consciousness from the exertion.

A feeling of flying. Delicious weightlessness during which even the unbearable pressure in her head seemed to lighten for a moment, before the sharp and winding trauma of a hard landing on unyielding ground. Her stiff limbs screamed at the impact.

She must be rolling, as grit filled her slack mouth, dust compacted her nostrils, and sharp stones and vegetation scratched and sliced at her uncovered skin. Suddenly, a greater agony than any she'd experienced so far, a million needles inserting themselves into her from chest to hips. What fresh horror was this? She tried to open her eyes, but they were gummed shut with Lord only knew what vileness. Presently, she understood she was finally, mercifully still. The tumbling, tightening terror was over, but a fresh torture seemed just beginning. The forest of sharp points made their deeply embedded presence aggressively known at the minutest physical twitch. Such was its rigidity, whatever material now bound her restricted her ability to breathe deeply. Unable to draw in sufficient oxygen, it didn't take long to lose her fragile grip on consciousness once more...

LEAVING

Once he was well enough to sit up, and could dispense with the itchy oxygen tube that rubbed the tops of his ears and made his upper lip sweat, his mother, pale and grim, placed a box of salvaged personal items onto his lap, pitifully little to indicate three lives lived in the destroyed building.

Photograph albums, mostly ruined. One leather-bound folder was the baby's album, with a two-page spread for each month of the child's first year. Only one page of pictures was completed: in hospital, coming home, meeting his bigger cousins, being sniffed by the curious dog and everybody laughing.

One page…

Plenty of time to fill those plastic sleeves with his son's first smile, first jar of baby rice, first roll over on the rug before the fireplace, first attempts at crawling, first cruising forays around the furniture in preparation for those first magical unsupported steps. Plenty of time…

He stacked the other albums to one side of the cardboard box, unopened. Not yet. Later.

Wedding picture still in its frame, glass broken, photograph beneath bubbled and rippled with the heat but still recognisably them. It had been on Jo's dressing table in the bedroom, next to the mirror where she'd used to sit and brush her long hair. The bedroom…where his wife and son had been trapped when the wildfire did its terrible worst. How was it fair that this picture had survived when they had not? He stacked the photograph against the albums, its broken face hidden from his sight.

He assumed there was nothing else of note in the box. He retrieved a pair of his spurs, metal blackened, leather straps burnt away, useless. Beneath them was a small wad of folded tissue. He bunched it in his fist, irrationally angry. Had someone thought these shabby, boxed remains of a once-happy life were *trash*? He was about to discard it amid the congealed remains of his untouched dinner, when his clenching fingers detected a hard centre in the ball of softness. He unpicked the layers and discovered Jo's wedding ring, cleaned and polished. It sat small and shiny in the centre of his calloused palm. His mother shifted nervously in the plastic chair next to the bed. Before he thought too deeply about it, he pushed the small ring onto his left little finger. It stuck at the knuckle, then slid down and sat comfortably against his own wedding band. He wasn't certain, but thought he detected a slight lessening of tension in his mother's erect form. She made no comment, so neither did he. He moved his fingers to click the two rings together, then nodded once, and continued with the box.

He withdrew another item, one partially melted baby bootee. His body spasmed and the tiny shoe fell from his trembling fingers. Jo had bought them even though he'd said it was crazy, the kid'd be too small to wear them for six months or more. She'd laughed, agreed, insisted, and he'd put them in the cart with the sardonic observation that they *really* didn't have to buy every stitch of clothing to see the kid through to college before it was even born. She'd pouted playfully and flounced off with as much sass as a girl can manage at eight months gone. Dumb idea or not, she'd got her way, of course. They'd bought the bootees and countless other unnecessary items too. All gone now. A waste. All of it a waste. The sweet little shoes his beautiful boy would never grow into. The empty pages of a baby album that would never be filled.

His voice remained a hoarse croak, his vocal chords damaged, but he managed to whisper, "I can't look at this now, Momma. Maybe keep it...you know...for sometime later...?"

They made brief, significant eye-contact, and his mother slid the box off the bed onto the floor, pushing it out of sight. Once he knew it was gone he felt able to take a breath. His chest still hurt, his throat hurt, his eyes hurt, his mind, his heart, his guts, his soul...

His mother was speaking, hesitantly, "Vernon was asking what you want done with the damaged land?"

Gage thought of his brother-in-law, big, solid, dependable; a man of action, not words. While everyone else wrung their hands and fretted over the best thing to do, Vernon got his head down and worked the problem.

"Tell Vern to decide. He and Jan'll do the right thing."

His mother forced a prim smile and patted his bandaged forearm condescendingly with soft fingers. Did she truly expect him to give a shit about the farm? What did it matter? Vernon could run it without him.

She persisted, "And soon, you can come home to us while *you* decide...what's...*next* for you..."

He closed his prickling eyes and eased his sore body carefully back against the propped pillows, whispering, "I told you, Momma, I can't think about it now."

His mother pursed her lips disapprovingly, took a breath and counselled patiently, "Gage, you're twenty-nine years old. You might live until you're ninety. Refusing to acknowledge that you have the good fortune of a future will not bring Joelle or Ryan back. When Daddy died, did I decide my life was over? I miss him every day, and I'm sure you do too, but we didn't make him sick, any more than we made that fire roll through our land. What just happened was awful, cruel, unjust, but it's not your fault – "

"It *is*!" His damaged voice cracked and squeaked like a pubescent boy's as he wailed, "I could've got them out of the house! I *should've* – "

The fury of his mother's retort shocked him into silence. She pounded her fists manically on the metal rail around the hospital bed, "Shoulda, woulda, coulda – stop this, Gage! Stop hiding! You have to deal with what *is*, not what might have been! It's too late, honey, you can't change it! You *have* to think about what comes *next*!"

Next. He grunted humourlessly. There was no next. Next had vanished in the split second of that explosion. There was only the unbearable misery of now.

****

He tried, and not only to please his mother. He understood he was twenty-nine, not ninety-nine, that life would continue and he must find a way to live it tolerably well. The months ground interminably on, but the guilt at his survival refused to abate. If anything, it deepened the more he endeavoured to push it away.

Gradually, his health improved. He became stronger, his natural physicality returning to almost what it had been before the fire. He turned thirty. It didn't feel like a milestone. Thirty years old: no wife, no family, nothing to look forward to but more of the tormenting same as he'd endured for the last nine months. He began to blame the farm for everything, as if it alone was responsible for preventing his full recovery. He dreaded waking up in his single bed in the tiny box room, listening to the morning sounds of Janice's happy brood beyond the bedroom door. He resented the chores that became more meaninglessly onerous with every day. Finally, he decided if the hurt wouldn't leave him, he must leave it instead.

A tent, a sleeping bag, some clothes, his hunting knife, his father's fishing rod, plus the practical stuff: pots, pans, cutlery, headtorch, shotgun, axe, toolkit. Right down one end of his rucksack, wrapped in a towel, the rippled wedding photograph and his son's half-melted bootee. He didn't tell anyone he was taking those. His mother presented him with a packet of plain postcards and exhorted him to write. Janice gave him a small, framed photograph of them all on the porch steps. Vernon, like a huge, benevolent Buddha, sat in the centre with a grinning toddler on each knee and his ever-faithful Blue-Heeler, Lacey, lying at his feet. Gage's mother sat on one side, holding a photograph of his father in her lap. His little sister was on the other, beaming proudly, slim fingers curled around her husband's bulging bicep. Gage had smiled and playfully pinched his sister's arm, "It's a long vacation, Janny. I'm hardly gonna forget what y'all look like." He'd noticed the quick, nervous glance pass between husband and wife. Had they decided he was never coming back?

Truck packed, he kissed the chubby faces of his gorgeous little nieces, patted the dog's soft head, hugged his mother tight, cupped his already-crying baby sister's cheek in one palm, and clasped his brother-in-law's mighty shoulder with the other, trying to grin.

"Back before you know it."

His mouth smiled, but his forever-damaged voice cracked over the words.

He got in the truck fast, and drove away waving and honking the horn as if he were embarking on the best and most exciting adventure ever, when really what he was doing was running away.

In the rearview mirror, he could see his mother wiping her eyes with a blue handkerchief. The barking dog and waving babies started after the truck, running into the clouds of dust thrown up by his departure. His brother-in-law raised one massive arm in farewell, gently folding the sobbing Janice against his chest with the other. They'd be all right without him. They had Vern to take care of them.

****

He drove for three days on two stale sandwiches and four cups of coffee, only pulling off the road for gas or to find a secluded spot to hole-up for the night. The weight of nameless anxiety pressed upon him as if he was being buried alive, the tightness in his chest leaving him struggling to manage a deep breath. He spent more time with his eyes glued to the rearview mirror than he did watching the road ahead. What if he kept driving to the ends of the earth and it made no difference? Might he just as well have stayed home, surrounded by people who treasured him and whom he cherished just as fiercely? But he knew he was a baleful presence in their contented midst. He was well-aware that interacting with him in his current state pained his mother, upset Janice, worried Vernon, and confused his small nieces. Hell, he even made the animals edgy! Stand brooding too long in the stables and he caused the horses to turn in agitated circles, trying to evade whatever malignance pulsed unbidden from him. He wanted to purge himself of the rawness of this guilty grief so he could return home freer, lighter and better able to participate in normal family life with his previous good humour. When she looked at her adult son, was it paranoid to think he could see disappointment in his mother's previously proud eyes? Was he no longer the man she'd raised him to be? The idea he was letting everyone down stung him. Had they all breathed a sigh of relief as his truck turned down the curve of the driveway and disappeared from sight?

He was looking in the rearview mirror again, hunted eyes staring back at him from a gaunt, prematurely-aged face he barely recognised as his own. Abruptly, he saw what he must do. Slamming on the brakes, he brought the truck to such a sudden halt that the seatbelt tugged sharply across his collarbone and left a red weal at the base of his neck. He dived out as if the vehicle were an action-movie prop set for imminent destruction, yanked his rucksack after him, slammed the door, and plunged down the opposite bank towards a river curling like a ribbon of mercury through the valley below.

Despite his blundering urgency, it took over half an hour of quad-shredding strides through thigh-deep grass to reach the bank. Panting, sweating, he collapsed to his knees and scooped handfuls of the icy mountain meltwater, slurping with impatient need. Thirst slaked, heart hammering with exertion, shuddering uncontrollably with what could only be fear, he fumbled the rolled towel from the bottom of his bag and spilled its precious cargo onto his dusty lap. The photograph: blackened, rippled, ruined. One tiny shoe his son had never worn: mostly melted, no good to anyone. Why had he attached such significance to these two items?

He clicked the two wedding rings together as if rubber-stamping his radical decision, took an item in each hand, strode into the centre of the freezing, shallow river, and released both from his trembling fingers into the fast-flowing current.

For a while he could detect them, bobbing along with the passage of the water. Then he realised he could no longer make out the little shoe, and wasn't sure whether the light was reflecting off the shiny surface of the photograph or simply bouncing off the water where the picture had just been. He squinted into the climbing sun, straining to focus, gradually accepting they were irretrievably gone.

He sloshed back to the bank, tugged at his boots and emptied a gush of water from each, peeled off his saturated socks and wrung them out, then knelt barefoot at the water's edge like a pilgrim before a shrine, and bawled the way he'd longed to since that horrific September night stole his beloved wife and beautiful boy.

By the time he crested the hill and arrived back at the truck, the sun was high, the crickets in full crackling cry, and mid-morning heat haze shimmered before his swollen eyes. He slumped in the hot truck and caressed the thin gold band around the little finger of his left hand. Then he sat up purposefully, pushed the key into the ignition and pulled away, tyres spurting loose gravel as they sought purchase on the weather-eroded surface.

****

It was liberating to be free of the constant demands of the ranch. He'd barely ventured more than a couple of hundred miles from home his entire life. Born and bred to be a farmer, he was tethered to the land tradition dictated must pass from one generation of Rutters to the next. He didn't resent that; indeed, until a few months ago, had never doubted his willingness to shoulder the burden. Having to face the increasing likelihood that the Rutter name would die with him had consequently hurt more than he could reasonably explain, as if he'd failed the intrepid and hard-working generations who'd gone before. At least the family tree would survive through his baby sister. Janice may be a Reynolds by marriage, but Rutter blood flowed in her veins. His rambunctious little nieces were now the future of the farm. The purpose of Gage's life had certainly changed the night of the fire, but he was determined to rediscover a reason to draw breath every day…otherwise, what was the point? He might as well find the nearest canyon-edge and drive straight off the side.

He decided to go somewhere completely new to him. Already into his third decade on the planet and he'd never so much as seen the beach, let alone felt warm sand between his bare toes or swum in the ocean. Travelling ever-further from the only home he'd known, he concluded he felt mostly okay. Not excited or delighted, or fascinated or adventurous. Just okay. A tentative peace settled over his embattled soul, and he tried to accept things for what they were rather than what he yearned for them to be. Not that it was easy to be a stranger out here on the road. Extreme embarrassment at the stares his terrible burns and damaged voice attracted in gas stations, diners and stores made him actively seek out the lonelier places, the emptier routes, and voluntarily pitch camp rather than check into Motels. He didn't stop and visit the towns he passed through unless he needed supplies, or the weather deteriorated and he craved a warm, dry night in a proper bed, a decent shower and somewhere to do his laundry.

It got hot. Gage was no stranger to working in the ninety-degree heat of the Western midsummer, but was adapted to the thin, dry air of the high plains. He found himself quickly drained by the unremitting humidity of the sticky South. He lost weight pouring sweat all day, filling himself up on water alone. He stopped too infrequently for meals because he couldn't bear the feel of anything but shorts and sandals on his overheating body, and hated the horrified double-takes when he got out of the truck bare-chested and people clocked the unsightly scars traversing his left-hand side from forehead to shin. Over the past couple of fragile years, he'd voluntarily withdrawn from gawking, nudging society to the point where he was now accustomed only to his patient family and mile upon mile of nothing but cows and horses, grass and sky. Most folks probably wouldn't notice the detail of a soft exchange between husband and wife in a diner, as their toddlers smeared more ice-cream across their cherubic faces than they ever got into their rosebud mouths, but Gage found he couldn't tune stuff like that out, no matter how hard he tried. Helplessly compelled to drink in every nuance of intimate human interaction with the desperation of a hot horse slurping at a water trough, Gage sometimes felt himself going so crazy with loss and longing he wanted to screw up his eyes, cover his ears, and scream at them all to stop. Just stop. Stop loving one another so vocally. Stop being so obviously happy. Stop allowing your adorable little children to beam the way his precious nieces did, their round cheeks like apples pinkening in the summer sun. His boy had never learned to smile. He hadn't lived long enough.

The only remedy for the threatening insanity was to get back on the road and concentrate unwaveringly on the boring, grey avenue of winding asphalt until the agony abated.

He drove. It was okay. There was enough to look at, he could croak along to the radio without anyone complaining like they did when he tried to sing at home, and if he never got where he was going, he didn't ever have to go back.

Fortunately, the United States was a vast country, but he was passing into Florida already. Then what? Stop, turn and face the demons that clearly still pursued him despite his best efforts to be rid of them? He didn't want to have to make up his mind, but he also knew he was rapidly running out of road.

BODY

Late afternoon on a deserted stretch of highway, perpetual heat haze shimmering in front of the truck until the whole panorama turned to liquid before his blurring eyes. He swigged the last of the water from his plastic bottle and tossed it onto the seat beside him. All he seemed to do down here was drink, sweat and pee. He needed to go again now but wasn't about to make the same mistake as earlier. Out of the truck with no one around, a carload of girls had gone by as soon as he'd begun to urinate, squealing from the windows and honking the horn. Some guys probably would have found it funny, but Gage wasn't in the frame of mind to deal with women passing vocal judgement upon his body, even from a speeding car.

At the next likely-looking exit, he turned off the highway and down a dusty track running perpendicular to it, bumping along for a hundred yards or so until he was certain no one could see him from the road. He got out of the truck and mooched to the edge of the scrubby undergrowth. As he stood there, peeing forcefully, he realised the rushing sound he could hear wasn't tyres on the highway or wind in the trees. It was too constant and rhythmic, waxing and waning with the predictability of waves breaking on a shore!

Over the past few weeks, Gage had discovered he very much liked the beach. He'd spent many of his recent hours just sitting on the sand and staring at the sunlight sparkling on the moving water, hypnotised by it in the same way the scudding clouds in the huge sky of home used to capture his imagination as a small child. He'd wonder where the shapes had been and where they were going. He thought the same about the waves he watched roll in. Where had they begun, and what submerged secrets had they passed over on their journey to break on the shore before his sandy feet?

Bladder emptied, he stepped back onto the road and only then realised he'd managed to pee onto his own uncovered toes. Gross. And he'd finished all his water so he couldn't even rinse them. That decided him. He wound up the windows, locked the truck, slid the keys into his pocket, and marched briskly in the direction of the rushing sound, sandals slapping and kicking up puffs of dust.

The track stopped abruptly. He could hear the sea and catch glimpses of twinkling blue through the bushes, but there was no clear path between this disused road and the ocean. Cheated of the sensory pleasure of cool water on his hot and dirty feet, Gage prowled back and forth along the hedgeline seeking a way through, eventually deciding he'd have to make one. Wriggling as carefully as he was able, trying to avoid scratching his half-naked body on protruding branches, he corkscrewed himself out onto a spit of coral and rock, a light dusting of white sand creating a beach no more than ten feet long, lapped by the lazy ebb tide. Gage grinned with satisfaction at having achieved his objective, flicked off his sandals and paddled back and forth in the shallows, appreciating the childlike diversion of playing in the sea by himself. Squelching from the water and enjoying the wet sand squidging between his toes, he pottered unhurriedly back up the beach to retrieve his shoes, absorbed in picking up and examining shells and skimming the occasional stone. Back at the jutting spit of rock, he jammed his flip-flops into the pockets of his shorts and climbed the few feet to look around.

To the other side of the rock was a much smoother half-moon of sand, at the opposite end of which was a large and fine-looking villa on an open area of lawn, ringed by stands of swaying palm trees. Gage regarded the house with a twinge of jealousy. What must it cost to purchase a home of that size and grandeur in such a secluded location, with its own extensive stretch of beautiful beach? Probably more money than he'd see in a lifetime. As with all the high-quality houses he'd passed on the southern-Florida leg of his extended sojourn, it was all closed up for the boiling off-season, storm shutters down, no vehicles on the drive, no furniture on the terrace, a cover across the pool.

As Gage stood and stared with unconcealed envy at the empty mansion and what he really coveted, a gorgeous beach of his very own, he realised there were tracks across the otherwise-pristine sand. They came out of the undergrowth five hundred yards down the beach from the house, curved around in a snake of trodden sand for only ten yards or so, and reentered the forest a mere twenty feet from where he was standing. His first thought was that it might be a sea crocodile, finding a place to hole up and wait for some unsuspecting food to scuttle by…but closer examination from his vantage point suggested regular indentations very much like the footprints he'd just left across the secret beach behind him. If the house was all closed up for the impending tropical summer, then who'd been in the woods that were supposed to be private?

The footprints were above the line of deposited seaweed denoting high-water mark, so it was impossible to know how long they'd been there, but it was their location that troubled Gage. The highway was bordered on both sides by thick vegetation, meaning that whoever left the footprints had willingly fought their way through perhaps a quarter mile of dense growth from roadside to beach, only to walk the shortest distance along it and dive straight back into the woods again. What was the point of that? If you were looking for a place to hunker down out of sight and swig your liquor unmolested, you'd only need to get a few feet into the hedge to be completely obscured from passing cars. If you were wild with passion for your latest girl, you'd hardly take the risk of her ardour waning by dragging her on a jungle trek when a quick squeeze under the dense bushes right by the roadside would give you all the privacy you needed. The incongruity of those unexplained footprints bothered Gage sufficiently for him to decide on a little uncharacteristic trespassing. A landowner himself, he usually greatly respected the sanctity of other people's property. He therefore made no negative judgement as he slid down the other side of the rock onto the private beach and found regimented lines of upright stakes marching at intervals from trees to waterline, swags of barbed wire strung between them to denote the boundary.

From down here on the sand, the dents in the beach were obviously two sets of footprints. Gage supposed he should just let it go. Whoever'd unrolled these swirls of vicious wire and staked them in place in the sand clearly wanted to keep people out, so he should probably take the hint and get going…?

Feeling guilty at what he was doing, Gage put on his sandals and hugged tight to the treeline, gingerly lifting his long legs over the fencing. Old links of partially broken stakes and severely rusted wire were scattered haphazardly among the trees, dislodged during the last storm season. He picked his way cautiously between them, anxious not to get caught on the razor-sharp barbs. Where the footsteps penetrated the undergrowth, the land dropped to a steep gulley, then climbed up a shallower bank back towards the highway. As he'd suspected, the cover was too dense to make out the road. He also couldn't see his truck, which he knew was a very short distance away to his right. Why come here? For what? A hard, hot, uncomfortable trudge from the roadside, through the jungle of foliage, down the shallow opposite bank, across the gulley, up this much-steeper hill and onto a beach they left metres later? Gage wiped his wrist across his sweating forehead and sighed. Was he simply thankful to have something else to occupy his mind?

His roaming gaze absently followed one particular tangle of the broken fence. It curled strikingly like a backcombed quiff, stakes hanging artistically in the air at intervals as if they were roman numerals on a giant clock-face. Abruptly, the swirl suddenly disappeared down the forested slope, the wooden pickets stabbing at an extreme angle into the bank, suggesting they braced a weight lower down. Curious, he padded over to the trail of wire, squatted to prevent himself tumbling headfirst, gripped one of the firmly embedded posts in his fist, and craned over the edge.

Directly beneath, so close he could almost touch them, the soles of two little shoes pointed up the bank towards him.

****

Gage started, slipped, instinctively grabbed at the fence to steady himself, and squawked in pain as a knot of sharp wire pierced his palm. Unbalanced, he thudded onto his side in the sandy dirt, hurt hand held protectively against his stomach.

He could see tanned female legs extending from the shoes and down the bank. Mercifully, her head and shoulders were obscured by overhanging bushes, but he could clearly see that the barbed wire wound several times around the body, encasing the wet-suited figure from ribs to hips. Gage rubbed a thumb over the single throbbing lump in the centre of his own palm as he gaped in dismay at the intense purple circles of dried blood around each of the numerous puncture wounds, shockingly bright against the pale yellow of the long-sleeved rash vest. A surfer drowned at sea and swept ashore, tangling in the wire as waves battered the land? But the last extreme weather event with a tide capable of depositing a body this far up the beach would have been months ago, during the previous hurricane season. In such oppressive heat, decomposition would surely happen fast, and this body clearly hadn't yet spent sufficient time in the gulley for the process to advance…so what the hell had he just found, a goddam *murder* victim?

Gage rolled his shivering, terrified body onto forearms and knees and vomited a puddle of watery bile onto the parched sand, which instantly absorbed the moisture to leave only a bubbling crust on the surface. He rocked back onto his heels and dragged a shaking palm across his lips. He needed to calm down and reason this out. He had to raise the alarm, but where? Clearly, the closest house was empty. He had a cellphone, but didn't stop in Motels often enough to ensure he kept the battery charged. By the road signs he'd passed, he was roughly midway between two small settlements. He could go back to the diner he'd passed and ask someone for assistance, but the cops would require basic information. Willing or not, he had to examine the body to at least report approximate age and other such relevant details. There could be a wallet or purse down in that gulley holding the key to her identity. It struck him she could even have a working cellphone on which he could call for help! Spurred on by this remote possibility, Gage edged down the slope until he was level with the body, apprehensively pushing aside the greenery hiding her face. One involuntary sob escaped him as he saw her long, blonde hair trailing across the forest floor, tangled with twigs and clumped with congealed blood. As Gage pushed a branch away, a snagged lock looped free and curled around his wrist. He recoiled in horror, shaking his hand frantically, body shuddering. It was how Joelle's hair had felt, silky, smooth and soft, slipping deliciously across his bare skin. He retched again but his stomach was empty. He spat repeatedly, the vile-tasting phlegm sticking to his dry lips. Taking deep breaths, getting the burgeoning panic under shaky control, he crawled back to her side and rubbed at the film of compacted blood, sand and soil coating her face. To his astonishment, as his faltering fingers wiped the revolting mask from her mouth, the tip of a swollen tongue protruded and attempted to moisten the cracked and filthy lips. She was *ALIVE*!

ALIVE

Mind utterly blank, frozen with fear, Gage gradually realised he had to do something other than slump and stare at this dreadful sight. Not knowing if she could hear or understand him, he nevertheless stroked her hair gently with his grimy left hand and whispered in his almost-vanished voice, "It's okay, it's okay," but of course it wasn't, and he needed to decide what to do, quickly. His fingers groped for her pulse. Faint, more tentative flutter than confident beat. He had no idea if moving her was wise, only that he couldn't abandon her here to go for help. A twenty-minute drive back to the nearest town, further delay awaiting the arrival of the cops or an ambulance, directing them here – it would all take time she doubtless didn't have. To save her, he had to do this himself.

A rough plan was taking shape in Gage's mind. He tugged his bunch of keys from his pocket. There was a multitool on his keyring. He kept stroking, comforting, whispering, "I'm gonna cut you free. Don't worry, sugar, I'm here to rescue you."

Gage fumbled his penknife off the keyring and flicked out the most-likely attachment, distractedly wiping at his now constant flow of agitated tears. Steadying trembling hands and churning guts, he bent to his task, using the woefully inadequate knife to slice back and forth on the rusting wire until it weakened enough to give way across the fulcrum of the blade. He tried to ensure minimal movement of the metal, first snapping each end where it joined onto the fence and only then attempting to cut her free in sections, sliding the evil spikes from her injured skin as he went. It took forever. His legs throbbed from kneeling so long on the uneven ground. Sharp pains shot through his feet as he braced them against the camber of the slope to stop himself slipping. His stomach muscles were in knots with the effort of holding his body stable above her, keeping his movements small and controlled. His neck and shoulders ached with the continuous sawing motion, back and forth with the skinny blade across the rusty wire until it mercifully surrendered and snapped. Occasionally, he wasn't quick enough to catch the rebounding links between his fingers and the barbs plunged further into her skin, making her whimper in pain. At these moments, Gage instantly stopped cutting and caressed her cheek with his hot hand. When she felt his touch, her eyelids fluttered but didn't open, and she didn't speak.

Completing his removal of the wire embedded in her front, Gage steeled himself to lift the near-lifeless woman. He slid a palm under the small of her back and supported her blood-caked head with the other, "I'm gonna sit you up, okay? I need to do your back now. I'll be as careful as I can, I promise. You're doing real well. It'll soon be over." Gage wasn't sure whether he was telling her or himself.

Slowly lifting her to rest against his chest, gently easing the lengths of wire one by one from her back, strands of her hair tickled his bare skin and a vivid memory assailed him: his laughing wife ambushing him in the hayloft of the biggest barn when she knew they'd be alone, flying blonde locks gleaming like threads of gold in the shafts of sunlight, that same glossy curtain falling forward and obscuring her face as his fingers pressed into the naked flesh of her hips, rocking her with the rhythmic upward thrusts of his pelvis as she straddled him.

This was the closest he'd been to a woman since…since… Suppressing the image, Gage inched the final foot of cut wire free of her skin, feeling again for the pulse. Flooded with relief to still detect the irregular beat beneath his clammy fingers, he held her body to his for a moment more. Weakened with pain, blood loss, probable dehydration and heaven only knew what else, if she were now to lose her battle, at least she'd sense his presence in this sinister place. Even as he cradled her, his keen eyes assessed the opposite bank, knowing he had to climb it with the dead weight of the unconscious girl in his arms. He had a fairly good idea where the truck was, but couldn't waste valuable time and energy staggering about in the undergrowth getting his bearings. How to pick a target and aim straight for it…? Of course, the remote locking! When activated, it flashed the indicators and blipped the horn. If he put his keys in his hand before he started off, he could repeatedly operate the mechanism and use the sound of the horn to navigate directly back to the truck! He held the key aloft, double-clicked the button, and was rewarded by a satisfyingly loud honk closer to his current position than he could have hoped.

He slipped the keyring over his forefinger and slid his wide palms under her buttocks, lifting her firmly against his body as one might carry a sleeping child, trying to hook her legs over his hips to spread the weight. He pivoted from sore knees to an unsteady crouch, counted to three in his head, and pushed upward with every ounce of latent energy in his quads and hamstrings. Overbalancing and tottering sideways down the steepness of the bank, his immediate thought was that he would tumble headlong and flatten her beneath him! When by some miracle he remained upright, he felt brave enough to use the remaining slope to his advantage, breaking into a cautious downhill trot to build momentum for the upward climb. As his feet hit the gulley floor, his legs drove hard, muscles humming with the effort, striding as wide as he could up the opposite bank to get to the top before his strength failed. A couple of times his dusty feet twisted in his flip-flops. Senses sharpened by coursing adrenaline, he had the presence of mind to leap instantly onto the other leg and keep powering away. By the time he reached the top of the bank, he was dripping sweat and heaving for breath, spent legs quivering. He paused, panted loud and deep, and blipped the button in his palm once more. Another loud honk a few metres further to his right. Turning sideways to protect her as much as possible from the scratching branches, he plunged into the hedge, pushing with all his remaining might against the springy undergrowth like a football player driving for a touchdown, crashing onto the track feet from his vehicle, staggering forward and thudding his back against the truck's hot bodywork.

He scrabbled the passenger door open, flopping awkwardly onto the edge of the seat, holding her tight to his chest with one shuddering arm and thrashing blindly behind him with the other, pushing the detritus of drinks bottles and food wrappers into the footwell. Fingertips at full stretch, he plucked a towel from the chaotic pile in the back, flattening it out across the front bench seat. Although his legs nearly gave way beneath him as he forced himself to stand, he struggled upright, turned, and leant over the seat with her injured head cupped in his palm like a newborn. He placed her on the towel with tender care, scuttled round to the driver's side, gripped its top corners and used it to slide her comatose form across the worn leather until he was confident he could close the passenger door. He needed her to be in the front so he could monitor her heartbeat and breathing as he drove. Given how faint her pulse already was, and following the extreme trauma of his rough and ready rescue attempt, Gage was convinced he'd shortly be pulling over at the side of the highway to start CPR. He just prayed he'd get nearer some useful help before that happened. Pulling his camping pillow from the back, he gently supported her head, slithered onto the driver's seat, plonked the pillow in his lap and eased her down. Did the tension in her broken little body lessen as her head lolled across the cushion? Fearing the worst, Gage licked his fingers and hovered them close to her lips. The softest whisper of breath cooled the moisture on his skin. The pulse at her neck was present but dangerously weak. He stroked her matted hair with his sweat-slick palm, "Hold on, baby. Just hold on..."

Gage started the engine, rammed the truck into 'Drive' and hit the highway.

LOGAN

Logan swung the car in a carelessly wide arc and paused with unconcealed impatience at the gates for the security guy to check his ID and numberplate.

"You know it's me, for Chrissake, Charlie!"

"Doin' my job, Mr Logan."

"Yes, yes, a little faster, huh? Some of us have *real* work to do."

As the gates swung open before him, Logan gunned the engine aggressively. The rear wheels span uselessly on the loose, dusty surface, then bit unexpectedly and shot him off abruptly on the diagonal. He swore, grabbed the wheel and wrestled it straight, inches away from hitting a tree on the right-hand side of the long driveway. Flushing with furious humiliation, he drove on without slowing or glancing back at Charlie, who was doubtless revelling in such an immediate and rib-tickling dose of karma. What did he matter? He was the gate-guy. He was nobody.

Logan pulled up before the house and leapt dynamically from the air-conditioned interior of the car. The Florida heat smacked him like a damp flannel. The day was still, the enervating humidity already uncomfortably high even though it was barely ten a.m.

He took the shallow steps to the front door in one bound, knocked authoritatively, and was admitted without preamble into the welcome, dim coolness. He waved away the housekeeper's supervision and saw himself down the corridor to the Atlantic vista, turning right and pausing before the chalky limewash of the study's double-doors. He checked the knot of his tie, tugged at the cuffs of his shirt to straighten the sleeves, brushed microscopic lint from one lapel of his suit jacket, and knocked three times with respectful confidence.

"Come."

Logan opened both doors simultaneously, considering any opportunity to make an entrance worth taking. The boss sat on a leather couch to one side of the grandiose desk, the coffee table before him obscured by an inch-deep spread of weekend papers. The Governor wore linen slacks, espadrilles, no socks, and an open-necked polo shirt. Logan noted with distaste that the V of suntanned skin at his septuagenarian throat was wrinkled, leathery and loose. The French doors before him stood open to the rear veranda and the long, straight lawn. Beyond that, nothing but sky and glittering sea, deep blue in the morning sunlight. Two Golden Retrievers formed panting parentheses on the cool terracotta tiles to either side of the coffee table. They didn't even bother lifting their heads as Logan entered.

The boss looked up from his paper and smiled warmly, "Robert."

"Good morning, sir."

The Governor took in the expensive woollen suit, tightly fastened tie, highly polished shoes, and looked somewhat pained, given the mercury hovered at ninety and the humidity was already building inexorably to the inevitable late-afternoon storm.

"It's Saturday, Robert."

"It is, sir."

"Do you *own* any casual clothes?"

Logan's brows knitted in momentary bewilderment. The Governor flapped his paper with a hint of frustration and sighed, "Never mind. Help yourself to coffee."

Logan nodded earnestly, pivoted on his heel with the formality of a soldier on parade, and marched over to the sideboard to pour himself a coffee, plopping in two cubes of sugar and stirring briskly with intense concentration on the tiny cup in his big hand. He perched stiffly on an armchair opposite the boss, eyes scanning the various headlines he could see, trying to read them upside-down. In the end, the Governor put him out of his misery, "Help yourself, Robert."

"Thank you, sir – "

"Only for Heaven's sake take off your jacket. You're making me feel too hot just looking at you!"

"Yessir."

Logan stood immediately, removed his jacket, and laid it as tenderly as one might a sleeping baby over the back of the chair, before leaning forward to riffle through the papers. The Governor watched him distractedly, unaware he was frowning. Unwaveringly loyal, unquestionably obedient, without doubt the most useful and reliable employee on the entire staff, there was nevertheless something odd about Robert. The Governor had seen a lot of himself in Robert when he'd recruited him. Another determined, self-made individual deliberately cocking-a-snook at the established ways of doing things, elevating himself without the assistance of either wealth or social status. Sick mother, broken home, financing his own Law degree and achieving scores his more privileged rivals would have sold a kidney for, the Governor admired a grafter...and Robert Logan was the hardest worker he'd met since entering politics. Everybody else coasted, backstabbed, brown-nosed and operated. They didn't put the effort in, just blamed one another when nothing changed. Robert rode roughshod over every convention to actually get things done. He didn't give a damn whether people liked him for it or not. Robert Logan didn't see colleagues, he saw obstacles. Secretly, the Governor rather envied his ability to stand alone. He'd promoted the youngster with indecent speed. He knew elbows nudged, eyebrows waggled and faces smirked behind his back. They thought Robert was his little boyfriend. The Governor could only imagine what his indomitable wife of forty-three years would have to say about *those* rumours if she knew! Notwithstanding the young man's inability to relax, and his tendency to rub people up the wrong way, the Governor liked the cut of Robert's jib, the thrust of his determined character, his refusal to be cowed or beaten, his complete self-contained independence. Just because Robert eschewed friendships and wasn't afraid of causing offence didn't mean he was doing anything wrong. Besides, ruffling feathers seemed to be a notable, electable quality in a politician these days! He entrusted an increasing amount to Robert regardless of the whispering, gradually coming to view him as the only genuine rock in their disingenuous world. Everything about his dedicated young aide was *so* perfect the Governor found himself turning a deliberate blind eye to overtly spiteful tittle-tattle, actively dismissing it as petty resentment on the part of those who'd been passed over in favour of his high-performing protégé. But at the back of his mind lurked a troubling unease. In public life, methods counted as much as results, and there didn't appear to be a point beyond which the young lawyer would not go to carry out his remit. Robert just didn't seem to possess the natural off-switch that dwelt intuitively within everyone else he knew.

The Governor realised he was staring, and returned his full attention to his paper before the younger man became aware of it. He thought no more about the behavioural quirks of Robert Logan until he noticed his employee was standing again, excusing himself, exhibiting his strange mix of deference and arrogance…and something more, surprising and uncharacteristic agitation, "Excuse me, sir. I just need to make a telephone call."

"Robert?" The Governor looked up at him in kindly concern, gesturing to the newspaper rolled to a tube in Logan's large fist, "Bad news?"

"Um…no, sir. The date, sir. The date on the paper. I forgot. My mother's birthday, sir."

The Governor smiled, inexpressibly relieved to see Robert betraying a hint of human frailty for once. He never usually forgot anything. It was funny to think of Robert having a mother.

"Well, can't have that, now, can we? You must call her straight away. Be sure to give her my very best wishes along with yours."

"Very kind and understanding of you, sir."

Robert was across the office so fast his shiny shoes barely touched the ground. The Governor waited until he was definitely alone before daring to chuckle. Robert didn't like being laughed at.

Study door closed quietly behind him, Logan sprinted as fast as absolute silence would allow across the wide dining room, down the steps to the sunken kitchen, through the door into the laundry, and out onto the gravel area beyond the back door, where the boxed air conditioners hummed rhythmically as they rotated in their metal cages. He dialled a number from memory and paced anxiously, beating his thigh distractedly with the rolled-up paper in time to the whirr of the fans.

"Hello?"

"It's me. Our unwelcome visitor is all over the local paper! Have you seen it?"

"No…"

"Where are you?"

"At home. It's Saturday."

"Well, go out and get a copy!"

"What's it say?"

"She's front page! She's a reporter. Works at the paper, apparently. Went home from work last Tuesday night saying something about following up a lead and – surprise, surprise – never showed for work again Wednesday morning. No trace of her having been home, neighbours haven't seen her since, car discovered parked off the highway opposite the Marina – "

"Shit! What was a *reporter* doing poking around?"

"According to her editor, she had a lead on a big story…and I quote, 'a political exposé of State significance'…then she vanished. His article's implying it's no coincidence. What do you think about that?"

"I told you, we just walked around the side of the house and she was there! Scared the shit out of the both of us!"

"Did you get rid?"

"Yup."

"So, this isn't going to come back and bite us now the cops are on the case?"

"No, we took her all the way over to – "

"Don't tell me! Best I don't know. Just reassure me it's dealt with."

"It's dealt with, Mr Logan, sir. I think she was dead before we even dumped her. She won't be tellin' nobody nothin'.""

"Let's be doubly sure, shall we? The implication of this very sparse article is that she hadn't seen fit to share her findings, whatever they may have been, with any of her workmates. Probably didn't want them stealing her story."

"What makes you so sure?"

"It's the goddam local rag! If they had a scoop, they'd be printing it, missing colleague or not."

"I guess so…"

"You said she was fixated on the basement?"

"Yeah, sitting on the grass trying to lever the window open."

"Unless you *knew*, you wouldn't bother with that, would you? You'd try to get in the house, look around upstairs maybe? You wouldn't start in the basement."

"Meaning?"

"She's either watched the house for a while, or someone's tipped her off. I've just got this feeling that, dead or not, she isn't out of our hair yet. We need to shut this down, fast, before another nosey reporter takes up the slack. Know anyone in local law enforcement down here?"

"Yeah, I do, as it happens."

"Any favours you can call in? We need to be kept abreast of the police activity somehow."

"Sure…I got just the guy…"

"Good. I'd like to know how the whole 'missing persons' investigation is progressing. I want to know the millisecond they find anything of note, particularly an unidentified female body in the middle of nowhere. If you can, get inside her house and search it. I want laptop, notebooks, memory sticks, photos –"

"Yeah, yeah. Don't worry. He's ex-military. We served together. Did some shit he ain't going to want getting out. I'll be as far in with the cops as I want to get."

"Excellent, Tyler! You know, you constantly surprise me. I start believing you're useless and then you spill a gem like that!"

"Thanks…I guess. What about Floyd?"

"Tell Floyd to keep a *very* low profile, get on with his goddam job, and try not to think for himself. Shit seems to happen when he does."

"I'll warn him."

"See that you do. In the meantime, I'm going to pay this editor a visit. She's gotta have given him something to go on, otherwise how did he know it was 'a political exposé'? That particular choice of words is just a little too close to home, don't you think?"

"Who you gonna say you are?"

Logan paused, considered, and a vulpine smile suffused his chiselled features, "Hmmm…whaddya think? Vice Squad, maybe? That should rattle his cage…"

MAL

Images.

Click.

Lines and lines of shots of the beaming Governor waving to supporters. Numerous official, posed portraits. Standard wood-panelled office, flag prominently placed, reins of State governance in a reassuringly safe and capable pair of hands. The guy was up there with Santa Claus for universal approval and cuddly approachability. If any of what she'd suggested last Monday night was even *remotely* true...! But he couldn't print a thing, not without proof, and he'd told her, probably rather too aggressively, that she'd struggle to obtain it. She'd left wearing the expression that made him mad both with exasperation at her obstinacy and delight at her spark. The face that declared, 'Think I'm incapable, do you? I'll show you, you pompous, sexist old fool.' And then she'd disappeared, and now he was powerless to do anything but stare at pictures of the State Governor of Florida and fret ceaselessly over what he knew. The allegations she'd unloaded during that revelatory conversation circled his head and stopped him sleeping. Frantic with worry but desperate to act, he knew he had to do *something*...

Terrified, it had taken him days to decide what that something should be. Eventually, he'd used his tin-pot paper to publish a purely factual article on the disappearance of a missing local woman, who just happened to be his lead reporter…oh, and the closest thing to a daughter he'd ever had. It wasn't much – a four-page spread to a circulation of a few thousand households – but it applied a salve of purpose to a pain the like of which he hadn't felt since losing his darling wife to cancer five years before. Looking through his open office door directly at the desk stripped bare by the investigating cops, it felt as if she'd already been erased from existence. Everything that might be considered evidence, from polaroid photographs to notebooks and clippings, had been catalogued and carted away in bags and boxes. There was nothing left but an empty in-tray, and a chair with the internal foam padding spilling from splits in the fabric.

Glen, hastily and necessarily promoted to lead reporter, and trying to keep a lid on how delighted he was about it in front of his obviously bereft editor, stuck his head around the habitually open door, "Boss?"

Mal sighed, lifted his eyes from examination of the computer screen, and tried to seem as interested as he'd usually be, "What can I do for you?"

Glen looked uncharacteristically edgy, which instantly sharpened Mal's attention, "Someone to see you. Another cop. Different unit."

Glen glanced behind him to where the visitor obviously waited, inched his head further into the office to ensure he was unobserved, and mouthed, "Vice Squad."

"Vice?" Mal's stomach tightened. Glen couldn't know the significance of this, and Mal was loathe to tell him. It had crossed his mind to give Glen the background on everything he knew and just let the energetic youngster run with it, but he didn't dare release the incendiary secret. Convinced he'd already lost one reporter to this story; he wasn't about to risk the neck of another. He pushed at the edge of his monitor to tilt the screen away from prying eyes, tried to assume a nonchalant attitude in his chair like a man with absolutely nothing to hide, and nodded calmly to Glen, "Okay, show him in."

Glen was about to address the visitor when the tall, well-groomed man strode impatiently past him to occupy a commanding position in the centre of Mal's worn office rug. Glen stood in the doorway and opened and closed his mouth like a ventriloquist's dummy, both affronted and intimidated.

Mal waved a casual hand, "Thank you, Glen. Could you close the door, please?"

Still gawping at the imposing stranger, Glen stumbled backwards out of the office, shutting the door so clumsily behind him that the badly fitting glass pane rattled loudly.

Mal attempted a cautious smile and indicated the empty chair before the desk with an open palm. The man tutted audibly, perched on the very edge of the seat as if having to accede to Mal's wishes was a huge waste of his valuable time, flashed the tin, and snapped, "Quantick. Vice. Your article. It made me wonder whether you're in possession of vital information you're deliberately withholding. You know that's an offence, right?"

Mal blinked, almost as startled as Glen had been. This guy sure cut to the chase. Determined not to betray a hint of disquiet, Mal leant back slowly, resting his elbows on the arms of his chair, steepling his fingers and pressing the pads firmly together to stop his hands shaking too noticeably.

"Detective…Quantick, did you say? My article is a compilation of all the facts we have concerning the recent disappearance of a much missed and highly valued member of the newspaper's staff. I'm sure you can appreciate, we couldn't sit back and do nothing when our friend and colleague might be injured, or in danger…? Someone could have witnessed something relevant to the police investigation. What we printed is intended to maybe jog a memory or two. We're using our position to raise awareness in the community. She's still missing. How can I withhold what I don't know?"

The cop's disconcertingly dark eyes glittered chillingly. He said nothing. Mal waited it out, holding his nerve, staring back, not volunteering anything more. The silence lengthened. Outside the door, the newsroom buzzed with talking voices, ringing telephones, clattering keyboards, chuntering printers. Mal's heart was whacking so hard against his ribs he was sure half the street could hear it. The pressure inside the tiny room intensified until Mal could no longer endure it. The first to drop his eyes, they darted compulsively back to the computer screen, focusing on the photographs of the smiling Governor, delaying the inevitable moment he'd have to meet the glacial gaze of the Vice cop once more. One particular shot suddenly caught his eye. For an instant, he couldn't understand what had captured his attention so completely. It was only the Governor addressing supporters at a Tallahassee rally during his recent election campaign, finger aloft as he energetically drove home a crowd-pleasing point. Then, he realised *why* the image had leapt out at him from a sea of similar pictures. There, in the background of a photograph he'd stared at repeatedly over the last few days, was a man Mal recognised. Unless he was very much mistaken, the figure in the shadows over the Governor's left shoulder was Vice Squad Detective Quantick! He tried to compare the faces without making it obvious he was flitting between man and screen. Same hard, cold expression. Same sensible haircut. Identical, erect form – broad shoulders, straight back, lofted chin – it was *him*, no question! Malcolm Lawrence was a hard-bitten, cynical old hack. He'd been around the block and back again, and he didn't spook easily. Usually, he thrived on a good mystery, one that got him out of bed in the morning and kept him plugging on day after day when, at his time of life, he should really be doing a little more fishing for yellowtail and a little less digging for dirt. However, this stank worse than a dead skunk down a storm-drain. Given the explosive secrets he'd been told, what possible reason could a Vice cop have for standing next to the State Governor on a rally podium five hundred miles away from here…unless he was undercover? Might it ease the terrible internal pressure to blurt out everything and hope he and this cruel-eyed cop were on the same side? Sorely tempted, instinct nevertheless held him back. Quantick's thorny manner pierced his reporter's sixth sense like a wasp sting. Until he could be absolutely sure the cop was safe to talk to, he just had to get rid of him, fast, before the guy wheedled anything out of him it might be deadly to reveal.

Standing, pushing his chair back, Mal politely indicated the door, "Well, if there's nothing else, Detective…?"

The cop shot up powerfully as if he had pistons for legs, towering over Mal's short, rotund frame, "Why is it I get the impression you're hiding something, Mr Lawrence?"

Rendered reckless by a flash of fury, Mal parried the question with one of his own, "What's the whereabouts of a missing reporter got to do with Vice?"

A twitch in the guy's jaw as if he was grinding his teeth in frustration, "I assume you understand the penalty for impeding an investigation – "

"I've made a full statement, Detective! We *all* have!" Mal indicated the crowded office beyond his door with an expansive sweep of his arm.

The cop's nostrils twitched as if he too had caught a whiff of Mal's metaphorical skunk, and his upper lip curled, revealing white and even teeth, "I'm here to discuss your article, not your statement."

The picture of innocence, Mal protested, "My article is a plea for witnesses to the disappearance of my lead reporter – "

"Who was working on – and I quote *you* – 'a political exposé of State significance'."

"And I repeat, Detective, because I simply do not see the connection, what does *any* of that have to do with the Vice Squad?"

"*I* am asking the questions, Mr Lawrence. The implication of your article is that her investigation was a contributory factor in her disappearance, if not the sole cause of it!"

"Detective Quantick, my article reports the facts of her disappearance as we know them," Mal ticked the points off on his fingers, "*When* I last spoke to her, *what* she was working on at the time, *where* she was last seen..."

"The facts?"

"Yes, as I know them. I reported what she told me. *All* she told me! She provided me with no article to print, and no evidence or proof of any allegations. She was investigating a lead into a story. What I printed is what I was told. It may or may not have a bearing on her disappearance, I can't say. I have no information, no briefing notes, no evidence, no proof...no political story, Detective! Nothing at all. *My* story is that my lead reporter is missing, and we are all frantic with worry about her."

"But *someone* made an allegation with a political hook? Something 'of State significance'? That's pretty specific."

"We'd all be in court Monday through Friday if we printed every piece of salacious gossip we got told. You can't just believe a source. You have to investigate. A man in your position must know that."

"Who were her sources?"

"I don't know. Confidential. She protected her network. Investigative journalism's a competitive field, even amongst colleagues on the same paper...even way down here off the edge of the world! Everyone's looking for the career-defining scoop that's going to catapult them to the big time. No one releases information about what they've got until they're ready to print an article."

"And was she ready? Where would that information be?"

"I've told you all I know, Detective. Whatever she was working on would be with her computer, her notebooks..."

"I need to take a look at her desk."

"Your colleagues have taken everything – "

"I might uncover something they missed. I'm coming at this from a different angle."

No kidding... Mal gazed unblinkingly at the cop's inscrutable features. His heart was still going like a freight train. Any second now, he was sure it would burst from his chest like an express from a tunnel. He watched the muscle jump in the cop's smooth cheek, thought of the image on the computer screen, and wondered whether the guy might be as keyed-up as he was. He took a calculated risk, beamed expansively, and said, "Well, *sure*, Detective! If you feel you need to. Anything to assist the investigation. We just want her back, you know? As we are always in possession of sensitive material in a newsroom, if I could just see the search warrant you've brought with you...?"

Mal raised his eyebrows, held out his hand, and let the question hang in the sultry air over the cluttered desk. The stalemate lasted probably no more than three seconds, but it felt like an hour. This time, Quantick was the first to crack, and Mal registered the terrifying triumph of a temporary victory. The cop's eyes roamed back and forth across the grubby carpet, mind obviously racing, eventually concluding his unconventional shakedown had run its course and glaring venomously at Mal's flushed and perspiring face, "Your 'Uncle Buck' routine might fool those idiots from the Sherriff's department, but I see what's going on here, and I don't like it. Be *very* careful, Mr Lawrence. Obstruct me and you'll regret it. I have an important job to do. *Don't* get in my way."

He left as abruptly as he'd arrived, and Mal subsided into his chair, groaning as if he'd just gone ten rounds with Tyson. An indecently short interval elapsed before Glen was back in the doorway, eyes shining. Mal reflected that with a little more polish and the guile only experience could deliver, Glen had the makings of a fine reporter, mostly because he was a nosey little bastard.

"Boss, you okay? What did he want?"

"Information."

"What information? We've already told the cops everything we know…?"

Ashamed at withholding the truth from Glen, Mal avoided eye contact, instead stabbing ineptly at the mouse buttons like he was playing Space Invaders, "Goddam it, Glen, how do you make a picture bigger?"

"Zoom in, Boss. Here…"

Glen politely elbowed him out of the way, took control, and swiftly enlarged the relevant shot.

"Who's that, Glen?"

Glen answered with some suspicion, as if it might be a trick question, "The Governor of Florida…?"

"No, no!" Mal poked the screen with a thick, stubby forefinger, "Who's *that*?"

Glen peered, gasped, recoiled from the screen to gawp at Mal as if he'd seen a ghost, "Whoa…"

"What's the date of that photograph? My eyesight…! The print's so small…"

"It says last year at the bottom there."

"So, answer me this, Glen. What's a local Vice cop from the Florida Keys doing standing no more'n six feet behind the Governor-elect on the campaign trail, all the way up in Tallahassee a year ago?"

"I can't answer that."

"No, I don't expect you to. The way to do this is to consider all the questions that come to mind and seek to establish facts connected to them. So, think, Glen. What possible explanations could there be?"

"Um…"

"Come on, Glen! You're lead reporter now. Step up. Use that brain of yours."

"Er…okay…okay…how about this? He wasn't a cop then, but he is now. Maybe he worked for the Governor, and then he left, and now he's a cop."

"Okay, there's a starting point. That's the first thing you look into. Write it down. Next?"

"Um…well…the other thing that springs to mind is that maybe he's an *undercover* cop…but that would imply there's something screwy going on in the Governor's office. Surely that's not likely?"

"Anything's possible, Glen. The longer you do this job, the more you'll realise truth is way stranger than fiction most of the time. That's your next angle. Has anyone working for the Governor in the last couple of years had reason to attract the attention of the Vice Squad?" Mal hesitated, weighed up the risk of articulating the thought uppermost in his mind, and went for it anyway, "Maybe even the Governor himself."

Glen looked positively scandalised, "Surely you can't be suggesting he's crooked or something? He seems so...so..."

"Glen, he's a politician! Don't be naïve. Anyway, all we're doing at the moment is compiling a list of hypotheses. Then, you're going to go away and test them against available evidence."

"I guess..."

"Next question?"

"He's...he's...not a cop?"

"Good man!"

"Well, what *is* he if he's not a cop?"

"*Why* are you asking *me*? Come on, Glen, think!" Oh, he *missed* her! He missed her nimble intellect, her fearlessness, her stubborn refusal to be deviated from her objective. A jolt of emotional pain walloped Mal so hard that he winced aloud. Fortunately, Glen was too absorbed to notice.

"There was something about him, right? What did you think of him, Boss?"

"I thought he was a psycho! Why, what are you driving at?"

Glen tapped a knuckle on the monitor, "He was like Action Man, wasn't he? A plastic dolly with a stick-on haircut. Just flat-out *weird*...like those guys at High School who were always straight-A students, but you knew darn well it was because they were bullying the geek to copy his homework."

Mal beamed at him in open admiration. Getting Glen to knuckle down and concentrate that butterfly mind of his was like swimming through molasses, but the boy always got there in the end, unerringly pinpointing the one detail no one else had noticed.

"Glen, that's it!"

"What's 'it'?"

"Sober suit, boring haircut, clean-shaven, deliberately invisible! Why might that be, huh?"

Glen grinned back just as wide, "Because he doesn't *want* you to remember him."

"Exactly! If he's a local cop, then I'm Oprah Winfrey!"

"Okay, then who is he?"

"Who knows? Who cares? A Fed, maybe? What matters is that he was in here lying and trying to intimidate information out of me about our girl. Either he's an undercover Fed keeping tabs on someone in the Governor's office...or..."

"Shit, or he's asking questions on the Governor's behalf!"

"Yeah, that had crossed my mind too."

"What do we do now?"

"Well, you've got your list, Glen. Start working your way through it. Don't discount anything...but remember I won't print a syllable we can't prove, all right? We don't have the financial resources to face the Governor's Office in court."

"Sure thing, Mal!"

The young man scampered from the office like a beagle after a scent. Mal slumped in his chair, trembling hands loosely gripping the edge of the desk, agile mind racing. He *couldn't* tell Glen, not yet. What they'd just brainstormed would occupy the lad for a while, eliminating their more outlandish theories and narrowing down lines of enquiry. It certainly wouldn't do any harm to ensure she'd been on the right track before her disappearance, and such low-key investigation would keep Glen out of trouble for the foreseeable future. In the meantime, Mal knew he'd have to embark upon some definitely dangerous digging of his own. If he hadn't been completely convinced of her story before, he sure was starting to believe her now.

SCARRED

When she stared down at her arms, laid flat over the tight-pulled coverlet, they were dotted with dressings, small squares of wadding taped at intervals over her skin like a human chequerboard. There was a cannula in the back of her bruised left hand, a clear tube trailing from it and looping behind her. Craning her head back against the propped pillows, she followed the tube all the way to a swollen bag of clear liquid on a hook above the bed. Squinting to determine what was being administered, she caught sight of a whiteboard on the wall. Scribbled in red marker was 'Room 5, JANE DOE'.

Jane Doe? She was a *Jane Doe*? Horrified, she tried to sit up, wriggling ineffectually within the tightly tucked confines of the bedding, slipping on the overstarched sheets. Her limbs simply wouldn't obey. Her body felt encased in concrete from neck to ankles. Attempts to lift her head off the pillows produced the same sensation as imbibing one too many Martinis. The room tipped disconcertingly and she was forced to temper the speed and violence of her movement, tugging gingerly on the blankets to release her legs, ease them slowly around, stretch her toes towards the floor. In the far-left corner of the room the bathroom door stood ajar, enabling her to see daylight outside. This room was dark, the window-blinds closed, a single anglepoise lamp spilling an inadequate circle of dim yellow light over the nightstand.

Her reaching feet found the cool linoleum. She planted them wide apart and tipped herself forwards, sliding her aching bottom off the mattress and taking full weight on unsteady legs that felt disconnected from her body. She raised her woozy head by degrees, anxious not to bring on a fainting fit, eyes focusing gradually on the room.

To her utter astonishment, in the shadow beyond the pool of insufficient light, a rangy man snored rhythmically in a plastic wing-backed chair. He wore frayed jeans, scuffed sneakers and a grubby t-shirt, so clearly wasn't a member of medical staff keeping her under observation. His tousled blonde hair needed a cut. It was too long over his ears, and the front flopped down and nearly covered his eyes. She stood stock-still, held her breath, and wondered what on earth was happening. Carving across his left cheekbone, over a severely-misshapen left ear, traversing his jawline, covering his neck and disappearing under the collar of his shirt, reappearing to circle his bicep, wind down his forearm and curl across the back of his relaxed hand where it dangled over the arm of the chair, were an unsettlingly-livid patchwork of rippling red scars from extensive burns. Nothing in his fearsome appearance, threadbare clothing or informal attitude gave her any clues as to his identity or the reason for his presence. He slouched and slept, long legs splayed across the floor, fringe falling over his eyes like a little boy's. He wore no jewellery but a wedding band and, unusually, another gold ring on the pinky finger next to it.

How had she wound up in hospital with a mysterious married man who'd clearly been unable to identify her, yet snoozed feet away as if he had every right to be here? Indefinable panic gripped her. He looked like a thug, and he was blocking her passage to the door. She couldn't move any further from the bed. Already, she could feel the cannula tugging uncomfortably, the tube pulling at full stretch from its hook to where she stood. Behind the scarred man's chair was a well-lit corridor, up and down which uniformed nurses occasionally flitted. She tried to call out to them, but no sound escaped except a clicking of the saliva in her throat. Terrified now, desperate for someone – even him – to explain what was happening, she cast about frantically, snatched up an empty plastic cup from the nightstand, and beat it repeatedly against the wood.

The scarred man started in mid-snore, jerking upright in his chair, eyes snapping open, mouth agape when he beheld her standing beside the bed in her hospital smock and bashing hell out of the nightstand for all she was worth. She stopped hitting the cupboard and stood shivering and gasping before him.

The scarred man spoke, his voice no more than a rasping whisper, like sandpaper scratching over rusting iron, "You're awake! Are you all right? Should you be standing up?"

His gentle, hazel gaze held hers. He didn't attempt to menace her. His attitude was one of cautious relief, as if he'd been awaiting this moment unconvinced it would ever arrive. She tried to ask what was happening but couldn't summon a single sound from her straining larynx. Eventually, she raised a wavering finger and pointed it unsteadily towards his face. He smiled shyly, and the frightening features were instantly transformed, "Hey. Do you remember me? Can you tell me what happened to you?"

Black spots burst and spread before her blurring vision, her body swaying alarmingly past the point of balance. The scarred man instantly sprang forward, scooped up her collapsing figure and sat her carefully onto the bed, holding her swimming head against his shoulder, whispering, "Ohhh-Kayyy… Just keep still for a little while. Don't try to do too much. You've had a rough few days as far as we can figure out. You've woken up a couple of times and been really confused. Do you remember anything about it at all?"

A whine of anguish. *No.*

"Okay. Don't get upset. Just stay still. You were all caught up in barbed wire. Do you remember *that*?"

Holy shit, the tiny squares all over her arms! She couldn't recall a *single thing…*

"I found you. You were near the beach in your wetsuit. I cut you loose. You had one heck of a head wound. You were severely dehydrated, had lost a lot of blood, were in extreme shock, and covered in bruises, all over! Your bottom and legs, your shoulder blades, the back of your head. The doctors said it was as if you'd spent a long time stuck in one position. Did you get trapped somewhere? Did you capsize a boat, lose your surfboard, get swept out to sea or something?"

Again, all she could produce by way of reaction to these revelations was that ridiculous nasal whimper like an injured puppy. Not being able to remember anything of what he'd described was distressing enough, but the inability to speak was immeasurably more disturbing. She groped around her throat and face seeking evidence of obvious injury, finding none. Her lips felt revolting, rough, scabbed and peeling. What must she look like? The tears came fast and uncontrollably then, the sobs no less intense for being virtually mute. The scarred man held and shushed her, stroking the tumbling tears off her cheeks with the pads of his big thumbs. It crossed her mind that if he was supposed to be intimidating, he was terrible at it. She clawed with frustration at the skin of her neck, "Shhh, okay…don't hurt yourself any more than you are already. Can't talk, huh?"

She shook her head furiously. The movement hurt so much her tears ceased abruptly as she closed her eyes and waited for the jolt of self-inflicted agony to pass.

Again, the low, gravelly growl, "Perhaps because you spent a long time in saltwater…or the dehydration, maybe? Hey, I'm no expert. Want me to get the nurse?"

This time, she waved her hand rather than move her head. What she wanted was for him to remain here, supporting her exhausted body in his comforting embrace, reassuring her by his mellow presence.

"How about a warm drink? A nice, milky coffee with lots of sugar? Would you like that?"

A warm drink. Yes, that would be nice. Perhaps it would lubricate her paralysed vocal chords and allow her to manage a few words? She made herself stop sniffling and upturn a grateful smile. She wondered how long he'd slept in the uncomfortable-looking chair, and what his wife thought about it.

"Are you okay to sit here while I go tell someone you're awake? Right by the Nurses Station, there's a big ol' machine that does okay coffee for a hospital. Believe me, last couple of years I've sampled enough hospital coffee to last a lifetime." He indicated the scarring, "I was in a wildfire back home. That's what screwed up my voice and made me so beautiful."

She smiled again, sympathetically touched his burnt hand with the tips of her fingers, and pointed to the bathroom and the drip.

"Need to go?"

Yes.

"Okay. I'll unhook the drip and you'll have to carry it in there with you. Sure you don't want the nurse?"

Another negative wave of the hand.

"I can see you're an independent woman." He winked, and she grinned. It was impossible not to. When you looked past the dreadful disfigurement, he was gentle, sweet and charming.

He reached over the bed with a long arm to unhook the bag and pass it to her to hold, "Shall I carry you, or you wanna walk?"

She pointed very firmly at the floor.

"Yes Ma'am. Okay, perhaps I'll support you for my own peace of mind, and we can go slowly. Happy with that?"

Thumbs up.

"Great. Arm around my waist, and I'll put my arm around yours. We'll stand up on three and just walk right on over to the bathroom like it's nothing."

It wasn't nothing. It was hard work controlling her rubbery legs, her heavy head swam, and without his support she wouldn't have made it, but make it they did, all the way to a toilet surrounded by enough grab rails to equip a retirement home. The scarred man took the drip bag from her and laid it carefully on the adjacent sill. The window stood slightly open, the warm Keys breeze blowing steadily into the little room. They looked at one another, suddenly shy. He reversed smartly towards the door, muttering, "I guess you'll be okay to do the next bit alone, right? I've just gotta tell someone you're awake and then I'll be right back. Even last night, the doctor said you might be in and out of consciousness for days more. They won't believe it when I say you're out of bed! Guess I shoulda had twenty bucks on it with him, huh?"

She shrugged and groped for the grab-handles either side of her.

"Back in a minute." He closed the door, and left her to pee in private.

****

Gage thundered down the corridor and thudded into the high counter encircling the Nurses Station. A nurse whose nametag said 'Patty' looked up at him in surprise, "Are you all right, sir?"

"Jane Doe? Room 5? Awake! I mean, *wide* awake, out of bed, and having a pee in the bathroom *right now*!"

Gage's excitement was infectious. Patty stared, momentarily thrown by the unexpected outburst, then beamed, snatched up the nearest phone, tapped in a number and replaced the receiver, "Wow, that's great news! I've just paged the duty doctor. As soon as he's down, we'll get him to come straight in and see her. How does she seem?"

"Confused…bit shaken…and she can't talk. At all."

"Really?" Patty bustled to the folder tucked in the pigeonhole labelled 5, flipped it open with a practised flick of her wrist, whipped her biro from her breast pocket with brisk efficiency, and scribbled notes as Gage talked.

"I was asleep in the chair, and then I heard this banging noise. I woke up, and there she was standing beside the bed whacking the nightstand with a cup to attract my attention."

"How long ago?"

"Five minutes...?"

"Okay...and generally?"

"Um...woozy...unsteady on her feet but very determined to walk to the bathroom. Distressed she can't talk. I asked her if she wanted a coffee to drink and she was smiling, nodding. She seems pretty alert considering she's been out of it for days. Oh, I had to unhook the drip so she could pee. I just put it on the windowsill next to the toilet."

"That's fine. How much had gone through, did you notice?"

"Half, maybe?"

"Okay," scribbling another comment, noting the time, initialling her entry in the folder, "I just have to complete this task– I won't be long – and then I'll come down and check her over before the doctor arrives. Did she want help in the bathroom?"

"No. She wanted to get on with it herself. I did ask if she wanted the nurse and she indicated not."

"Fine."

"Why do you think she can't talk?"

"That's not a question for me; that's one for the doctor…but it's likely something to do with her head injury. Does she have motor problems?"

"What…?"

"Are her limbs going all over the place like the Hippy Shake?" Patty did a demonstration that owed less to medicine and more to hip-hop, making Gage snort with mirth, "Yeah…flailing legs, waving arms…"

"It can make you do all sorts of screwy stuff if the signals between brain and body are interrupted in some way. She might have extensive swelling, bruising. As I said, the doctor can assess it and probably explain it better."

"Bet he ain't such a smooth mover, though."

Patty sniggered, reached under the desk and withdrew a battered copy of the local paper, "We've got some news for you, too. I was going to get the doctor to tell you during his regular round today, but as she's woken up already it's probably useful for you to know now. Look at this. It's from Saturday. Someone left it in the Family Room. We nearly put it in the trash! We've informed the police."

Patty pushed the paper onto the counter in front of Gage. Saturday's headline read LOCAL REPORTER STILL MISSING, and beneath it was a smiling picture of Jane…only he must stop calling her that, because her name was Kennedy McKendrick, and she'd been missing since last Tuesday night. She'd worked ten years at the paper, was their lead reporter, and had been investigating a big story with a political angle. The article heavily implied it was the reason for her disappearance. Unnerved, recalling that helpless, broken, trapped little body, Gage blurted, "Are the cops on their way?"

Patty glanced at her watch, "I reported it when I got on shift a couple of hours ago and saw the paper. They said they'd send somebody. Given she was still comatose when I made the call, I guess they didn't see much point in rushing straight over."

"But…did you read this article?" Gage whipped distractedly through its sensationalist content.

"I did, yeah."

"And you don't think she's in any danger? Doesn't this imply what happened to her was deliberate rather than an accident?"

"You can't believe everything they put in the papers! Surely all that's for the cops to figure out?"

"Yeah…I guess… I'd better get back. Can I borrow this?"

"Take it. It was going in the trash anyway."

"Thanks. Might jog her memory."

"If you need some help, call us. Press the button above the bed or holler up the hall. I'll be right down. The doctor won't be much longer…and probably neither will the cops."

"Much obliged, Ma'am."

Gage turned away, tucking the dog-eared paper under his arm and hurrying further down the corridor to the coffee machine. As he stood impatiently waiting for the partially blocked nozzle to trickle the correct measure of coffee into each cup, he was aware of darkly clad figures passing behind him. He turned hopefully, in case it was the cops arriving, but it was only two guys in suits asking directions at the Nurses Station. One of Patty's colleagues was leaning out over the counter, pointing helpfully. Gage thought no more about the men, anxious to get back in case Jane – Kennedy – needed more help in the bathroom than her pride would admit. Preoccupied with not spilling the drinks, Gage was halfway back up the hall before he noticed the two men in front of him were also making a suspiciously brisk beeline for the open door of Room 5. Watching surreptitiously, pretending to still be intent upon the coffee cups, Gage saw them pause in the doorway, peer inside, exchange a muttered word and stride off again, heads inclined toward one another as they continued down the corridor, gabbling urgently.

Gage sped up as much as he could. Anxiety knotted his belly. The skim-read text of the alarming article circled his head. The suspicious-looking men had stopped a few yards further down the corridor, backs to Gage. Faces close together, muttering, gesturing, they were clearly disagreeing over their next move. Gage suspected the girl was still in the bathroom, the room deserted, and their plan gone to hell as a result. Patty the nurse had called the cops barely two hours ago. Now, here were two guys who didn't look at all like any law enforcement he'd ever encountered, acting suspiciously right outside the room of an investigative reporter with a 'political exposé' on her to-do list? After nothing happening for days but tense and silent observation of the mysterious comatose woman in the deliberately darkened room, suddenly events were following one another with a speed too incredible to be coincidental. Either that, or he'd watched way too much Netflix.

In his worn sneakers, Gage was able to creep down the last few feet of corridor without as much as a squeak of rubber sole on linoleum floor. Eyes glued to the men, he waited until their backs were definitely turned and slipped into the darkened room. He put the coffees on the nightstand and shot across to the bathroom door, tapping urgently, "Hey, it's me. You okay?"

A nerve-jangling delay…and the door opened. She stood with a toothbrush in her hand and foam around her lips, supporting herself on the basin.

"Sorry. I got you a coffee…and you're gonna want to take a look at this." He shoved the paper at her. She took it, audibly gasping at her photograph on the front page.

"Stay in here for a minute. There's a couple of suspicious guys down the hall. I caught them hanging around the doorway here. I'm just gonna check the coast is clear. In the meantime, read that article. It's pretty full-on! It might all come flooding back. Don't come out 'til I tell you, okay?"

Nodding. Eyes flicking between his serious expression and the newspaper headline.

He pulled the door to, tiptoed to the bedside, snapped off the light, and plunged the whole room into shadow. He heard them coming back, brisk, clipped strides in their fancy shoes on the polished floor of the corridor. The bigger guy stopped outside, leaning casually against the wall like he was waiting for a bus, eyeballing the Nurses Station with limited subtlety. The shorter of the two, a wiry weasel of a man, glanced left and right and dived through the door of Room 5 straight into Gage, who stood motionless in the dimness between doorway and bed.

"Aah!" The guy recoiled as if Gage was an exhibit in a house of horrors. Gage drawled conversationally, "Kinda dark in here, ain't it? I think you might have the wrong room, buddy."

The weasel tried to dart sideways to get a look at the bed, but Gage anticipated the movement and sidestepped with him, blocking his view, "Like I said, I think you got the *wrong room*."

The guy tensed, and Gage considered his options. He couldn't yell for help. These days, all that came out of his mouth when he tried to shout was a soundless exhalation of the sort that cleaned your glasses. If the weasel went for him, he decided he'd throw both hot coffees in his face, swing as many punches as he could manage before the bigger sidekick joined the party, and hope to God someone noticed the commotion before they did to him what he was beginning to suspect they'd already done to poor Kennedy McKendrick. He squared his stance and waited for the little guy to make his move. Resolute, his scars lending him a nightmarish aura in the shaft of light spilling from the corridor, Gage projected a more formidable image than he appreciated. He was thin these days – omnipresent misery had killed most of his appetite – but he was muscular, powerful, accustomed to hard physical labour in challenging conditions, and he emitted inner strength from every pore. The weasel evidently thought better of tangling with the threatening stranger, instead scuttling from the darkness of Room 5 into the well-lit corridor, bumping hard into his loitering colleague, who span sharply around, startled.

"My bad," the little guy cocked his head towards the Nurses Station, "I thought the chick said Room 5, but I guess I heard her wrong."

Gage swaggered forward with false bravado as the two men backed away, reaching the door and grasping the handle firmly in his trembling fist, "I guess you did. Have a nice day."

He swung the door very firmly shut in the weasel's face, threw the bolt, and pelted over to the bathroom, "Kennedy? You okay? I don't know who those guys were, but I didn't like 'em! Did you sneak a look? Seen them before anywhere?"

Silence. No discernible movement on the other side of the door. Perhaps she'd fallen over and couldn't call for help?

"Kennedy, are you all right? I'm concerned about you, okay? Are you decent? I'm coming in…"

Gage pushed the handle, stepped inside, and skidded on the drip bag, which was split and leaking its contents all over the bathroom floor. The plastic tube had been violently detached, the bathroom window was wide open, and Kennedy McKendrick was gone!

TAKEN

Stomach tight with terror, Gage lurched across the slippery floor to the open window, leaning out. Four feet beneath, in the sandy soil of the recently watered shrubbery, a set of small footprints were clearly visible in the damp mud, leading diagonally in the direction of the parking lot. Gage squinted into the sun glinting blindingly off the roofs of the parked cars, spotting the slight, blonde figure in her hospital smock staggering in circles, bumping between vehicles like a pinball. Without thinking, Gage clambered after her, landing clumsily in the flowerbed. Pelting across the parking lot to catch her up, he slid his hands under her elbows to support her toppling figure. She was panicking, breath shuddering and whistling through parted lips, tears tracking her drawn cheeks, newspaper still flapping in her little fist. She whirled around as she felt his touch, instantly falling, injured brain unable to command her unstable body to react with any speed or agility. Gage caught her before she hit the tarmac, wrapping his arms around her and hissing urgently, "Kennedy, it's okay! It's only Gage. Remember me? I found you. I brought you to hospital. Do you remember?"

She didn't reply, but her bruised left hand clutched a fistful of his t-shirt and clung on determinedly. The cannula was still in the vein, the drip tube dangling a few inches of useless, stretched and severed plastic down her arm, making Gage feel mildly queasy at the sight of it.

"Did you rip that tube yourself? Kennedy, you need to be in bed. You're very sick! You can't be out here. Let me take you back inside – "

Frantic shaking of her injured head, lolling as if her neck couldn't support its weight, desperate pushing at his chest to free herself from his embrace, limbs juddering uncontrollably.

"Kennedy, please relax! It's okay. How about we just go sit in my truck for a minute? You need to rest, not get excited…"

Calming, clinging to him.

"It's right over here," Gage steered her slowly across the hot asphalt, warning, "It probably ain't great in there. I've barely been back to it since the afternoon I found you."

He unlocked it and helped her carefully inside. The footwell was littered with rubbish. The interior smelled ripe and stale. Getting in the driver's side, he used the camping pillow – still stained with her blood – to prop her head and neck so she could lean back and stretch her legs along the front bench seat.

"Comfy?" He tried an encouraging smile, took her burning bare feet into his lap, and rubbed off the mud of the flowerbed and grit of the sun-baked parking lot with his work-roughened fingers. She whimpered, slapped the paper across her lap, and smacked it with the back of her hand, as if punishing it for the disruption it had caused.

Gage patted her shin reassuringly, lifted the paper, and asked, "Can I read this again?"

A feeble nod.

"You okay? Need me to fetch somebody now?"

No answer.

"Those guys…know 'em? Seen 'em before? What made you run?"

Too weak to sit up, she instead pushed at the buckle of his belt with her reaching toes.

"Belt? The buckle? A belt buckle on one of them? The little guy? Seen it before?"

Again, just one cautious nod.

"Where?"

She waved a hand vaguely.

"Was it distinctive? I didn't notice. What did it look like?"

She hooked her thumbs together and flapped her fingers.

"A bird? Like an eagle or something? But you don't remember where you've seen it before? Don't remember their faces?"

Gage rubbed an open palm across the stubble on his chin, grunting, "Those guys looked like hoodlums to me."

He tapped his knuckles on the paper, "You read this, right? This political story your editor refers to, is there any chance you're onto something serious and you don't even know it? I mean, with the text of this article, he's implying pretty heavily that you are, isn't he? 'State significance', what does that mean? Is there a chance you told him what you knew before you hit your head and forgot it all?"

She was about to reply when he noticed her eyes focus on something behind him and widen in alarm. She pointed anxiously, the broken drip tube swinging creepily back and forth. Gage turned his head, following the path of the trembling finger.

There they were at her bathroom window, Rocky and Bullwinkle. They'd be comical if this whole situation wasn't so disturbing. Short and slight, big and fat, just like the old cartoon, their unmistakeable silhouettes peered out at the mess of jumbled footprints in the dirt, gawking left and right for a glimpse of their quarry. A few seconds of heated discussion at the open window before the two of them ducked back inside. Gage pushed the key into the ignition and started the truck's engine, "I locked the hospital room door! Didn't hold 'em long, did it? They *really* want to meet you, huh. Something tells me we're safer outta here for a coupla hours. I'll straighten it out with the staff later. I just think, right now, it's better to be where those two ain't."

****

The movement and stench of the dirty truck made her nauseous, so she rolled down the window to feel the breeze on her face, closed her eyes, and concentrated on holding her head still. The next thing she knew was waking to the scarred man scrabbling in the footwell beside her, retrieving rubbish and shoving it into a bulging plastic bag. He grinned sheepishly, "Hi. Just cleaning up the apartment to impress you. I don't have girls over a whole lot, as you can probably tell. We're at the beach! You wanna get out or do you feel unwell? Want me to just take you back to hospital?"

She tried to sit up, couldn't, and a wave of hopelessness washed over her – *can't move, can't talk, can't even remember anything about this seemingly-gentle man and why I'm here with him.*

Her face crumpled, the tears welled…and a rough palm caressed her cheek, "Shhh, don't cry, you'll make me feel bad. I'm trying my best here. Classy date in a stylish limo, romantic afternoon on the beach…? You gotta humour my pathetic efforts or I'll cry too…"

She smiled despite her frustration, gave up trying to force her body to do something it wouldn't, and flopped back onto the pillow again, eyes closed. She heard the click, thump and rustle of him fishing for something in the glove box, and felt the warmth of his body very close to hers, "I'll pick you up, and we'll just go sit in the shade and watch the ocean for a while. How does that sound?"

He could be anyone! He could be dangerous! She looked at his smiling face, his kind eyes. She trusted him. Was that foolish?

"Ready?"

Again, her thin little hand reached up and clutched at the fabric of his t-shirt.

"Bring your newspaper."

He carried her with confidence and care, placing her carefully on the sand beneath the gnarled bronze trunk of a Gumbo-Limbo tree. She sat between his bent knees, his body curving protectively around her back. He didn't seem to mind her leaning against him, and resting the weight of her unbearably heavy head in the hollow between his neck and shoulder.

"Still okay?"

A nod.

"Good. I like the beach. I'm thirty, and I'd never seen the ocean 'til a few weeks' ago! Can't get enough of it now. I'm from out West. We got prairies, forests, mountains, but no seaside."

She slid her hand across the back of his and tapped a finger onto his wedding ring.

"What?"

She tried to say, 'where's your wife', couldn't, and cast helplessly about her for a way to make him understand.

Brow furrowed, he watched her for a moment, then asked, "You want to know about my wife?"

Yes!

"Right…what sort of thing do you want me to tell you?"

She flapped the front of her hospital smock and pointed to the cannula and the squares of dressings.

"What does she think about me being in hospital with you instead of at home with her? Is she shredding all my shirts and boiling my pet rabbit as we speak?"

She grinned, rocking her hand. *Something like that.*

"She's not, you'll be relieved to know. If I had a rabbit, he'd be just fine."

He glanced down at the sand, suddenly a lot less jocular and self-assured, "I'm…widowed. The fire…"

He gestured to the terrible scars, "I got all burned-up, but I made it."

He clicked the two rings together absently as he whispered, "My wife wasn't so lucky."

His straining voice faded to nothing as his throat closed over with suppressed emotion. She couldn't move her head to look at him, but nevertheless felt his quickening breathing at her back. She slid her fingers between his and held on. It took several moments, but gradually his rapid heart rate slowed, his erratic breathing steadied, and she felt his body relax against hers once more.

She gestured around them: the tree, the sand, the ocean.

"What am I doing here?"

Yes.

"I'm on vacation, I guess, although it doesn't feel like one. My baby son died in the fire too. He was only a few days old. I've found it very hard to get over losing them both. You got any kids?"

She shook her head, swaying woozily at the movement. She might not be able to remember much, but was confident she'd recall something as significant as marriage and motherhood.

He nodded, didn't comment, continued, "To cut a very long story short, I'm so wrapped up in the past it's screwing up my chance of a future. I'm taking some time away from home to put a lid on it and learn how to move on. Not to forget them, just to convince myself life's still worth living without them in it. To see that there's a world beyond the farm gate. Running into you's done me a favour, really. It's made me quit worrying about myself, because all I've done these last few days is fret over you. It sure has kept my mind occupied."

She wondered what he'd done for her, what had dragged him to the hospital room of a stranger – that is, if they *were* strangers to one another. Oh, *why* couldn't she remember!

Grateful to him simply for providing reassurance when everything seemed so enormous and mystifying, she pulled his fist firmly against her chest, wrapped both her hands around it, and squeezed as hard as she could, trying to articulate her gratitude through that single, inadequate gesture.

He pushed his face into her hair, and whispered, "I'm okay… Thank you for giving a shit."

He rocked onto one hip and withdrew a pen and an unopened packet of postcards from the back pocket of his jeans, passing them to her, "I thought we could jot some notes about what's going on here. Might help us make sense of it. You're the journalist, so you can do the writing."

Her usual dexterity completely absent, she eventually had to pass the sealed packet back to him in defeat. He peeled it open and slid out a couple of cards, "My Momma bought these. I'm supposed to be writing home. As you can see, the whole staying-in-touch thing ain't going so well. If I don't think about home and family, then I don't think about them…Joelle, and Ryan. It's the coward's way to fix the problem, but at the moment it's all I can manage. I'm hoping eventually I'll deal with it somehow, and then I'll be able to go back. Right now, just the idea of writing a postcard to my mother scares the crap outta me."

She poked his chest.

"What? Me? My name? Again?"

Write it.

He wrote in spiky capitals: **GAGE.**

She nodded, and pushed the card into the sand beside her leg. She knew he'd already told her. She wondered how many times.

"And you're called Kennedy. It's unusual. You're the first Kennedy I've ever met. Are you named after the President?"

An exasperated exhalation.

Embarrassed, Gage retorted, "What?"

She was accustomed to writing frequently and extensively. Her usual handwriting was a breezy, looping swirl of confidently flowing prose, but what stuttered from the nib of the pen onto the white postcard took considerable effort and shocked her deeply. It didn't look like her writing at all. What it resembled was the shaky messages her long-deceased grandmother had used to put in birthday cards.

Kennedy's sense of self-worth was founded upon being an active, fit, strong, stubbornly unstoppable thirty-four-year-old woman capable of anything she set her mind to. Determined not to panic over what appeared to be a comprehensive deterioration of all her faculties, she very firmly assured herself this latest distressing aberration was as temporary as the loss of speech and, tongue protruding with concentration, scrawled: **Kennedy Space Center. Dad did Comms. Was a space nut. Frustrated astronaut.**

"Did he work at the Space Center?"

Yes.

"Wow. Have you been there?"

Yes.

"Amazing! You have a cool name, Kennedy!"

She grinned, bashfully flattered by his enthusiasm.

"So, you *can* remember your family. Is there anybody you want me to call? Someone who'll be worried about you? Mom? Dad? Boyfriend?"

It was a strange sensation to blush and well-up at the same time. She wrote: **No one to call. Dad's dead. Mom's not interested.**

"I'm sorry to hear that. No other family? Brothers and sisters? No guy going crazy waiting for you to come home?"

There's no one. I do get boyfriends sometimes, I'm not totally weird...but I can't seem to keep them for long.

"What do you do?"

Tick 'em off, I guess. Ask them, not me.

He chuckled, and teased, "How about me? Have I managed to make any impression on you yet? Got my name embedded up there now?"

Oh…no…already it was gone! It took her a beat too long to recall the card and grope for it in the sand, reddening again.

"Your short-term memory's real shot, huh."

She was too distressed to respond.

"I'm not *that* offended," he ribbed gently, indicating the newspaper and tactfully suggesting, "Just skim through that again to refresh your thoughts. Let's see what we can figure out between the two of us. Make a list. You can't remember their faces, but you do remember the little guy's belt buckle?"

What guys? Wait, a belt buckle, now that *was* familiar. An eagle…yes, she remembered that.

"You can't remember how you wound up hurt? You don't remember me finding you, or getting to hospital?"

A frown. A shake of the head.

"But you can remember your job as a reporter, your editor on this paper, your parents, your personal life, all the long-term stuff?"

Yes.

"Well, that's a start. So, *think*, Kennedy-Space-Center, what possible political story could you be investigating way down here? Corruption? Environmental damage? Something to do with fishing? What's the perennial news story? What are you always writing articles about?"

She considered, then haltingly wrote: **Tourism, Property Development, Traffic Problems, Ocean Pollution, Hurricanes...**

"Okay...so might it be something to do with misappropriation of hurricane relief money? Some kind of public-funding scandal?"

She shrugged.

"Those hoodlums *knew* you were in that hospital! The longer I think about it, the more convinced I become that if they were cops, when I got in their way back there, they would've shown me their ID and demanded I comply. Instead, they acted real suspicious and pretty incompetent. A couple of bungling heavies doing a job for the big boss like something out of a bad gangster movie! The article suggests you got a tip-off. Can you remember where from?"

A groan of defeat.

"Never mind, we'll come back to that. Add 'tip-off' to your list. Okay, according to the paper, you got a tip, you followed it up, found out somehow that the dirty dealings you'd uncovered – it unhelpfully doesn't say what they are – had a political connection. You told your editor, and vanished. It looks very much as if someone with some influence is trying to shut you up, Kennedy. They called in the heavies, who did goodness knows what to you, took you to the woods near the highway, dumped you, and expected you to die. You didn't. Instead, I found you and took you to hospital, and now whoever-it-is knows you're still alive and is trying to finish the job. *How* do they know?"

She simply stared at him, too shattered for nimble thinking.

"I've got a theory about it. The Nurse on duty saw this paper, joined the dots and called the cops…but they never showed. Instead, our two suited and booted buddies rocked up. It might be a coincidence, but…?"

Dirty Cop?

"Exactly. So is that your political story, police corruption?"

She didn't know. She couldn't remember anything! Her hands flopped heavily into her lap. She was useless!

"Hey…don't get upset. All we're doing is bouncing ideas around. Nothing says any of them are correct. Stuck at the back of your head somewhere is the answer to all this. I wonder how we shake it to the front? What worries me is, if we're right, whoever did all this to you doesn't know you can't talk and doesn't know you can't remember, so they're going to keep trying to silence you until they succeed…and if the cops are corrupt, they ain't gonna protect you!"

The nib scratched erratically across the card: **No Hospital then! Don't take me back!**

"I have to take you back."

No. Sitting duck in Hospital! Safer with you.

"Kennedy, I'm a farmer, not an action-hero! What about your medical care?"

You're overreacting! I can lie low. Rest. Recover. Remember.

"You only properly woke up a few hours ago! You've been in and out of consciousness for days… It could take weeks for you to recover from what happened to you! What if you have a relapse or a seizure, something I have no idea how to deal with?"

Safer with you than in Hospital.

"Baby, I got a dirty truck and basic first aid! I know nothing about head injuries or serious trauma! We can't even keep your cuts properly clean. No. We *have* to go back."

What about the danger? What about those guys?

"I understand…but you're in even greater danger out here. You could get a serious infection! In hospital they can care for your medical needs properly."

Her handwriting was becoming increasingly haywire, but he managed to decipher: **I'm at risk in Hospital.**

"We don't know that for sure. Everything I've suggested is hypothetical…but I admit it does all look mighty suspicious. The good thing is we spotted those idiots a mile off – they weren't exactly subtle – and that was before we were even aware you might be in danger. Now we'll be ten times more vigilant. I got rid of 'em once, I can do it again! I will do everything in my power to protect you…but *in hospital*, okay? I'm not arguing with you about this, Kennedy! We're going back."

Resigned despite her perturbation, knowing what he said made sense, she let him lift her off the sand and carry her limp body back to the truck.

As they turned onto the road again, she tugged at his sleeve and rubbed her stomach, indicating hunger.

"Really? Okay. If we see a good place, I'll stop and get us something. I guess I'm peckish too. Take-out, right? You can't exactly waltz into a restaurant dressed like that!"

He indicated the hospital smock, her dirty bare feet, the patchwork of tiny dressings. She frowned, too drained to respond, rested her head back on the pillow, and fell asleep in seconds.

When she next awoke, Gage was manoeuvring the truck into a shady parking spot a long line of parked cars down from a roadside food shack.

"Awake?"

A soft murmur that transformed into a smile as he suggested, "Lobster-tail? Fries? Still mad at me? Still think I'm overreacting?"

She wasn't sure what he was talking about.

He watched her keenly, then asked softly, "What's my name?"

She hesitated, glanced around the truck for a clue, and spotted the card sitting on top of the newspaper. She knew the word written on it was his name, but it was too far away to read. She reached for it, and his strong hand closed firmly around her wrist, preventing her, "*Without* looking at your cheat card!"

She didn't know. Tears of shame rushed into her eyes. She turned her flushed face away from him. He brushed a stray lock of hair off her cheek, reasoning gently, "You have memory loss, confusion, problems with movement. You're exhausted from what you've been through. That's why we're on our way back to hospital now. I'm not trying to be an asshole; I'm trying to look out for you!"

Touched, she reached up and cupped his scarred jaw in her hand. The skin felt papery and odd, dry and rippled under her fingertips. His eyes pleaded with her, "Still mad?"

Somehow, that was impossible.

"Buddies? Lobster-tail and fries?"

She beamed.

"I'm locking you in. For your own safety…and because I don't trust you not to run away again the moment my back is turned."

She was suddenly seized with the impulse to hug him, but he was too far away, and she couldn't sit up quickly enough to catch him before he moved, "Back in a minute. Behave yourself."

Gage fidgeted nervously in line at the popular stall, instinctively averting his unusual appearance from two cops demolishing a burger each and flirting with the long-suffering girl wiping tables. He tried not to notice how much the man behind the counter stared at his scars as he paid for the warm, deliciously aromatic parcels of food, schlepping back along the line of hot cars to the shade where he'd left his truck, unbearably boiling in his jeans. He'd put them on days ago, the air conditioning inside the hospital making him chilly as he'd sat for hours on end watching Kennedy's immobile features and praying she'd stir. Directly in front of him, another truck was turning from its roadside parking space and trying to rejoin the unceasing flow of rush-hour traffic. Gage leant wearily against the door of the parked police car and waited for the truck to move out of his way. Suddenly, the squad car's radio crackled into life and through the open window, Gage heard the horrifying intelligence that during their two-hour absence from hospital, he had effortlessly metamorphosed from Good Samaritan into ruthless kidnapper!

FUGITIVES

Gage's legs buckled and he sagged helplessly against the squad car, accidentally dropping both packets of food in the dust at his feet as the shock turned his limbs to spaghetti. As he bent shakily to retrieve them, he glanced surreptitiously back up the road towards the cops, wondering if their personal radios were on, and whether they were simultaneously hearing the details of his and Kennedy's descriptions being comprehensively relayed by the relentless voice. The cops didn't immediately leap up from the picnic table and chase him down the line of parked cars, so Gage rescued the food and hurried back to the truck, clambering in. Tossing the increasingly battered food wraps onto the seat between them, he slid his hands around the hips of the soundly sleeping Kennedy and eased her down until her body was too low to be glimpsed through the window. He couldn't perform an illegal U-turn in front of two cops, however intent they were on their snack break, so had no option but to drive right past them. Luckily, the unbroken stream of vehicles on the busy highway would mean his truck would soon be obscured by another, and another, and on and on in the ceaseless homeward-bound flow…but it only took one of them to look up from the table and spot his easily recognisable face, or notice his out-of-state licence plate. He just had to go for it. There was no alternative. As unobtrusively as he could, he inched out persistently until another driver yielded. Sedately, with barely a crunch of tyre on gravel, Gage accelerated smoothly onto the highway. The agonising creep towards the seated cops was the longest hundred yards of his life. The blood surged so loudly in his ears it even drowned out the rushing of the air past the wide-open windows. Thank God his burns were on the left-hand side of his body. If the cops glanced up, they'd just see an average-looking guy driving a boring blue truck. He simply had to hold his nerve and hope they enjoyed eating and flirting way more than fighting crime. Desperate not to attract any attention whatsoever, Gage stared fixedly ahead through the windshield. To his utter dismay, as he drew level with the shack, the cars in front suddenly began to slow, "Oh no, no, no, no, no, no…" Gage lifted reluctantly off the accelerator, whole body juddering with tension, heart hammering in fear as the truck crawled past the food stall at a maximum ten miles an hour, "Come on…keep going, just keep going…please…"

Someone up there had his back. The cars inched along torturously for over five hundred yards but never came to a complete halt, and the impatient guy in the Chevy behind was tailgating so close you'd have struggled to slide one of Momma's postcards between the fenders of their two vehicles, fortuitously concealing Gage's distinctive licence plate. He pictured Joelle interceding on his behalf, imagining her tossing her ponytail over her shoulder, parting the clouds, and demanding, 'Hey, Big-Guy, you see what's goin' on down there? Cut my husband a little slack, willya? He may be a chump, but he ain't no criminal!'

Gage dared to sneak a look in the rearview mirror. There was the shack, the tables, the line getting longer as more people decided to grab a bite on their way home and wait for the heaviest jams to clear…and the cops, still eating, still yakking, not showing the slightest inclination to conduct a high-speed pursuit. Trembling, Gage slumped in the seat and drove on robotically, paying scant attention to the road ahead, t-shirt sticking uncomfortably to the sweat on his back.

The milometer racked up another six before the traffic thinned and Gage found a place he considered safe to stop. Turning off the highway, the violent rocking of the truck across uneven ground woke Kennedy, who blinked in bewilderment. Once confident they were concealed from the road, Gage turned off the engine and sank his whirling head onto the hot steering wheel, groaning aloud. He couldn't think straight. Complete panic paralysed his brain like a cramping muscle. He thought he might throw up.

A gentle touch to the back of his bowed head.

Kennedy.

He jolted up abruptly, making her recoil in alarm and slither away from him across the seat.

"I'm in deep shit! I got the food, walked back past a parked cop car, the window was open, and the radio started going crazy! Reports of the abduction of a female patient from the hospital, a local reporter called Kennedy McKendrick. Heard of her? Some psycho's kidnapped her, apparently, in his blue Dodge, last seen on hospital CCTV leaving the parking lot in a southerly direction. My licence plate, my fucking *description*, and I don't exactly blend in, do I? I shoulda just taken you straight back inside the moment you got out that window! That's what my instinct told me to do, and yet I ignored it, and look at the goddam trouble I'm in now! I didn't kidnap you, Kennedy McKendrick. If anything, you kidnapped me!"

Rounding on her, red-faced with fury and fright, Gage sighed and relented. She looked so small and vulnerable squashed up against the door of the truck, acres of bench seat between them, mute and petrified. Why was he bothering going nuts at her when she doubtless had absolutely no idea what he was talking about? Gently, he ventured, "Kennedy, do you know where you are?"

Fear in her eyes.

"Never mind. You definitely know my name. Can you remember it?"

He detected the flicker of recognition. Her face scrunched with physical effort, panting, "Guh…?"

"Guh…? Gay…? Gage?" he prompted, trying to be patient with her, knowing she wasn't doing this on purpose.

"Yuh."

"Do you know *who* I am, *why* you're here with me?"

Slow shaking of her head.

"I'm a farmer from Wyoming. I'm on a sort of a vacation, driving around seeing a little of the country. I found you in a ditch between the beach and the highway. You were in a wetsuit. You had some real bad injuries and no ID. No one knew who you were or where you'd come from. Then, this afternoon, one of the nurses at the hospital showed me this newspaper. It says you're a reporter. There's an article written by your editor, a guy called Malcolm

Lawrence. Do you remember him? It contains allegations about the reason for your disappearance. Seems you winding up in those woods with your head caved in wasn't an accident."

Gage lifted the paper from the seat between them and pushed it into her lap. She started at the sight of her photograph on the front page and Gage was overcome by futility. Why was he bothering to explain? In an hour, this conversation would be gone the way of every other they'd had today, invisible in the impenetrable fog of her confusion.

"Your short-term memory has been affected by your head injury. We've been through this a couple of times this afternoon already, and you've forgotten."

He tried to keep the accusatory note from his voice because he knew he was being unreasonable, but couldn't help how he felt inside. He was meant to be on vacation, fixing his life instead of permanently screwing it up beyond all recognition! It was his own fault. He should simply have taken her to safety, entrusted her to medical care and got back on the road, but that small, battered, motionless body had called to him without uttering a word. He'd been unable to leave. The couple of hours he'd intended to stay, just to reassure himself she was stable and out of immediate danger, had turned into a night by her bedside, the following day, and the one after. By then, he knew he wasn't going anywhere. He couldn't contemplate abandoning her to wake alone, in a place where no one even knew her name. He'd remembered the moment his own eyes had first opened in a hospital room, daylight reflecting the panes of the opposite window into a stretched rectangle on the white ceiling above his bed.

He'd gradually been able to focus on faces, and the relief in beholding them had been profound. His brother-in-law, jaw set, standing at the foot of the bed with hands in pockets and shoulders hunched. Sitting to one side, his sister, face puffy and blotched with crying, chewing at her bottom lip until it looked red and sore. To the other, his mother, ashen with anxiety and grief. He'd read the truth in her eyes. That was when he'd known for sure. He had survived. So had the beloved group of individuals ranged around his bed...but not his wife...and not his boy. His throat had hurt so much he couldn't speak. He'd thought if he could cry that might relieve the swelling agony pressing on his heart, but try as he might to force the emotion out, all that had escaped was a tiny whimper like the whine of a dog. He didn't know then that he'd never look, sound or feel the same again. He only knew the sunlight streaming in through the window made his head ache. His eyes were quite dry, so he'd closed them, hoping they'd never reopen.

He shook his head violently, as if the motion would disrupt the vivid memory like erasing a drawing on an Etch-A-Sketch.

She was still reading feverishly, gaping in horror and amazement.

Gage picked up the shakily-scribbled postcards and placed them in her lap, "These are the notes you made on the beach about an hour ago. Do you remember that?"

She blinked in confusion.

Gage rubbed his temples in a circular motion with sweaty fingers, seeking to dispel the throbbing tension-headache.

"This is hard, Kennedy. You can't remember. You can't talk.
We're not getting anywhere…and now the cops are after me for
something I haven't done. You need to go back to hospital, but right
now I'm not sure I'm brave enough to take you. See those notes?
There's every chance this is about police corruption or something
similar. We don't know if the cops are legit or whether all this
'kidnap' crap is a stunt to get me out of the way. If you know
something you're not supposed to, and I'm safely locked in a jail
cell, they can do what they like to you and no one will be there to
cause a rumpus."

Kennedy was flicking clumsily through the postcards, consuming
their content voraciously.

She tried to speak again. Her lips formed shapes but her throat failed
to push out the sound. She gave up on talking and reached for the
cards and pen once more: **A trap?**

"The article implies you have some pretty serious evidence about
something major…but you can't remember what it is, can you?"
She fidgeted pensively and didn't answer.

"No. So, neither of us can make an informed judgement about
whether we're in genuine danger or not. All we have to go on is this
article, the state of you when I found you, and those hoodlums who
scared you so bad you ripped off your own drip-tube and climbed
out a window to escape them. Do you remember doing that?"
She turned to him, wide-eyed, hooking her thumbs together and
miming a bird.

"Yeah, a bird on the belt buckle of the smaller guy. You knew you'd
seen them before, and the mere sight of them terrified you enough to

jump out a window when you'd barely regained consciousness! My problem is how we assess the danger we're potentially in if we have no idea what we're playing with! I need information, Kennedy, and you can't provide it right now. I'm not blaming you for that, it's just a fact…and we have no idea how long you'll take to get your memory back, *if* you ever do! All we have to go on is this article, and it could be made up to sell newspapers, right?"

She considered, head cocked, then set to writing, pouting with absorption: **Mal doesn't make things up. That's not how he rolls.**

"So, you've fed him a story?"

There's a good chance of it, yes.

"How do we find out if he knows more than he's letting on?"

Ask him.

"Kennedy, get real! If he's printing salacious allegations, he's as likely to be under observation as you are! He might be next on the list for a visit from our gangster buddies. The cops are circulating the licence plate of my truck! I can't exactly chauffeur you down the freeway to your editor's place so we can cosy up and swap notes. We'll be pulled over in five seconds! Since you woke up a matter of hours ago, life's got real serious, real fast. That can't be coincidence! We've *got* to keep a low profile!"

She flapped the paper insistently: **Mal clearly has information. I've obviously told him something. I might have told him a lot more than he's printed, but he's had to hold it back because you need to prove stuff to safely put it out there.**

"How can we find out one way or another?"

I told you, talk to him.

"And I told you, that's not easy to achieve. Got a cellphone on you?"

Naked but for the hospital smock and paper panties, she scowled reproachfully at him.

Gage backed down, "Sorry, I was being facetious. I have one in the glove box there but it's flat as a pancake…and we daren't go out in public any place to plug it in and charge it up. Like I said, we gotta stay under the radar here. Checking into a Motel just to charge a cellphone isn't the most intelligent thing we can do right now. Your buddy's article implies this is huge and scandalous…there's every chance his calls are being monitored in case you get in touch. I know it sounds like something out of a spy movie, but everything's going so wrong so fast, it can't just be bad luck! You've clearly made a dangerous enemy. I'm talking the kind of person who silences a journalist by beating her senseless and dumping her body. The sort of nutjob who dispatches two thugs to a *hospital* to finish what they started. Do you see why I'm afraid?"

I'm afraid too.

"I know you want to contact your buddy, but it's not wise. What we need to do is get the hell out of the Keys. We need to put some serious distance between us and this shitstorm."

What will that do?

"Huh? It'll stop us getting arrested, killed – "

No, it won't. It won't fix anything.

"Kennedy, honey, you're not thinking straight – "

She slapped her palm flat on the seat between them, the ripped cannula tube flicking like a horsewhip. Scrawling frenziedly, the barely legible text meandering across the postcard like a trekking trail up a mountain, she admonished; Don't you 'honey' me, you patronising idiot! The way to find the answers you want is to go to the man we know has some information: Mal! I've evidently told him something. It's a start. It's all we've got.

"We can't – "

Slap! We CAN! I agree we should be cautious. I agree we're up against forces we don't understand…so we have to deal with what we know, right? We know those bad guys were at the hospital, so we should stay away from there. We also know the cops are looking for you, and we don't know if we can trust them, so we need to be secret, and vigilant. Beyond that, all I know is that if you run from things, they have a habit of following. My Dad did that. Instead of admitting he'd screwed up and trying to rebuild things with my Mom, he ran away. We ended up down here in the Keys in a crappy trailer, while he drank himself to death in the sunshine, hid from real life, and blamed everybody else for the mess we were in. I learned you can run but you can't hide. Eventually, you have to turn and face down whatever's after you, regardless of whether the demon's in your head or at your back. If you don't, it never leaves you.

Unnerved, Gage whined, "Kennedy, I'm a farmer. I'm not some superhero special agent! I can't fly by the seat of my pants like this! I'm also not a doctor. I can't take care of you."

Her shrewd blue eyes fixed upon his: And yet that's exactly what you are doing. By what you've said, you saved my life. I'm only sorry I can't remember.

"I don't think you'd want to remember. It wasn't nice. I…I just happened to find you…" Gage was blushing increasingly beetroot under the intensity of her disarming gaze. He felt like a coward and a fool.

Kennedy was still writing, concentrating intently like a second grader: I'm sorry you've been dragged into whatever's going on here. I know it's a lot to ask after all you've done already, but please can you get me to Mal? Then, if you want to leave the Keys, that's up to you. Please just help me contact him. Help me get there so I can solve this mystery and fix this mess and I'll never ask anything else of you ever again. Despite my stupid memory, I promise I will never forget it. The faster we can get to Mal, the sooner you'll be free of me forever. Please, Gage The Farmer. I can't do this without you. Please.

THE WANTED MAN

The derelict cabin in which they chose to hide had perhaps once been someone's vacation home. Nestled on a private plot, damaged by hurricane and flood, it was now abandoned to the elements. The garden was choked with overgrown planting and debris swept in on the highest storm-surges: broken spars of wooden decking, snapped tree branches, sections of torn fencing, plastic patio furniture, oil drums spotted with saltwater corrosion, and numerous lengths of ripped rope still connected to round polystyrene sailing floats, sun-baked and crumbling like wheels of maturing cheese nibbled by armies of rodents. The most striking addition was an upended speedboat balanced between the trees like a monolith, bow pointing skyward, a huge hole smashed in its fibreglass hull, through which the regenerating vegetation already sprouted.

Rotten, roofless, with broken windows and collapsing superstructure, other desperate humans had nevertheless taken refuge in the cabin as they were doing. Empty liquor bottles and food packets littered the leaf-strewn floors. Some furniture remained. Rattan chairs and wooden bookshelves black with mildew, and one room sporting a rusting iron bedstead in its centre. Gage yanked a fallen palm frond from the jungle of undergrowth nearest the door. Its dry foliage rustling stiffly, he wielded it vigorously like a broom, pushing the vile detritus of food waste, beer cans and wrinkled condoms to the edges of the room, a grimace on his face, "Gross."

He glanced across at Kennedy, who was subsiding wearily against a wall, on the verge of physical collapse.

He shot outside, frantically tugging and freeing further interwoven fronds, dragging them through the narrow doorway and flattening them as best he could across the cleared floor to create improvised rush-matting.

Kennedy pointed weakly at the ground.

"Hold on. Two more seconds." Gage pelted to the truck and returned promptly with two thick blankets, laying them on top of his rudimentary palm-leaf mat, "These stink some, but I'd still rather sit on them than that." He indicated the swept pile of vileness in the corner with disgust, and supported Kennedy's unsteady passage across the room to their makeshift camp, gently lowering her onto the blanket and sliding the grimy pillow under her spinning head.

"Once it gets dark, I'll make a fire. The smoke won't be so noticeable then."

Her eyes were already closing. Gage shook her awake, pushing the food parcel under her nose, "Eat this before you fall asleep. We've had nothing all day. If we're on the run, we need to keep our strength up."

She ate lying on her back, staring glassily at the sky where the ceiling should have been, watching it turn from bright blue to deep pink, milky rose and dusty grey as the evening light faded. She was glad of the food, and the lukewarm lobster and soggy fries tasted better than she'd expected them to. Staying awake to eat consumed all her remaining strength. Eyes closed, she heard Gage bustling back and forth, bringing in fuel and setting the fire, her nostrils detecting the sharp scent of the first burning twigs as the flames caught and blossomed. She was aware of his body next to hers on the mat, and the rustling of the foil packet as he unwrapped and consumed his own meal. She supposed she must have drifted, as she remembered nothing for a while until she sensed the weight of the second rug being laid over her, "Sorry about the smell. I never noticed until I got away from home how much everything I own reeks of horse."

She managed a dreamy half-smile in response, and he laid a warm hand on her forehead as if administering a blessing, "Just rest now. We'll figure out how deep in the shit we are tomorrow."

Gage boiled his camping kettle, made himself a coffee, envied her seemingly serene sleep, then tamped down the glowing fire, curled his body to hers and, despite his disquiet, succumbed speedily to uneasy slumber of his own, strong fingers gripping the cool metal of the loaded shotgun resting across his hip.

****

Violent branch-cracking in the tree canopy directly above woke Gage with a start, and had him scrabbling to his knees and jamming the butt of the shotgun into his shoulder, whipping around to face the door, convinced a ring of gun-toting cops had just busted through it! When he realised what it was – a bird, only a bird – he wilted with relief, trembling hands placing the gun on the floor beside him with exaggerated care. He needed to calm down or he was going to wind up shooting something out of unhinged panic.

He turned to Kennedy. She breathed deeply, still sound asleep, exhausted by the toll this ordeal was taking on her damaged body. He lifted her nearest skinny wrist and checked her pulse, finding it steady and strong despite all she'd endured. She was a survivor, no question. An indomitable character with unquenchable spirit. Gage re-covered her solicitously with the dislodged blanket and stepped softly to the barricaded door, sliding aside the rotting armchair he'd placed across it, peering cautiously out. Coast clear, beach and sea deserted, he stumbled outside and peed lengthily against the side of the house. He turned to face the rising sun as it peeked over the horizon, shooting its first fingers of glittering light across the calm dawn water.

The world looked the same. The flitting birds still called. Gentle waves still lapped the sandy shore. The eternal Florida sun still shone. Had yesterday even *happened*?

Dawn advanced and Gage simply stared, slack-jawed and stultified, suddenly picturing his long-dead father appearing before him on the empty beach, playfully slapping his fingers down on the brim of Gage's hat so it dropped over his teenage eyes and startled him from his troubled reverie, chuckling and counselling, "The way to fix a worry, son, is to give your hands a head start, and let your head catch up once it's good and ready."

Dad had been a straightforward, pragmatic man who invariably knew what to do for the best. Shelve the problem, get working, and suddenly the answer you'd been seeking would appear, like clearing a rock fall on a mountain pass. It never failed. Gage took the advice, got busy, and hoped his unquiet mind would settle.

Tiptoeing back inside with an armful of fuel, he reinvigorated the campfire, put on a kettle for coffee, another pan for washing, and concentrated on Kennedy's peaceful expression as he waited for both to boil. How much of yesterday would she remember?

If she had no memory of her desperate plea for his help, should he seize the opportunity to bluff her and just get them both out of Florida as fast as he could? Even contemplating it made him feel grubby. The idea of betraying her trust left a worse taste in his mouth than the stale saliva of yesterday's lobster-tail. He must do right by her, because that's what he'd promised last night. Despite her injuries and fuddled confusion, Kennedy's spirit was staunch and her reasoning sound. He didn't agree with what she wanted to do, but he respected her bravery. He even grudgingly admired her obduracy too. Pride wouldn't allow him to reveal the extent of his own foreboding, and so their decision was made. He would remain for as long as it took to reach Malcolm Lawrence, the man who might have all the answers, even though it meant they had to stick around here a lot longer than he was comfortable with – wanted by the cops, hunted by the bad guys – until they could get close enough to make undetected contact. Following the publication of his article, it was naïve not to assume Mal was now a person of interest to all sides, and doubtless under close observation. How could they *possibly* get near him? Gage groaned inwardly. He was ignoring his own remedy for mental distress! The water was already boiling merrily. Gage quickly made himself a coffee, gingerly lifted the second pan off the heat and carried it carefully. Jobs first and thinking later, when Kennedy awoke.

Outside, he uncovered the truck he'd camouflaged with broken branches and fallen palm leaves, riffled through his stuff for clean clothes, stood in the sand by the open truck doors, and strip-washed his sweaty, grime-caked body in the welcome hot water. Feeling fresher and more comfortable, he chomped a couple of cereal bars from his food stash, chugged down his cooling coffee, brushed his teeth, and devoted effort to cleaning out the vile interior of the truck, returning his belongings to some semblance of order instead of simply tossing everything from dirty underwear to spent beer cans over his shoulder into the back seat to add to the tumbled chaos. Personal grooming, cleanliness and pride in himself hadn't really mattered much since the fire, but he didn't want Kennedy thinking he was a slob. It was rather nice to suddenly feel embarrassed again. It meant he *cared*.

He sat in the front seat and tried to tune the radio to a local station. Eventually, he found a breakfast show and waited for the 5.30am news broadcast. There was one mention, almost in passing, regarding the possible abduction of a newspaper reporter from a local hospital…and no detail on his physical description, vehicle or licence plate like there'd been on the police transmission. Not too bad. That meant he only had to watch out for cops. No one else would be looking for him or his truck. Kennedy, however, was a more complicated problem. Dotted with dressings, that revolting, flapping cannula tube still in the back of her hand, and clothed only in a filthy hospital smock. He searched his clean belongings and found a t-shirt he hardly wore because it was too small, and a pair of shorts that were a little snug in the waistband for comfort. He had no underwear suitable for a woman, of course, but at least they could ditch the horrible smock. Gage flicked off the radio, re-camouflaged the truck, gathered up his carefully selected bundle, the half-empty pail of warm water, and went to wake Kennedy with renewed purpose in his long-legged stride.

****

The delighted beam of recognition when she opened her eyes and beheld him was as encouraging as it was enchanting. Of course, she immediately tried to speak, a faint *Guh* noise emanated from her throat.

"You talking?"

Gage agitated the fire and put the kettle back on the heat. She smiled and strained to push out more sound, pointing at him, "Guh. Guh."

"You remembered! Zero prompting!"

Unexpectedly overcome by a surge of emotion, Gage glanced away, coughing and sniffing self-consciously, fussing unnecessarily over the fire until the incomprehensible moment passed. Why should he care whether she recalled his name or not? It made little difference to their predicament. He poured her a coffee, helped her sit up, and gave her two of the cereal bars from his dwindling food supply.

"Can you remember yesterday? The problem with the cops and everything?"

She waggled her hand. *Some.*

"I'll go over it all again – what happened, what we've decided – but first we need to get you a little more sorted. Number one, *that's* coming out!"

He pointed at the cannula. She frowned, grimaced, and shook her head firmly.

"Kennedy, it's a highway for bacterial infection! Besides, flapping around, it makes my stomach turn. It's coming out."

She clapped her other hand over the top of it.

"Leave that in there, live like this for much longer, and you'll have septicaemia within the week! It won't matter who's after us, and why, and whether you've got a big, exciting story to tell the world, because you'll be dead from blood poisoning!"

She glared venomously at him but Gage feigned indifference, all the while preparing a dressing from his rudimentary first-aid kit. He gave her time to mull it over, topping up the washing pail with fresh hot water from the kettle.

"What we doin', Kennedy? You growin' a pair?"

She was about to react angrily, before beholding the twinkle in his eye and throwing her food-wrapper at him instead.

He eased her gently back onto the rug, "Lie down in case this makes you feel funny…and don't watch me do it. *I'm* sure gonna keep my eyes shut the whole time!"

She thumped him good-naturedly on the shoulder, and Gage took immense heart from the surprising strength behind the swipe. Rigid with tension, very deliberately averting her eyes and bunching the blanket in her other fist, she surrendered to the unavoidable.

Gage extracted the tube from her hand with one sharp and highly unprofessional yank, and pressed the prepared dressing onto the wound as hard as he was able, ignoring her whimpers of discomfort, wrapping the bandage as tight as possible to maintain pressure and staunch any blood flow. He tossed the vile tube onto the fire, where it swiftly began to melt and drip blue plastic onto the red-hot embers. "It's done. You okay?"

A wan smile.

"You did good. Smarts, huh?"

"Yuh."

"Sorry. Like I said yesterday, I'm no doctor."

She patted his knee, smiled again, and asked for help to sit up, "Pih."

"Say again?"

"Pih. Pih!"

"Pih? P-something? Pee!"

"Yuh."

"Need to go now?"

"Yuh."

"I peed outside, but I guess you won't want to do that. How about the other room? We ain't exactly going to hang out in there. You could hold onto that bed frame."

"Yuh."

"Okay. Come on."

Gage helped her to what must once have been a pleasant bedroom with a sea view, and chivalrously turned his back so she could urinate, then returned her to their mat and spread out the items from his bundle.

"Priority is that you stay clean and infection-free, because we have no medicine and no knowledge of what to do. So, we have to do our best to keep your cuts covered and clean until they're healed. Here's warm water. Use anything in my washbag. There's a clean-ish flannel in there, and a new toothbrush in its packaging – you have that. They're now giving out the report of your abduction on the local news, so we need to make you look as little like an escaped patient as possible. That means losing that smock. These are my smallest t-shirt and tightest pair of shorts. They're clean. You need to get out of the smock, have a really thorough wash, and put this stuff on, okay?"

"Nnnoww?"

Gage grinned, "Don't worry, I ain't gonna supervise! I'll go outside. You bang the spoon on the kettle when you're done, and then we need to figure out how we're going to contact this editor of yours without getting nabbed by the cops or the bad guys. Sit and read that paper again, and all those notes. You'll realise we can't just rock up at his front door and expect no one to be watching or waiting for us. We need a proper plan of action."

When he was summoned back inside, he found her leaning against one wall trying to wash her filthy feet in the pail. She'd tied the t-shirt in a knot around her waist, but it was still enormous, the sleeves flapping halfway down her forearms like a Japanese kimono. The shorts barely clung on at her hips, an expanse of hospital-issue paper panty puffing out above the waistband. On Kennedy, the legs of the shorts resembled culottes, finishing mid-calf. Gage couldn't help but chuckle at the sight, "Uh-oh, it's all way too big! That outfit's almost as obvious as leaving you in the smock. Before we do anything else, we need to get you some clothes."

"Yuh."

"Here, these are my thickest socks. Double them over and wear them like shoes. They'll protect your feet a bit. Feel fresher?"

She pushed a hand into matted locks that had been cursorily washed by the nurses but were far from clean. Gage took another bandage from the kit, cut off a section with his penknife, and Kennedy looped it around her hair, pulling to make a ponytail.

"Do for now?"

"Yuh."

"Right. We need to move on, Kennedy. We shouldn't stay in one place too long."

Gage squatted before the fire, rolled up the discarded smock, pushed it onto the hottest embers, and pressed it down. The synthetic material caught instantly, flaring quickly, then melting and singeing subtly with a blueish flame, edges blackening and crisping like burning toast. Once confident the energy of the blaze was spent, Gage gathered up their belongings and repacked the truck, returning to scoop Kennedy up with ease as she wobbled towards the door, carrying her outside and turning her towards the risen sun, "A lovely day to be on the run!"

She lifted her face to the increasing warmth of the powerful rays, and waggled his damaged earlobe affectionately, a teasing admonition for his flippancy.

He beamed. His ear tingled deliciously where she'd tickled it. He thought he might never wash that bit of himself again.

He stood her carefully on the sand by the passenger door of the truck. She climbed inside with more agility than he'd expected. Encouraged by this morning's apparent progress, he swiftly got into the driver's side, started the engine, and turned to her, "Right, clothes! We'll stop at the first decent place we see. I'll go in and get you whatever I can, and then we'll find somewhere new to hunker down and plan our covert approach to your buddy."

She jabbed her own chest with a proprietorial forefinger.

"You, shopping? Be serious! Look at you!"

She jutted her chin in defiance.

"No! You look like a person who climbed out a hospital window and spent the night in a pile of trash! You *cannot* go in a store, particularly not dressed like that. You need to tell me your size and I'll go in. Right now, I look the less freaky of the two of us. You'll just have to wear whatever I get and not complain if it doesn't match."

Suppose...

"I'm sorry. I know you'd probably much rather pick, but it's too risky. You can barely talk. You're still real unsteady on your feet. You've got bandages all over...and your outfit is hideous!"

She signed resignedly, grinned weakly, and rubbed her forehead with her bandaged hand.

"Headache?"

"Yuh."

"Lie down." Gage shoved the blood-stained camping pillow inside another of his clean t-shirts, "Here, lie flat. Put your feet in my lap if you want. Rest your head on this. Just relax. Sleep some more if you need to. I'll wake you up when I find a safe place to camp. You should probably stay out of sight when I'm in the clothes store anyway. You're so much more alert than yesterday, but you shouldn't overdo it."

"Guh."

"What?"

"Thunk."

"Don't rush to 'thunk' me. We're still in as much trouble as we were last night."

She sniggered, the air whistling out of her nose as it wrinkled with the soundless laughter. It made Gage grin despite his apprehension. "Go to sleep now."

Too early for shoppers but past the commuter rush-hour, his eyes roamed constantly from mirrors to windshield and back again, scanning the quiet road for anything that looked remotely like a cop car. He stopped at the first roadside clothing store they came to, encouraged because one window contained mannequins in lingerie, and the other, models in various summer outfits. He could do it all in one stop. Parking parallel with the road so the truck was less noticeable, he reversed tight up to a trash can, hiding the licence plate. He cut the engine and shook Kennedy awake, shoving a postcard at her.

"I'm at a store that looks like it's got everything. Write down your sizes for underwear, clothes and shoes. I'll get whatever I can."

She passed back the card. Gage squinted at the haywire scribble, "You were writing more clearly yesterday."

She held the bandaged hand over her eyes as if the sun was too bright. Gage thought of the darkened hospital room, reached for a towel from the back, and put it across her face.

"Headache bad, right?"

A groan from under the towel.

"Just sleep. I won't be long."

He got out of the truck, locked her in, and strolled into the store with the assumed nonchalance of the wanted man.

****

As the deserted parking lot suggested, the small store was empty but for the assistant, who was busy undoing boxes in the stockroom and hooking new garments onto hangers ready for display. As he opened the door, it hit and pinged a small bell, making her look around, "Well, hello there! Do you need any help, or are you happy to browse?"

Gage calculated speedily. It would be preferable to help himself, take his selections to the counter, pay his cash, and spend as little time as possible interacting with this woman, but he'd never bought ladies' clothes in his life. If Joelle had ever wanted anything, she'd asked him for the money and got it herself. As for lingerie, he had no idea where to start! The more time the truck spent parked at the side of the highway, the greater the chance of a cop cruising past and spotting it. He'd be quicker if he asked the woman to help him. Gage steeled himself for the usual involuntary reaction when a stranger caught sight of his scars, smiled as sweetly as he was able, and growled huskily, "If you wouldn't mind helping me, Ma'am, I'd be so grateful. A friend of mine is very ill, she's staying at our place while she recuperates, and my wife's sent me out to get some basics to tide her over. She lost everything in the last hurricane. She's not well enough to go shopping for herself yet, but I've no idea what to

110

get. I was hoping you could choose for me. She needs underwear, shoes, clothes. If I tell you her sizes, can you…um…rescue me, Ma'am?"

Gage gave it his all, puppy-dog eyes, boyish grin, trying to flex every muscle he had at the same time until he feared he'd either fart or faint with the effort. It had used to work, before he was married, before the fire took everything from his looks to his confidence. The intervening years rolled effortlessly away as the middle-aged woman melted, simpering, fiddling with her hair and fumbling with the hangers as she selected suitable items. When he had several sets of clothes and lingerie, sneakers, flip-flops, a hairbrush, and two of the large, elastic loops Joelle had favoured to tie up her hair, Gage beamed his satisfaction, profusely thanked his new best friend Lorelei for her patient assistance, and suggested he'd better get home before his wife thought he'd left her for another woman. He winked, and Lorelei giggled and blushed. Ringing up the sale, she kept sneaking shy glances at him from beneath lashes over-clogged with dark mascara. Gage made sure to lean on the counter with his right elbow – to display only the undamaged side of his face – smile as suggestively as he could, and look her up and down openly as if she was the best thing he'd seen all week, while inside his head screamed, 'Come *on*! How long does it *take*, goddamit?!'

A retro-style radio sat on a high shelf behind the counter, tuned to the same station Gage had heard this morning. There were a few inane commercials, the odd banal interjection from the idiot DJ, and a combination of old favourites and new hits to while away the working day. Gage had been dimly aware of it throughout his time in the shop, but hadn't paid much attention, just more white noise encroaching upon his world of worry. As his new conquest painstakingly removed each item from its hanger, typed its price into her old-fashioned cash-register pretending she didn't need the glasses resting in her dyed hair, then folded them with overly-considerate care and slid them individually into a large paper bag with twine handles, Gage was resisting the urge to look over his shoulder and check the truck. He didn't want to draw attention to it. As the woman bustled in back to find the boxed sneakers rather than the display pair, Gage's wandering attention was recaptured by horrifyingly familiar words emanating from the radio.

'...removed her from hospital without the consent of the medical team caring for her extensive injuries. It is unclear whether Ms McKendrick left willingly or under duress. Police would urgently like to trace this man. CCTV footage and statements from hospital staff describe him as over six feet tall, of lean build, with fair hair. He was last seen driving a light blue Dodge Ram with Wyoming licence plates. The left-hand side of his face, his neck, and left arm are described as 'extensively scarred'. Members of the public with any information are asked to call the Monroe County Sherriff on 305-664..."

Lorelei, on her knees in the stockroom edging out the correct shoe box, heard this too, and was unable to suppress an unintentional squeak of alarm. Mind racing, she turned to see if the man had noticed, and screamed aloud as she found him filling the stockroom doorway.

OUT-OF-STATE PLATES

This was it. This was how it ended. The horrors in the paper that you tutted over as you ate your breakfast. The things that only happened to other people were about to happen to *her*! Strangled by a psycho when all she'd been trying to do was turn an honest buck since that asshole Vinny split and took their savings with him. Throat tight with trepidation, she managed to croak, "Please…"

Grim-faced, the psycho wrenched the 'phone off the wall, tugging the cable clean out of the plaster. Petrified, Lorelei tried to cry quietly, desperate not to incite him to greater violence.

In his low, rasping whisper, he demanded, "Got a cellphone on you?"

She hesitated. He took a step closer, "Don't make me search you, Lorelei."

She took it from her back pocket and held it out, body shaking uncontrollably. He took it without touching her, tossing it onto the floor and stamping on it expressionlessly until the screen shattered and the case cracked. He pointed to the shoebox at her feet, "Are those the right ones?"

She nodded, mute with terror.

"Kick 'em over."

She pushed her pump against the shoe box, and it skidded along the laminate to stop at his feet. Eyes never leaving her face, he bent and retrieved it. Tucking the box under his arm, he reached into his pocket for his wallet, took out three $50 bills, placed them atop the nearest box, and whispered, "Believe me, Lorelei, it's not how it looks. Please can you go sit right up in the corner."

She complied, struggling down onto the cold floor, back to the wall, knees drawn up close to her chest, arms wrapped protectively around them. She looked up imploringly. He frowned, sorrow in his eyes, and jerked a thumb at the cash, "I hope that covers it. Thank you for your help, Ma'am."

Gage shot out of the stock room before she had time to get to her feet and follow him, slamming the door and wedging a chair under the handle to delay her escape. He snatched the paper bag of clothes off the counter and pelted from the store, flipping the sign on the door from OPEN to CLOSED as he passed it. He dived into the truck, tossed bag and shoebox into the footwell, and left the parking lot like he was in a Hollywood car chase, pulling out across the path of another car and forcing it to swerve sharply. The truck's violent motion almost rolled the sleeping Kennedy off the seat onto the floor. Gage made a frantic grab for the fat knot in the t-shirt and hauled her back, panting, "Wake up! Wake up *now*! We're in even deeper shit than we were before! I've got to talk to you! Wake up! Sit up!"

Kennedy struggled upright, clinging to the headrest as Gage sped up the road too fast, weaving about dangerously in the lane. Some cars honked at his road position. Other drivers made hand gestures or simply stared. Upon first waking, she still found lucid thought an immense struggle, as if her brain was a seized engine that wouldn't turn over, but she did know they were supposed to be keeping a low profile. Not understanding what had sparked his distress, Kennedy nevertheless comprehended they were attracting negative attention. She groped groggily across the bench seat to Gage's side and pointed at the fifty marker on the speedo. She indicated all the other drivers staring back at them. It sank in. He nodded, dropped back to a normal speed, but still writhed in his seat as if in the grip of demonic possession, eyes rolling left to right from mirrors to windshield, bulging with fright. Kennedy touched his arm lightly, and he jumped as if she'd slapped him. She made the sign for time-out.

"Are you crazy? We need to get away from that store! She *knows*! The woman behind the counter knows! I had to shut her in the stockroom! I trashed her 'phones! They're giving out my description on local radio, Kennedy! The truck. The licence plate. My *face*! I can dump the truck if I have to, but I can't dump my goddam face, no matter how much I might want to. I got the most recognisable face in Florida! This is *over*, Kennedy! I can't do this. It's only a matter of time…"

Again, she signed to stop.

"You're nuts; you know that? We've got to get away from that store!"

A shove of his shoulder. *Stop, and stop now.*

"Where?"

A down-at-heel collection of stalls, bars, restaurants and on-water activities was approaching on the right-hand side. Kennedy pointed.

"It's like you *want* to get caught! If you're changing your mind about this now, after all you've put me through! I told you I wasn't the guy for this job, but you insisted – "

Three sharp whacks with her open palm on the dash. *Stop! There! NOW!*

"Who the hell put you in charge?"

She bared her teeth and exhaled an approximation of a roar of frustration, forming a fist with her bandaged hand, thumping his thigh as hard as she could and yanking the wheel, making the truck lurch sideways, "Ow! Jesus, what are you doing, trying to roll us over? Okay, okay, I'm stopping, all right?"

He slowed, indicated as if nothing untoward had occurred – glancing in the mirror in time to see the driver behind shaking his head at their erratic behaviour – and rolled unassumingly into the dirt lot. Out of season, a smattering of cars still dotted it, but it was too early in the day for most of the food stands and bars. The parking lot was concealed from the highway by stands of tall trees with long, weeping branches, trailing foliage fluttering in the warm breeze. Gage reversed into a space to the rear of the lot, turned off the engine and rounded upon Kennedy, "Well? What now, Brains?"

She threw up her hands in frustration, pointing agitatedly back up the highway. He needed to tell her what was going on before she blew a blood vessel.

Gage wiped a hot palm down his sweating face and swung the bag of shopping onto the seat between them.

"I got your clothes! It was all going fine. I told her your sizes, she picked stuff out, I went to pay, and while she was in back getting your new sneakers, I suddenly heard your name on the radio! Local news was playing, and they started giving out details they hadn't said before. The truck, the plate…and then *me*. Height, build, hair colour…oh, and looks like Freddy Krueger on a bad day. They were giving out the local Sherriff's number for people to call if they'd seen anything! She clocked it, and then I knew I had to do something, fast. I got around the counter and into the stock room before she saw me coming, and pulled the 'phone out of the wall. That scared her pretty bad. I asked her to hand over her cell. I stamped on it, wrecked it! I put $150 on the side to cover the stuff in the bag – so I didn't exactly steal it – and I told her to sit on the floor as far away from the door as possible. I told her I was sorry, that it wasn't how it looked, and then I ran for it! I wedged a chair under the door handle so she'd struggle to get out, but as soon as she does, she's calling the cops…and yet you want to sit here, half a mile away from the scene of my latest misdemeanour – committed for *your* benefit once again – and dish about how I've spent my morning? We need to get *away*, Kennedy!"

"No!"

She reached into the glove box for the postcards, shaking the packet so several fell out onto the seat between them, snatching one up and scrawling: **Hide in plain sight. You were last seen speeding down the highway. No one will expect you to have stopped so close by. We're shielded from the road here. I just need a moment to get my head in gear. We need to think, not panic!**

"That's easy for you to say! You're not a kidnapper, and a…a…"

Kennedy, rummaging through the contents of the bag, smirked, and teasingly wrote: **A man who pays double what his shopping's worth?**

"Does nothing scare you?"

Plenty scares me…but living like this forever scares me more. I want my mind back, Gage. I used to be sharp! I used to be able to think my way out of anything…and now it takes me ten minutes to remember who I am, and who you are, and what the hell is happening. If I didn't have this newspaper and these cards to read, I'd be totally screwed. I hate feeling like this. I want it to stop – do you understand?

She slid across the seat until her body was inches from his, cupping his hot face in her cool little palms. The bandage on her left hand caught abrasively on his stubble.

"You remembered my name again without your cheat-card."

Her eyes bored unblinkingly into his. Gage held his breath, as if that would freeze the moment in time. It didn't, of course. She released him promptly to write again, but remained close enough for her shoulder to rub against his bicep.

Calm down. Think straight, because I'm finding it difficult to do that. I need you to do it for me. What will the cops see first if they spot us?

"The truck..? The licence plate..?"

So, we need a new truck.

"No problem! Why didn't you say so before? Wait right here, I'll just go buy one."

She rolled her eyes in annoyance at his petulant sarcasm.

Steal one.

"Hell, yeah! Why not? We'll just add it to the charge sheet!"

You haven't committed any crimes…except maybe locking a scared lady in a stock room. Gage, I need you to keep your head, because I get confused. I need you to be reliable.

"I warned you I don't have the life-experience for this."

Can you break into a truck? Can you start it without the key?

"No, of course I can't! What do you take me for?"

Shit. I can't either.

"See? We're screwed! We can't abandon the truck and continue on foot. We need transport…and this truck is packed with stuff that could help us out. I got water back there, a little food stash, lots of really useful camping equipment. If it comes to it, I got a shotgun too! Having a truck is a lifeline for us."

But we don't know how to steal one.

"No, we don't. So we're stuck with this one that the whole world's looking for, or nothing."

Gage flopped forward, elbows on the steering wheel, head in his hands, staring despairingly out through the windshield, mind a morass of confusion and dread…until…

"Hold on a second…! Look. One Dodge…two…three… Same model…all right here in this little parking lot!"

Why so many of the same?

"They're a real common truck."

Isn't that good? Needle in a haystack?

Gage smacked the steering wheel triumphantly with the heel of his hand, "It sure is, baby! I've had an idea…we don't swap the truck, we swap the *plates*. The cops are looking for a Wyoming plate, not a Florida one."

Right…so we have a plan?

"Yeah, maybe we do…"

Gage unclipped his multitool from his keyring, "Get out of the truck. You're my lookout."

As she struggled the door open and slithered off the high seat, Gage popped the hood, lifted and propped it, "Someone comes, slam the hood, got it?"

"Yuh."

He hurried round to the back of the truck, emerging seconds later with the distinctive Wyoming plate of the saddle bronc rider in his hand, "Ready to do this?"

"Yuh."

"I'm relying on you because I won't be able to watch."

Gage strolled casually over to the nearest truck, circled behind it, and came out shaking his head, mouthing, "Georgia."

He trotted to the next and ducked behind that instead. Suddenly, Kennedy noticed a retired couple turn down their line of cars and start walking directly towards where Gage was hiding! Alarmed, she stretched to unhook the arm that supported the hood, and was horrified to realise she couldn't reach it, even on tiptoe! She tried climbing onto the front fender without attracting too much attention, but hadn't yet recovered sufficient strength or balance. Unable to quickly think of another way to warn Gage short of sounding the horn, which was surely a last resort, she edged back down the side of the truck, out of sight of the couple, and waited to see where they'd go, praying their car wasn't a blue Dodge with Florida plates and a large, scarred cowboy squatting behind it with a screwdriver. Suddenly, the woman became very animated, pointing urgently towards the rear of the Dodge, squawking something at her husband that Kennedy couldn't make out. Mired in indecision, Kennedy was torn between remaining in hiding and creating some sort of diversion to give Gage time to escape. The husband, marching moodily ahead, walked the few steps back to his gesticulating wife. Kennedy watched their hot-tempered exchange, which contained a lot of aggressive body-language and plenty of frantic gesturing in Gage's direction. Decided, Kennedy edged open the passenger door of the truck and wriggled across the seat. She needed to start the ignition to sound the horn. Her reaching fingers fumbled under the steering column…where the hell were the keys? Gage must've taken them with him out of habit. They were probably in his pocket right now! She couldn't warn him!

Reversing back out of the truck, Kennedy dropped to hands and knees and crawled forward through the dust, trying to ignore how dirty her bandage was getting.

She peeked cautiously around the front of the truck. The couple were five cars away from Gage, woman pointing, husband glowering. Eventually, her argument won the day and he advanced towards the rear of the Dodge with set jaw and determined stride, as if preparing for a confrontation.

The husband walked right up to the truck, squeezed between it and the next-door vehicle, and strode around to the rear.

Sick with terror, Kennedy had absolutely no idea what to do.

A heart-thudding millisecond of suspense, and there he was. As the husband's footfalls crunched up one side of the truck, so Gage's sneakers tiptoed down the other at a stooping crouch, squatting behind the truck's long hood, level with the tyre so his feet couldn't be seen beneath the vehicle. He mouthed, "What's happening?" She frantically signalled him to keep still.

He nodded and lifted his t-shirt. Tucked into the waistband of his shorts was a 'Sunshine State' plate! Half-way there. At least he'd offloaded the dangerous out-of-state plate onto some other unsuspecting innocent. However, had the old guy's wife seen him do it?

The seconds ticked torturously away. Kennedy watched the husband's head at the rear of the truck. He wasn't checking the plate. He was peering over the low bushes behind the vehicle, into the other area of parking lot beyond. He paced impatiently back and forth, waiting for his wife to reach him. A mere forty-five-degree turn to his right would have revealed Gage, squatting motionless in the dust, back pressed against the vehicle, eyes fixed on her, waiting for a signal.

At length, the man's wife reached the truck and squeezed down the side of it to join him. They exchanged further gruff words before he grumpily pushed aside a portion of hedge, holding it out of the way for her to precede him regally through, and letting it swing back to cover the gap again. A moment later, there was the sound of car doors opening and closing, an engine barking into life and a vehicle pulling away, tyres popping on the stony surface.

Shaking with disbelief at the close shave, Kennedy tried unsuccessfully to pull herself up using the truck's tyre whilst simultaneously communicating an all-clear to Gage. He sprang up and pelted over, lifting her easily to her feet, and panting, "Jesus, what were they doing, fighting over where they'd left the car? That was way too close for comfort. Why didn't you slam the hood?" Kennedy extended a trembling arm to illustrate.

"Oh. Never thought of that. Okay, well, it doesn't matter now. Just get in the truck."

Gage shut the hood and went quickly to the rear of the vehicle. A moment's delay and he was back, clambering inside looking considerably calmer.

"I think that'll buy us some extra time. Okay, we need to find somewhere we can hole up until dark and come up with a plan for Project Mal."

He glanced over at her, "You don't look very well."

Wincing illustratively at the debilitating headache, she rubbed her pounding temples again.

Usually, his expression softened when he looked at her, but this time he merely snorted, shook his head testily, and snapped, "Oh yeah? You and me both, sugar! Let's get the hell outta here before any shadier shit happens."

JUNK MAIL

Lord, she was *cold*. The inch of filthy seawater swirling around her buttocks and legs was freezing. She couldn't stop shivering. She wanted to stand, to give herself some relief from the intense chill, but she couldn't move. She couldn't even waggle her feet or lift her hands from her lap. Her body was a solid block of icy agony. Suddenly, there was a noise. A washing, sploshing sound, as if someone was wading next to her. She opened her swollen eyes as much as she could, and twitched involuntarily on beholding a face inches from hers. A young man. Smooth-skinned, dark-haired, redolent of expensive cologne, and utterly out of place in the dank, oozing grime of her prison.

His glittering, black eyes pierced like daggers, and Kennedy instinctively jerked her head back, smacking her skull hard into the bridge of Gage's nose as he slept soundly behind her. He started, shooting upright, grabbing for the gun, wheeling around in terror, staggering sideways clutching at his head. With nothing to lean against, Kennedy rolled limply onto her back and lay still, staring up at the reddening dawn sky, unable to understand what had just happened. She turned her head to look over at Gage, who was crouching a metre or two away, gun at his feet, sniffing, wincing, and manipulating his sore and running nose, "Owww…you have a nightmare?"

She couldn't remember. There was an image imprinted in her mind, but she couldn't make sense of it. Just two cruel eyes boring unblinkingly into hers, charged with intense hatred.

****

"Hey, Kid!"

The boy couldn't hear him. He popped his gum and scuffed his toes in the dust.

Gage whistled, and the peroxide-blonde head snapped around.

"Hey! You!"

"You talkin' to me?"

"Is there anyone else here?"

The boy was curious, but wary, "Very funny, mister."

"Wanna make an easy fifty?"

"I don't know. Doin' what?"

"You wanna make fifty bucks or not?" Gage beckoned, his husky voice straining to be heard across the wide space between them, "Come over here."

The kid narrowed his eyes suspiciously, "I ain't no rent-boy!"

Gage chuckled. He hadn't even considered how this might appear, an older guy in a dark car at midnight, trying to attract a young man's attention at a deserted roadside pull-in. He smirked, and growled, "Relaax, sweet cheeks. You're not my type."

The boy puffed his chest and peacocked aggressively, "You sayin' I'm a faggot, mister?"

Gage rolled his eyes, and drawled, "Oh, Jeez, you want this fifty or not?"

"What I gotta do to get it?"

"Post this card here through that door there – the newspaper office."

"And that's it?"

"Yep. Money upfront."

"Why don't *you* do it?"

"That's my business."

"Money upfront?"

"That's what I said."

"Mister, you're dumb! How you gonna stop me tossing that card and just running off with your fifty?"

"This oughta do it."

The oiled and gleaming barrels of the shotgun slid out through the black square of open truck window to point directly at the teenager's heart. The kid took three steps smartly back across the dusty lay-by. Gage explained, "You'll walk straight over there and put the card in that mailbox, or I'll blow a hole in you as big as my dick…and trust me kiddo, that's a huge fucking hole. So, we got a deal or not?" Unsure what the gun-toting lunatic would do if he refused, the youth stuttered, "Yeah…yeah…sure, we got a deal. Gimme the stuff, man."

Gage held the items out of the truck window. The boy hesitated for a millisecond more, eyes flicking from the black barrels to the crisp $50 bill folded around the card, then darted forward, whipped them from the stranger's loose fingers, and pelted across the street before the mysterious man could change his mind, shoving the fifty into his pocket and the card through the letterbox. Gage saw the white rectangle flutter down inside the glass door. Satisfied, he put the shotgun on the seat next to him, started the truck's engine, but prudently left the headlights off. The boy glanced back nervously, then beat a swift retreat, skinny legs pumping. He didn't get far. A sudden blinding beam illuminated the kid like a searchlight against the fence, and a large car surged from the darkest corner of the newspaper's parking lot, accelerating hard and bearing down upon the terrified teenager. Gage didn't delay, but swiftly swung the unlit truck around and pulled back out onto the empty midnight highway. He watched the rearview mirror, observing two shadows leaping from the car and pouncing upon the boy. One big and fat, one short and wiry. His suspicions were confirmed: a stakeout of the newspaper office. He wondered whether they were dividing their time and watching Mal's house too. No matter. He had achieved his first objective. Kennedy's message had been delivered.

****

"Where?"

"Right outside the newspaper office! We were just sitting there, not expecting anything to happen – 'cos nothing's happened any of the other nights we've been there – and then this kid runs up, shoves a card through the door, and makes off like his ass is on fire!"

"What did you do?"

"Caught him up and asked him what he was doing. He wasn't over-keen on telling us at first…but Floyd persuaded him."

"I'll bet he did."

"After that, we couldn't shut him up! He said some guy in a truck with a shotgun and a screwed-up voice gave him fifty bucks to deliver a card. Said he'd shoot him if he didn't. We just laughed and said, 'Get real, kid, how's he gonna shoot you', and he turned around and pointed, 'He's parked right over there' – "

"You have *got* to be kidding!"

"It was *dark*! Floyd kept hold of the kid and I sprinted down to where he'd pointed, but the guy had split time I got there. In torchlight, there were tyre marks all over, but no way of telling which were his."

"Did the kid say there was a girl with him?"

"He didn't mention a girl…but it's the guy from the hospital, it has to be! I asked the kid if the guy had scars all over him, but he said he never saw his face, just the gun."

"Shit! You were parked feet away from him, Tyler!"

"I know, Mr Logan. I'm sorry…"

"What did you do with the kid…and please don't tell me you let Floyd handle it…?"

"We let him go, Mr Logan. He didn't know nothing. That guy just used him as his delivery-boy. He must've known we'd be watching."

"Who told him that, huh? Her? She's *supposed* to be dead in a ditch! Right now, I'm not feeling too confident of your crisis-management, Tyler."

"I understand, Mr Logan… I can sort it, don't worry."

"What about the card? Did the kid know what was on it?"

"He said he had no idea. I believed him. He just wanted to make a quick fifty."

"And now we have no way of finding out!"

"Well, we looked at it."

"*What?*"

"Through the glass door. It was just lying there on the mat with all the other mail."

"And?"

"It was like a kid's drawing! It made no sense!"

"A drawing of what?"

"Now, it was only lit up by the porchlight, but we used a flashlight too, and it looked to both of us like a rocketship, a flower, and a fishing rod."

"Well, what the hell does that mean? Are you sure that was what the kid put through the door?"

"No question, Mr Logan. We saw him do it. A white card…and that was the only white card on the mat. We thought it could be some kind of code…?"

"If that's a code, it's pretty fucking kooky! Mind you, this whole situation's totally whacko – I don't know why I'm so surprised. I guess you're right, Tyler, it could be some kind of message…but saying what?"

****

"Glen?"

"Yup?"

"Get your butt in here and look at this!"

Glen was in the doorway faster than if he'd been fired from a cannon.

"Shut the door. Sit down."

"What's happened? You look half-crazy!"

"This! In today's junk mail."

Mal passed the postcard across to Glen, who looked at both sides – one blank, the other containing three wonky images that looked as if they'd been drawn by a six-year-old – squinted in puzzlement, and handed it back.

"What's it supposed to be, junior drawing competition?"

"A message."

"What? Who from?"

"Kennedy, Glen! Who else?"

Glen's face crumpled in confusion, "But, she doesn't have kids…?"

Mal thumped the desk, irritated by Glen's obtuseness, "No, Glen…but according to the hospital, she has a bad head injury!"

"Huh? Are you saying *Kennedy* drew these pictures? Are you saying *she* put this through the door? I thought she'd been kidnapped?"

"I'm not saying anything, Glen. All I know is that brain injuries can interfere with your ability to do everyday things…like draw little doodles."

"I don't get it. How do you know this card is from Kennedy?"

"It's obvious, Glen! It says so!"

Glen picked it up again, looked hard, and placed it carefully back on the desk, venturing, "Boss, are you okay? There's no shame in admitting the stress of all this is getting to you. If you need to take a couple of days, we can cover –"

"Oh!" Mal snatched up the card in irritation, "Don't be so dense, Glen! You've got a first-class honours degree!"

"Boss, if Kennedy was going to communicate with you, don't you think she'd have just written a note?"

"Anyone can read a note, Glen."

"Boss, anyone can read this postcard!"

"Yes, they can...but even if they do, they won't understand it, will they? You don't."

"No, of course I don't, because it's three stupid pictures drawn by a kid and put through the door probably as some prank!"

"No, Glen, it's from Kennedy."

"Boss...I...I don't know how to say this...but...do you think you might be...um...losing a little perspective...?"

Mal ignored him, "I've got a summerhouse in my backyard, Glen. Right down the bottom by the canal. I sit there and fish late in the evenings when I've got things on my mind."

"Um...okay...?"

"A flower, Glen! A fishing rod!"

"Boss – "

"I'm right, Glen!"

"Sure. Explain the rocket...?"

"She's named after the Space Center, Glen! Her daddy wanted to be an astronaut, but he kept failing all the tests. He wasn't good enough, but he couldn't accept it. He drank himself into an early grave a very bitter and disappointed guy. Only a few people know that and I'm one of them. Why do you think she's so stubborn and pushy all the goddam time? First to arrive, last to leave? She's got this cloud over her from childhood. She doesn't want to follow in Daddy's footsteps and live her whole life as a monumental failure."

"Oh..."

"Kennedy's grown up with a paranoia of inadequacy. She's got a fear of being average because she watched what being just like everybody else did to her Dad."

"She's certainly far from average!"

"I know, Glen, I know…but this crap that circles her head makes her take dumb risks that get her into the kind of trouble she's in now, and in the ten years I've employed her, I've yet to figure out a way of controlling her. She's a law unto herself. Most of the time, I just have to sit back and let her hunt whatever it is she's got the scent of. Sometimes, I wish I had the power to stop her."

"So, she wants to meet you in the summerhouse at the bottom of your yard?"

"Looks that way, doesn't it?"

Glen was watching him keenly, "I wonder what's really at the root of this story? So far, I can't uncover anything suspicious apart from that guy, Quantick. Everything else to do with the Governor seems above-board, the way you'd expect it to be, except for him. I can't even establish if Kennedy's truly been kidnapped. If she has, then this note's not from her. It's an elaborate trap so her kidnappers can get their hands on you too! They might assume you know more than you're printing, like Quantick did!"

"And if she *hasn't* been kidnapped?"

"Then who's the guy on the hospital CCTV, her boyfriend or something?"

"You know as well as I do, she's perennially single. Too much of a handful for most guys to cope with! You wouldn't want to date her, would you?"

Glen pulled a face, "Too old for me. Too bossy. Too high-maintenance."

Mal chuckled.

"Well, if she hasn't been kidnapped, and the mystery guy is on her side, why doesn't she just go to the cops and explain?"

Again, Mal was tempted to blurt out what he knew, but still held back. He couldn't knowingly pull Glen into the mire along with him. Glen's ignorance remained his insurance.

"Maybe because of that Quantick-guy, who we now know definitely isn't a Vice cop, probably isn't a Fed either, but is quite obviously up to his neck in whatever's going on here."

"There's no one on the Governor's staff called Quantick, or anything else beginning with a Q."

"I think it's safe to say his spontaneous shakedown the other day was *not* conducted under his own name. Oh, if we could only find out who sent him here! If we could figure out who he's working for, we'd know if it was safe to talk to the cops or not!"

"Why wouldn't it be safe to talk to the cops? Mal, is this something to do with corruption?"

Something in Glen's expression made Mal feel guilty for lying to him. Defensively, he blurted, "All I know is it stinks…and I'm nervous."

Glen persisted, "I can't even find out if he's definitely employed by the Governor, under *any* name. Some of his aides have their pictures on his website, but – "

"Our boy's camera-shy, huh?"

Glen grinned, nodding wryly.

"He was probing way too hard to be a disinterested party…but was he digging for himself or somebody else?"

"I'll keep looking, Boss."

"Good man, Glen. I appreciate your dedication. Kennedy's life genuinely could depend on it."

"Do you really think so?"

"Yes, I do. Where did she go, Glen? One minute off chasing a lead, the next…? Suddenly, she's discovered in hospital! Then she's been kidnapped? Then she's putting notes through our door in the middle of the night?"

"Maybe…"

"I don't have any choice, Glen, I have to test this theory. If it's her, she could *really* need help, and I might be the only person who can provide it."

"So, what will you do?"

"I'll spend the foreseeable future doing a lot of late-night fishing. I can't see an alternative."

"You need to be careful, Boss. There's every chance this is a trap."

DELIVER…OR DIE

Arizona.

Inescapable dust.

Unbearable heat.

He hated it. It reminded him of the past.

He pulled his rental car up outside the tall gates of an Adobe-style compound, the rendered walls resembling moulded dirt, as if the whole place was one gigantic termite mound. An overweight guy in a cheap suit shuffled reluctantly from the shade to bend down at the window, "Yeah?"

"Bobby Levine. I'm here to see Mr Grafton. I called ahead. He is expecting me."

The gatekeeper raised unconvinced eyebrows, as if that's what they all said. The visitor persisted, "He…um…knew my mother. You tell him I'm here. Boh-bee Luh-veen. He'll *want* to see me. He *won't* appreciate you holding me up."

"Wait."

The guy loafed to the shaded sentry-post, picked up a 'phone off the desk next to a bank of flickering CCTV screens, conducted a brief conversation, then extended a casual arm out of the open door and waved the idling vehicle on.

The electric gates swung smoothly inward, and the rental car purred slowly up the landscaped drive, flowering cacti and desert foliage

artfully planted with such flair and imagination Bobby Levine
almost forgot what a dustbowl dump this really was.

Bobby had grown up the hard way, living in the back of a rusting
1970 Lincoln Continental as his Momma beat a well-worn path
between California's racetracks, loading the betting odds for Harry
Grafton. Harry had gone to Vietnam a law-abiding young idealist,
and returned firmly possessed of the conviction that only power and
ruthlessness mattered a damn if you wanted to get anywhere.
Subject to Uncle Harry's intimidating influence from before he
could talk, impressionable little Bobby Levine absorbed this pitiless
life lesson along with his ABC's. He also swiftly comprehended –
as he watched his mother slide a few hundred here and there from
Harry Grafton's takings under the baggy trunk carpet of the Lincoln,
and press a silencing finger to her glossy red lips – that perception
mattered more than reality. Folks believed what they chose and
heard what they wanted, regardless of a little detail like the truth. As
he grew, Bobby Levine patiently observed the situations in which he
found himself, and began to realise how best to manipulate them to
his advantage. He grifted as he drifted, state to state, city to city, job
to job, always with a fresh identity, a believable back-story and an
eye for the main chance. Winding up in Florida seeing out the
lucrative winter season fleecing half-cut idiots in hotel bars on
Saturday nights, and using his largely unsupervised City Hall
position to run a small-time postal lottery scam Monday to Friday,
the junior filing clerk began to realise just how much real estate the
Governor owned. A Key West property-developer who'd first
decided to run for local Mayor on a whim, effortlessly swept aside

all challengers on a tide of personality-driven popularity and elected not to stop there, the Governor had also continued to dabble in bricks and mortar on the side. Most of his property was down in the far south of his State, the tropical archipelago of the Florida Keys, tied up in seasonal condo rentals and exclusive luxury villas that stood empty for weeks at a time, when the climate was simply too hot for most folks to stand. That seemed a shame to Bobby Levine, especially when there was so much *potential* in empty property. True to form, Bobby didn't do anything straight away. He sat back, gave it some thought, and an idea began to take shape in his fertile brain. It would require effort, research, planning...but Bobby Levine was in no hurry. He enjoyed savouring things, seeing them through to fruition like a farmer patiently tending a growing crop. Bobby dug in, did the groundwork, bided his time and waited for the right opportunities. They came... Slowly, but they came. A few Central American vacations deliberately spent in the cheaper hotels, lingering too long not to attract attention in bars no sensible foreign tourist would ever frequent. The correct cautious conversation, a pertinent contact or two, and just the right amount of cash to change even the most suspicious mind began a network. A couple of guys with decent-sized vessels equipped for night fishing, who were having terrible trouble obtaining the permits they needed at the right price, strengthened it further. How fortunate when an enthusiastic young administrative official offered to expedite all the red tape on their behalf! The resourceful kid even found a way to waive the exorbitant permit fee altogether...in return for the odd under-the-radar favour. How could they possibly refuse? Careful, methodical,

Bobby Levine built his supply chain as precisely as he'd crafted Robert Logan's fictitious resumé. In the meantime, his inspired creation climbed the Florida political career ladder impressively fast. No one could believe they'd never noticed what a little superstar their graduate recruit was! With his outstanding qualifications, why was he not ensconced in a Boston corporate high-rise billing treble figures an hour? Why not in Atlanta playing legal hardball, placing football players for an eye-watering cut of a multi-million-dollar contract? Why not in LA getting the ridiculous kids of A-Listers off DUI charges for obscene fees? Because he'd had to stay in Florida. His Momma was sick, and she needed him. That humble admission made them love him even more. Intelligent, good-looking *and* principled. The fact she was long dead and had never visited Florida in all her life didn't trouble the conscience of Bobby Levine. Momma would want him to make his way exactly as she'd taught him, and Bobby well-knew no one could resist a handsome boy who loved his mother. Doors of opportunity swung ever wider before Robert Logan's rising star. The offices into which he routinely strutted for 'chats about his future' increased in plushness and prestige until he got where he needed to be, onto the personal staff of the Governor of Florida himself. Now, he was in a position to pull those disparate strands together into a coherent whole. Finally, Little Bobby Levine was a hair's breadth from being utterly in control of his own destiny, answerable to no master but himself. The Kennedy McKendrick problem was therefore a volatile explosive beneath his painstakingly constructed foundations. He'd come all the way out West to buy himself enough time to fix the interfering little bitch once and for all. No more leaving it to the hopeless bungling of Tyler and Floyd. They were useful, because they'd do any shit for the right amount of money without question or qualm, but Bobby Levine now saw that Kennedy McKendrick was one of those particularly thorny problems only *he* could solve.

He parked at the top of the sweeping drive, and was unnerved to see Harry Grafton himself appear at the front door to greet him, beaming genially. Bobby's stomach tightened instinctively. The more the old bastard grinned, the worse it usually was for the object of his affability. He hastened to get out of the car and stride with a confidence he didn't feel up the steps to stand before Harry, the one man who'd had the greatest influence upon the direction of Bobby Levine's unconventional life.

"It's been a long time, Bobby. Too long."

These days, Harry was clearly styling himself the Irish immigrant answer to Don Corleone, as he grasped Bobby's upper arms in his vice-like grip and yanked the young man's rigid body into a theatrical Mediterranean embrace, smacking overly wet kisses to both cheeks that Bobby was subsequently unable to wipe away. Revolted by the feel of the old man's saliva drying on his skin, Bobby fastened a false smile to features immobilised with tension, and managed, "Yes…Uncle Harry. Yes. Too long."

Harry clapped a giant palm forcefully between Bobby's shoulder blades, making him lurch forward in surprise, "I often think of your mother. So sad at the end, Bobby. Cancer is a cruel disease."

Grafton shook his fleshy head regretfully, and Bobby immediately sought to suppress the baseless fear that surfaced whenever Harry mentioned Momma. She'd always maintained her ignorance of his father's identity, which left Bobby Levine irrationally petrified it might be Harry Grafton himself. The notion he shared even a portion of his genes with this evil, sweating mass of blubber sickened him almost as much as the conviction that Harry *knew*.

Bruising as it was to confess any loss of control, however temporary, he couldn't fix the Kennedy McKendrick problem without assistance from Uncle Harry. He was here to throw himself upon the dubious mercy of the devil himself.

"Come in, Bobby."

"Thank you, sir."

Grafton ushered him inside, irritably waving away an approaching shirtsleeved thug brandishing a hand-held metal detector, "No need, Ray. Bobby's not packing…are you, Bobby?"

"No, Uncle Harry…I don't…" In Bobby's position, possession of a firearm would take some explaining. He was supposed to be a pen-pushing office-boy.

Harry grunted, "Fuck off, Ray."

Ray took offence at this, gave Bobby a dirty look as if he was responsible for the offhand treatment, and stood his ground so the visitor had to edge around him to follow Harry. Every time Bobby looked back, Ray's eyes were on him, watching him coldly along the length of the corridor.

Grafton led him down the cool, tiled hallway and out into a colonnaded courtyard bright with trailing bougainvillea. A fountain tinkled musically in its centre and, through an archway to his right, Bobby glimpsed the glittering artificial blue of a vast swimming pool. He wondered absently whether Harry had it drained and refilled after every drowning, or if his overfed body bobbed about in water cloudy with the swirling DNA of his victims until the filters did their work of sucking the evidence away. He shuddered, and Harry's heavy, clammy arm clasped him around the neck, "You can't be cold!"

"No…no…I…"

"A premonition, perhaps?" Harry chuckled nastily, and Bobby swallowed thickly.

"Come and sit down, Bobby. Sunshine or shade?"

"Shade, please." His imagination was already raging quite chaotically enough without giving himself heatstroke into the bargain.

"Over here," Harry steered him by the elbow to two armchairs with invitingly plump cushions, positioned beneath a flowering mimosa tree in an immense yellow pot.

"Your grounds are looking great, Uncle Harry."

"It's Joannie's thing, you know."

"Well, she sure has a flair for it."

"I'll tell her, Bobby. She'll be very touched. Most of the uneducated oafs who come through those gates wouldn't recognise a well-designed garden if they were buried in one!"

Grafton threw back his massive head and guffawed richly. The inside of his mouth was very pink, like raw steak. Bobby's troubled subconscious conjured a nightmarish image of naked corpses impaled on the ornamental stands of cacti, and he shuddered again before he could prevent it.

"You're not sick, are you, Bobby?"

"No. I'm just...tired. The journey...and I've been under some pressure recently."

"Well, you chose politics! Tough game, eh? Running for President yet?"

Bobby smirked tightly, and muttered, "Maybe next week," which made Harry roar again, before hefting his huge frame around in the chair and bellowing into the house, "Jimi! Get Bobby a cold drink, will you?"

A muffled, "Si, señor Grafton."

A couple of moments passed, during which Bobby pretended to relax and enjoy the tranquillity of the latest Mrs Grafton's labour-of-love. He supposed it could have been nice here – in the shade, listening to the trickling fountain and the desert wind disturbing the leaves of the potted trees – if he wasn't sitting a table's width from Harry, feeling the old reptile's eyes boring into him like skewers through his skin.

A young man of Hispanic appearance arrived with a jug of iced tea and two frosted glasses fresh from the icebox, their opaque, cold coating evaporating and cracking as it encountered the extreme Arizona heat.

"Thank you, Jimi."

"De nada, señor."

Jimi withdrew swiftly, and Harry cocked a thumb after him, "Can't see what the honky-tonk is in Washington about Mexicans. I employ cartloads of 'em like Jimenez there. They're willing, cheap, and they don't grouse about their goddam rights all the time.

They're just grateful for the work. Those drinks won't pour themselves, Bobby."

"Um…right…"

"On the 'phone, you said it was important. You've come all this way to see me in person…so you'd better spit it out."

"Yessir."

Bobby was ashamed of how much his hands shook as he poured the iced tea. It might have been the heat, or the recent lack of sleep, but vivid hallucinations of his own unclothed corpse displayed in various undignified positions around Joannie's garden oasis like ghoulish modern art, circled his head and impeded clear thinking. He pictured Ray's cold eyes staring after him up the hallway, "Are we alone?"

Harry spread his meaty hands wide, and asked mildly, "You see anyone else here?"

That wasn't an answer, but Bobby couldn't argue, so he proceeded cautiously, "It's hot in Florida."

"It's always hot in Florida, Bobby."

"But I need to…lower the temperature a little."

"Can I ask why?"

"Security reasons."

"Bobby, I'm a busy man. I don't have all afternoon to dance around the goddam point. It's almost as if you don't trust me! You requested this meeting. You wanted to talk, so talk. If you've changed your mind, get your bony ass onto an airplane and back to the beach. I don't have the patience for this smoke-and-mirrors bullshit."

"No, Uncle Harry. I didn't mean – "

"*Now*, Bobby."

"Um…yes…right…okay…um, after *Irma*, we discovered one of the houses we were using had sustained enough damage for some…merchandise to…um…leak out."

"Really," Harry couldn't have sounded less interested, more concerned with lighting his cigar than sympathising with Bobby's plight.

Bobby ploughed on, "I have reason to believe one of them spoke to the Press."

That got Harry's attention. He struggled his immense bulk forward in the chair, thrusting out his neck like a tortoise from its shell to grunt, "What?"

"First of all, one of my guys discovered a woman snooping around at a safehouse we'd been using for…um…storage. We subsequently found out she's an investigative reporter! Now, speculative articles have started appearing in the local papers. Every few days, there's another sensationalist splash. A little more is implied every time – "

"So, shut it down, Bobby! You're the Governor's bulldog. In his eyes you can do no wrong. Pull rank!"

"I *can't*. They know what they're doing. They're not printing anything I can pounce on through official channels. It's all suggestion, allegation, but it's sufficient to convince me they *know*."

"So, put the frighteners on 'em! Where's your balls, Bobby?"

"Believe me, I've done all that! I've got people under observation. I'm tracking leads. I'm doing everything I can without blowing my cover and jeopardising this whole operation it's taken me years to build...but I'm limited by my position."

"I thought your position was your power, Bobby?"

"It usually is, but this situation is becoming...delicate. I can't get too involved. I need to stay hands-off so I can't be implicated. I lose this peachy job and the whole network collapses like a house of cards! You wouldn't want that, would you? I can sort it, but I can't have the tap running and fix the leak at the same time. Do you see what I'm saying? It's becoming too dangerous to keep the supply-lines open. I need a temporary cessation – "

Harry raised a hand to silence him. Bobby stopped talking instantly and held his breath. Harry took a large swig of tea and ruminatively rolled an ice-cube around his mouth, piggy little eyes never leaving Bobby's drawn face.

The hot wind blew, the dry leaves rustled, the fountain tinkled, the ice-cube clinked dully off Harry's teeth, and Bobby's heart thumped like the bass drum in a military band.

"Bobby, you put me in a difficult position, son."

"I – "

"*No*. You had your chance to talk, Bobby. Now it's *my* turn. You wanted a seat at the big boy's table. You were most insistent, I seem to recall, assuring me my past reliability issues could be resolved by going solely through you. You were ideally placed to make my operation easier, slicker, and more profitable as a result. 'Move more, and move it quicker, and you can collect faster on your investment.' I distinctly remember your excellent pitch, Bobby, and you were right. I'm *so* satisfied with our arrangement I'm even content to turn a blind eye to what you're skimming off the top to line your own pockets. Armani, by the look of it. You're thorough and careful, just like your mother. I used to let her do the same because she never got too greedy…and I don't think you're greedy either. What I think you are, Bobby, is naïve. What makes you so sure I don't also have agreements of my own to honour? The chain doesn't stop with me, son. If you let me down, I let others down…and that simply isn't an option. Reputation is everything. You know that perhaps better than anyone else I deal with. Lose your caché and you've lost control. What do your Central American suppliers think about this temporary interruption in the free flow of trade?"

"I haven't – "

"No, I bet you haven't! They won't deal with you as *reasonably* as I will. You stop their income, refuse to take their product, and they'll be out for your blood, Bobby, I have no doubt."

"I approached you first, Uncle Harry."

"Of course you did. I'm the guy putting a fuckload of money in your hand."

"Hey –!"

"We *have* an agreement, Bobby. It *will* remain in place. Fail to deliver and I'll consider my needs better-served by appointing an *alternative* middleman."

Horrified, too indignant to remain silent, Bobby blurted recklessly, "It's *my* network! *I* put it in place! *I* control it! You wouldn't *have* this goddam super-slick arrangement if not for me! It's *mine* –!"

Suddenly, something caught the sunlight at the periphery of his vision, whipping down past his face. Bobby's quick brain identified it immediately.

Wire.

He'd taken this a step too far. He'd been unguardedly arrogant. He'd pissed off Harry Grafton and now he would be strangled where he sat.

Instinctively, he jerked up his arms to protect his neck, and his grabbing fingers caught at metal taut and sharp as a cheese-cutter, slicing deep channels into the flesh of his palms and making him cry out in pain. He pushed as hard as he could against the upward jerking of the wire, but was at a disadvantage, arms bent awkwardly, body reclined into the cavernous cushions, spluttering and struggling as the blood from his ribboned hands ran down his wrists and dripped onto his so-recently-pristine suit.

Harry tossed the half-smoked cigar across the courtyard, heedless of where it landed, leaping to his feet with surprising agility. His huge palms thudded heavily onto the arms of Bobby's chair as he loomed over him, wheezy voice revealing the effort such unaccustomed physicality had placed on his straining heart. Whoever it was behind the chair – Ray, it had to be Ray, with those hard, cold, dead eyes – temporarily paused in their attempts to slice clean through his hands and move onto his neck, while his villainous employer sought to express his utter contempt for Bobby's current conduct.

"I held your mother in very high esteem. What would she say now if she could hear you? She didn't raise no whinger, Bobby! Man up! Seems to me you're losing your shit over a bunch of goddam journalists!"

Harry chuckled malevolently, and sarcastically observed, "You'll never make it in politics if you can't control the press."

He reached forward, grasped fat handfuls of Bobby's ruined jacket, further soiling it with the damp marks of his sweating fists, and lifted the young man by his lapels to dangle painfully millimetres off the seat, suspended only by his once-expensive tailoring and the hideous wire slicing ever-deeper into his screaming flesh. Agonisingly snared, grimacing and grunting with the pain, Bobby hung from Grafton's fists and Ray's garrotte like the victim of a crucifixion, and waited for Harry to drive home his point. The man who might be his father lowered his round, red face so close to Bobby's that his spittle hit the young man's lips, and hissed, "Listen to *me*, Big Shot. I couldn't give less of a fuck about your 'negative publicity'. You made a *deal*. You have a job to do, merchandise to move, a network to service. You make your choice, Bobby, and you make it *right now*. Deliver...or die."

LATE-NIGHT FISHING

Gage snapped another small branch across his knee and fed the splintered thirds into the dying campfire, "They were watching the newspaper office, so chances are they'll be watching his house too. It ain't straightforward. I told you we wouldn't just be able to drive up to his door."

Lying on her side on the rug before the fire, pinched little face illuminated by the flickering light, Kennedy drew her knees into a foetal position, sighing heavily and massaging her pounding head with hot fingers. She'd been uncontrollably sick all afternoon and evening, and Gage had paced and fretted, by turns comforting her distress and chiding her overexertion. It was touching how his anxiety grew as the evening wore on and the reality of having to leave her side loomed, but he'd gone to deliver Mal's message because she'd begged him to.

She pictured the journey to Mal's house, the winding approach out through the newly constructed development of condos nearest the highway towards the older properties beyond, with their more-secluded settings amongst the mangroves rich with bird and marine life. Gage was right, they couldn't just drive down the only road and expect not to be seen. But this was the Florida Keys! It had just occurred to Kennedy's battered brain that they didn't have to arrive by road at all. Reanimated, she sat up abruptly, but her head reeled and she dropped awkwardly onto her shoulder, gasping at the pain of the unexpected fall. Gage was beside her in an instant, of course, "What are you trying to do, sit up?"

"Yeh."

"It's two a.m! You need to sleep!" He nevertheless put her arms around his neck and heaved her to a sitting position, but her head lolled backwards and black dots burst before her vision, the precursor to a fainting fit, "No…No…"

He lowered her tenderly, huge hand supporting her head until it could rest on the pillow again.

Eyes hooded with fatigue, she gazed steadily up at him, stretching a weak, shaking arm to push a palm against his firm pectoral muscle, and rub in an uncoordinated gesture of affection. Gage clasped the little hand between his warm fingers, massaging the joints with his thumb, murmuring, "Will you quit fighting this and rest? You're doing too much."

She smiled dreamily, allowing her eyes to close.

With no idea how long she'd drifted, she was jerked awake by the thud of Gage's fist in the dirt beside her as he burst out, "I'm such an asshole! I care more about not getting arrested than I do about your health. I'm torn between seeing this thing through like we've discussed and just cutting our losses and taking you straight back. I mean, I ain't exactly coping! I'm screwing up every step of the way so far! Take a look at that bandage. It's filthy! What about how sick you've been all afternoon? You're worse today than yesterday. What if you're even sicker tomorrow? What if you just steadily decline because I'm doing it all wrong and I don't even realise?"

Kennedy struggled onto one elbow and tugged insistently at the front of his t-shirt until he yielded, body sinking down over hers, their heads millimetres apart, eyes raking one another's faces. She brushed her hands around his jawline to clasp the back of his neck, little fingers sliding into his shaggy hair, touching her forehead, nose and lips to his disfigured cheek. Gage closed his eyes, wrapped his arms tight around her, and allowed his body to relax for the first time in days, resting his head on the pillow next to hers. Eventually, he whispered, "I've already failed one woman in my life. I can't do it again; the guilt would kill me. I have to do what's best for you, Kennedy, even if it goes against your wishes…and what's best for you right now might be returning you to hospital, whatever the consequences."

She rocked her upper body away from his, smiled kindly, and traced a tingling circle with a fingertip around his eye socket, sunken with lack of sleep, "Kayk."

"You want cake? Now? It's the middle of the night!"

"No. Kayk."

"I don't understand, Kennedy."

"Kayk! *Kayk!*" She mimed paddling, and Gage started to work it out, "You wanna go kayaking?"

She tapped him lightly on the chin with her index finger.

"You want *me* to go kayaking?"

"Us."

"What?"

Her little face scrunched with the effort of forcing out the sounds locked inside, "Mmmaaal!"

"Oh, I *see*, you want to kayak to Mal's!"

"Yeh!"

"Because his house backs on to the water?"

"Yeh."

Like an overbearing parent, he retorted, "You can barely stand up, you're not kayaking anywhere! Anyway, where are we gonna get a two-man kayak from? Oh, wait, don't tell me, we're gonna steal one, right?"

Kennedy poked out her tongue in retaliation for the sarcasm, and tried to explain, "Borr...borr..."

"'Borrow' one?"

"Yeh!"

"Like hell we are!"

Kennedy twinkled innocently, and Gage gazed at her shining face, hopelessly enchanted, "You're such a bad influence on me. My Momma would be scandalised if she could see me now."

Kennedy pressed a hushing finger to his lips and winked cheekily.

Gage chuckled, and teased, "When do you propose we commit our latest crime, Evil Genius, given it's nearly dawn, I've had no sleep, and we probably shouldn't do it in daylight? Maybe tomorrow, huh? We'll only go if you feel okay. Rest is the most important thing. The more rest you get, the better you seem to be. Our next problem, of course, is that we need to figure out where we can steal a kayak from."

She pointed proudly, nodded knowingly.

"Oh, you know a place, huh? Yeah, I'll bet you do! Is there somewhere near the crime scene we can stash the truck, by any chance?"

"Yeh."

Gage shook his head, unable to suppress the broad smile that suffused his weary features, "Holy shit, woman, here we go again!"

****

Moonlight glittering faintly on black ocean. The plastic tourist kayaks corralled together in the shallows beside the pontoon bobbed with the motion of the water and knocked against one another with dull thuds. Kennedy, crouching in the safety of the bushes a few feet away, joggled Gage's sleeve and pointed the way.

He nodded, shot from the shadows at a running crouch, and leapt with barely a splash into the knee-deep harbour. The sand was soft, and his feet sank into the unpleasantly gooey seabed. He was glad it was dark. He didn't want to see what he was paddling about in. He waded over to the line of two-man kayaks, stepping cautiously, jerking his reaching foot up every time a piece of weed wrapped his leg or his spreading toes discovered a sharp shell or jagged stone. He tugged at the tail of a suitable craft. It floated compliantly towards him, then stopped dead and would move no further. Desperate to be in and away as quickly as possible, unable to see what was stopping it in the dark, Gage tugged with increasing frustration until he realised Kennedy was on the jetty above him, his overstuffed rucksack of belongings dragged behind her, the heavy shotgun clutched awkwardly under her other arm.

Gage hissed furiously, "Kennedy, I told you to stay in the bushes!"

She exhaled in obvious exasperation at his hopelessness, and grunted, "Guh! Tie! *Tie!*"

"Huh?"

"Rup," She stopped, clenched her fists with pure frustration at her inability to speak fluently, and put everything she had into enunciating, "Rowwpe!"

"Rope? They're roped together?"

"Yeh!"

"Shit! Where?"

Gage impatiently nudged the kayaks apart with his driving knees, feeling frantically across the plastic surface of the closest one until he discovered a ring protruding from the nose, and through it, a taut and sticky rope. He slid his sharp hunting-knife from his pocket and sliced easily through the salt-encrusted fibres. The kayaks, so tightly bunched, spread apart like petals sprinkled on the surface of a puddle, some floating into the darkness under the jetty, others making a directionless bid for freedom into the open water behind them.

Gage waded to the side, pulling the chosen craft with him, spinning it to point out to sea, "Gimme the gun."

Kennedy sat, legs dangling, and lowered it down to him.

"Can you lift the bag?"

"No."

"Okay. Can you drag it over until I can reach the straps from down here?"

Kennedy complied, but he could see and hear the extreme effort it required in her weakened condition. Again, he found himself wondering what havoc tonight's adventure would wreak. Her speech was improving markedly by the moment, but seemingly at the expense of her physical health, which appeared to be declining as fast as her mental faculties recovered. Gage just hoped this Mal guy was all she'd built him up to be. If not, he truly had no idea what to do for the best.

He reached up, teetered the heavy bag on the edge of the deck, tightened his biceps and stomach muscles in anticipation, and swung it down into the rear of the kayak, which sank considerably. Gage had taken weight into account, but had also been unwilling to leave his most-personal possessions in the hidden truck, in case it was a while before he could return to it, if ever. He'd had to accept abandoning most of his good camping equipment and comprehensive toolkit, but wasn't prepared to leave the shotgun, his decent clothes, or items such as his binoculars or Janice's picture of the family. He'd also had to make room for Kennedy's new wardrobe within the already-bulging pack. He hoped they didn't ride so low they'd sink once out on the open water, where he couldn't see if there were jellyfish, sea-crocs, barracudas, or even benign manatees who might swim beneath the kayak and unwittingly roll them over into the black and sinister sea. Tucked next to the paddles in the cargo net at the back of the kayak were two lifejackets. Gage tugged one free of the net and passed it to Kennedy, "Put this on. No arguing."

He watched her pint-sized silhouette struggle into the cumbersome jacket and click the fastenings closed. Gage reached up like a father encouraging his little girl down off a high wall, "Ease forward.

Lower your hands towards my shoulders before you jump. I'll catch you."

She was shuffling her bruised and sore bottom slowly off the edge, too scared of falling to make the leap, when suddenly a bright light illuminated the shed at the far end of the jetty, and swung along its length towards them! They detected the purr of an engine and the pop and crunch of tyres on the gravel parking lot.

Kennedy gaped in horror as the travelling light sped relentlessly towards her, and flung herself without further delay at the alarmed and considerably distracted Gage. Instead of being caught confidently in strong arms, she thudded hard against his unprepared body and knocked him backwards into the water with a loud splash. The headlight rippled across the pontoon above them as Gage and Kennedy spluttered desperately to the surface. Huddled in the cool sea amongst the flotsam of untied kayaks, spitting out unpleasant mouthfuls of dirty saltwater, shivering, breath shallow, hearts thudding, they waited to be discovered.

The vehicle came to a halt. The engine stopped. The lights went out. Gage and Kennedy strained for the slam of a door and the crunch of a footfall over the sound of the slapping tidal water and the hollow impacts of free-floating kayaks.

They could hear traffic on the distant flyover, the slop and splash of waves hitting the jetty…and nothing else.

No footsteps.

No voices.

Kennedy looked at Gage. Gage looked at Kennedy. She raised her eyebrows and shrugged, teeth chattering.

Gage lowered his head to whisper in her ear, his breath warm on her chilled skin, "We can't sit here all night."

"No."

"I'll lift you up. You look. All right?"

"Yes."

Gage directed their tight-pressed bodies closer to the pontoon. He squatted in the water, guided her feet onto his thighs, supported her hips in his splayed palms, and counted, "One, two, three, up!" pushing out of the water so Kennedy's head and shoulders rose above the level of the deck. She leant on her elbows as best she could to take some of her weight off Gage, peering into the darkness.

Ten feet away, illuminated only by the blue light of a car stereo, a young couple kissed passionately in the front seats of a parked truck. As Kennedy watched, their lips parted long enough for the young man to slide the girl's t-shirt over her head to reveal a lace brassiere, before their bodies entwined once more. Kennedy pointed downwards, and Gage lowered her back into the water, demanding, "Well? Is it the cops?"

Kennedy twinkled mischievously and mimed the throes of exaggerated passion, crossing her arms over her chest and rubbing them up and down her body, as if in an amorous clinch.

Gage sniggered, "Someone's making out up there?"

"Yeh."

"Is it real hot and heavy?"

"Yeh."

"Lift me up so *I* can look!"

She rolled her eyes and splashed him with a scoop of water.

"Hey! Well, what now? I don't exactly want to hang here freezing my balls off 'til they finish."

"No. Go."

"They won't notice?"

Kennedy shook her head.

"Wow, they must really be going for it, huh?" Gage grinned wryly, and quipped, "Those were the days!"

Unbidden, a vision of his wife on their wedding night sprang into his mind, laughing hysterically as he fell up the stairs in their swanky hotel suite trying to get his pants off, blind drunk and animally aroused. He'd bragged to all his buddies that the carpet-burns on his knees were from his Honeymoon...just omitting to clarify how they'd really been sustained.

Such a melancholy expression settled on his face that Kennedy thought her heart would break. Not knowing what else to do but distract him, she reached forward and pushed at his shoulder, "Guh!"

He jumped, as if he'd quite forgotten where they were, "Oh! Sorry... Yeah, let's go. Here." He lifted her from the chilly water into the pleasantly balmy night air, plonking her clumsily onto the front seat of the kayak, hefting the rucksack forward and pushing it into the space before her feet. The nose of the craft dipped alarmingly, but Gage calculated Kennedy-plus-bag would roughly balance his weight once on the rear seat.

He gave Kennedy one paddle to hold, launched the other off into the dark water, straightened the free-floating kayak and waded out, pushing it before him.

"I'll paddle. You navigate."

He glanced behind them. He could see the outline of the car, the faint light within, the suggestion of moving figures. If he could barely see them, illuminated as they were by the interior light, then they definitely couldn't see him, an indistinct and distant shape on the dark, constantly-moving sea.

It was getting deeper now, reaching mid-thigh. Gage placed his hands on the side of the kayak, hopped his bottom crookedly over the lip, and wriggled onto the moulded plastic seat, folding his long legs into the craft, leaning forward and tapping Kennedy on the arm, "Paddle please, co-pilot."

She fed it over her shoulder into his hands, and he felt one fin to check he held it the right way round, dipping it into the water and sculling experimentally. The kayak surged smoothly forward and Gage nodded with satisfaction. Pretty well-balanced. Good. Now he just had to get them there.

In the insipid moonlight, the clumps of mangrove resembled a rolling landscape of uneven black hills. She pointed to the left, directly into the impenetrable wall of undergrowth. There must be a channel through the swamp that he couldn't yet see. He just had to trust she knew the way. Gage pushed the paddle into the water and powered them on into the dark.

****

Once into the mangroves and away from all hint of artificial light, Gage's eyes became more accustomed to the dimness, and he found the weak moon lit the way sufficiently well. To his relief, far from the journey being the anticipated complex twist of dark channels through dense undergrowth, Kennedy was taking them directly down a boat route with buoys marking left and right-hand lanes. Able to paddle comfortably along the wide river with leisure to look about him, Gage quickly started to get his bearings. Away to the far right, slightly behind their current course, he could see the taillights of vehicles on the distant, raised highway, although he could no longer hear the rush of the traffic. Directly ahead, the myriad twinkling lights showed the way. When they got close enough to differentiate individual buildings, Kennedy pointed to the right and they skirted the development, leaving lights and highway behind. The tight clumps of mangrove were more numerous here, the houses larger and further apart.

The main river narrowed, but the mouths of small channels became visible to either side, snaking off into the blackness. Kennedy sat more upright, peering as if searching for something. Abruptly, she raised her hand.

Stop!

Gage rammed the paddle vertically into the water and pulled back as firmly as he could. The kayak's brisk forward momentum stuttered, ceased, and they floated briefly in the tidal flow, bobbing persistently right on the current until Gage corrected their position, "What's the matter? Have we gone wrong?"

"No."

She pointed.

"Are you kidding? It's pitch dark in there!"

He wasn't afraid exactly, but…

There!

Kennedy McKendrick evidently wasn't bothered about a spooky little swamp. She had an objective to achieve. The furious, impatient jabbing of her pointing finger shamed him into steering towards her chosen route without audible protest. He couldn't deny the tightening of his guts in apprehension as the channel closed around them, the mangrove branches entangling overhead to create a natural tunnel. Gage couldn't shake the sensation of them slipping down the throat of an immense, black eel. Once into the monster's gaping maw, the moonlight didn't penetrate, and Gage was paddling nearly blind. He could just make out the narrow strip of water meandering confusingly before them, but couldn't see the branches above that arched and drooped across their path. He continually whacked his paddle as he lifted it, or misjudged the direction of the passage in the dark and wedged the nose of the kayak between mangrove roots that extended into the water like talons.

At first, every unexpected impact of paddle with unseen branch or startling lurch of kayak into invisible obstacle made him jump a millimetre or two off the plastic seat and caused his heart to pound violently. When it happened every six feet or so, it ceased to be frightening and began to madden him to the point where he could no longer contain his annoyance, "Jesus, Kennedy! What the hell did you bring us this way for? This'd be awkward enough in daylight!"

"Shhh!" Finger theatrically to her lips to communicate her point, she mimed the necessity for silence and urged him to slow down. They were barely moving anyway, so Gage sulkily thumped the oar across his damp lap, sick of paddling and getting nowhere, and glanced up moodily, amazed to see their irritating short-cut had delivered them into another wide boat channel, the other side of which was a man-made canal with a few substantial houses backing onto it.

Frustration forgotten, Gage whispered, "Over there?"

"Yeh."

"Which one?"

Most of the houses had lanterns on their jetties at the water's edge. Kennedy held up her hand, silhouetted against the artificial glow, and Gage counted her fingers, "One, two, three. Third one along?"

"Yeh."

"You realise once we're out in that channel, we're lit up like a Christmas tree. We've got to get into some cover as soon as possible. I know it's late, but someone could see us. We can't get complacent now when we've come this far being careful."

Kennedy pointed, "Wwwall."

"Okay. Fast across the channel, and up as tight against the retaining wall as we can get."

"Right."

Gage rolled his tired shoulders, and rocked his aching head from side to side, stiff neck pulling uncomfortably. He gripped the paddle firmly in both fists, "Ready? We going for this?"

"Yeh. Go! *Go!*"

****

Mal dozed fitfully on the sun lounger inside the summerhouse. His old bones creaked with the discomfort of inadequate support and unsuitable ergonomics. It was okay for an hour or two's snooze, but not to spend whole tense and watchful nights on, not at his age. He was starting to think Glen might have been right. It was a kid's drawing, and he'd so wanted it to be a communication from her that he'd started to join random dots to form a non-existent picture. What would Sally say if she could see him now, bent almost double with backache from nights sleeping on a chair in a shed, all because of an insane hunch? Darling Sally, his voice of reason, taken from him too soon, when he clearly still needed her to temper the madness. What he should do now was unfold himself from this chair, limp agonisingly up the lawn attempting to stretch the kinks out of his spine, and have a pleasant night's rest on his expensive, orthopaedic mattress. Nothing was going to happen out here.

He sat up with a grunt of discomfort, lower back tweaking painfully. The double-doors stood open, admitting night breeze into the close little shack. As Mal swung his legs around and prepared for the torturous ordeal of standing, a human shadow flitted across one of the opaque side windows.

Instantly alert, Mal groped desperately under the lounger for the baseball bat he'd taken the precaution of bringing in case Glen's theory was proved correct, that this was a plot to kidnap him too! His hand closed around the reassuring wooden shaft. He withdrew it from under the chair and gripped it firmly in front of him like a batter facing a pitch, trying to edge to his feet as silently as possible, for once little noticing the chorus of complaining pops, pulls and twinges.

The silhouette reappeared, creeping slowly around the water side of the summerhouse towards the open door. A big outline, tall and broad, clearly not Kennedy. Adrenaline pumping, physical limitations of sedentary late-middle-age temporarily forgotten, Mal squared his stance, raised the bat in both hands level with the approaching intruder's head, and got ready to swing.

THE MAN WITH ALL THE ANSWERS

Although telling himself he was prepared for anything, he was nevertheless not expecting what came through the door. A powerful bear of a man with wild hair and a ghastly patchwork of livid scars disfiguring his face. Mal exclaimed aloud at the shocking sight, took several involuntary backward steps, swung without conviction, and missed his target by miles. The undaunted stranger stepped closer, and Mal saw he balanced a shotgun in one massive fist. Convinced he was about to be menaced at gunpoint, Mal hoiked the baseball bat back up to shoulder level and swung again before the freak could get any nearer.

Suddenly, a smaller figure darted between the terrifying thug and the advancing weapon, a woman squeaking, "No!" and shoving frantic hands out to stop the bat in mid-air. As the travelling wood connected firmly with her lifting arms, she wheeled and staggered, her eyes rolled back in her head, and she collapsed to the floor between the two horrified men.

****

"I'm sorry! I didn't know, did I? What would you have done in my position?"

Mal was wringing his hands in tormented supplication.

Kennedy lay on the sun lounger, whey-faced and shaken. Gage stroked her hair, holding her hand and glaring coldly at the older man, growling, "I wouldn't go around swinging baseball bats at the heads of defenceless women."

"I wasn't swinging it at *her* head; I was swinging it at *yours*!"

"Whatever."

"Who *are* you?"

"A friend."

"Whose 'friend'?"

"Kennedy's friend, who else? I told you, I'm the guy who found her and took her to hospital. Why you have a problem with me, I don't know. I'm just trying to keep her safe."

"*SAFE*? Look at the state of her! She's filthy, covered in wounds…is that brown stuff in her hair blood?"

Gage rubbed cold fingers across tired eyes. Mal, their ostensible saviour, seemed suspicious, obstructive and cowardly. Gage was unwilling to trust him. What he really wanted to do right now was punch him to the ground.

Kennedy was trying to talk, "Mmmaal…"

Mal eased himself gingerly onto his knees like a man with back trouble, reaching for Kennedy's other hand, holding and patting it gently, "I'm here, sweetheart."

She smiled beseechingly at both men and pushed their two hands together, so the knuckles bumped. Gage grinned wryly, "Be friends, huh?"

"Yeh."

Gage jerked his head towards Mal, and grunted laconically, "But I don't trust him."

Indignant, Mal snapped, "Well, I don't trust you either!"

Gage shrugged indifferently, and Kennedy exhaled exasperation, bashing his chest ineffectually and pointing insistently at Mal, "Guh!"

"What's wrong with her speech?"

"She's had a head injury. It's affected her movement, her speech, her writing – "

Mal thought of the childlike drawing on the postcard.

"She's recovering fast, but she's still very sick and incredibly drained. She should be in hospital."

"So, why'd you take her out? I saw the CCTV footage on local news – "

"What, of me 'kidnapping' her?" Gage retorted with aggressive sarcasm, "What are they *actually* showing?"

"You, lifting her into your truck, driving away…"

"How convenient they're not showing the first part, where she was so terrified she pulled off her own drip and climbed out a window to escape the guys who were after her! I happened to be in the right place at the right time…or the wrong place at the wrong time, depending on how you look at it."

"Yeah…mighty coincidental you just showed up in the middle of nowhere…"

"What exactly are you saying?"

"Well, how do we know you are who you purport to be?"

"Jesus, how paranoid *are* you people? What the hell is going *on* here?"

Just as Mal opened his mouth to reply, Kennedy's pallid and feverish body spasmed, and she jerked up sharply, spraying a copious gush of watery vomit down all their fronts.

****

Gage had showered and changed. Bare-chested, he'd carefully bathed Kennedy in Mal's huge tub, cradling her shocked and shuddering body in his arms like a child as he'd sponged off the dirt and delicately shampooed her hair. The micropore tape securing the chequerboard of dressings gradually became soggy and limp in the warm, soapy water, detaching from her skin so the pads of wadding peeled off and bobbed around the bath. The puncture wounds looked surprisingly good considering how much her body had endured in the last few days, the skin around the points of penetration only light pink now rather than deep red, the holes scabbing over reassuringly. Her bruises were lightening from purplish-black to yellowish-green, body repairing with encouraging rapidity.

Touching her hair – rubbing the shampoo cautiously into it so as not to disturb the healing wound – reminded him of the night they'd let Joelle home from hospital, and she'd lain in the tub while he'd washed her hair for her, and Ryan had slept soundly on the bathroom floor next to him, swaddled in a blanket his mother had crocheted for her newest grandchild.

Clean for the first time in days, wearing Mal's bathrobe and wrapped tight in a blanket like a sushi-roll, Kennedy slept long and deep on Mal's big leather couch, while the two men sat uneasily opposite one another at the dining table. Eating a hastily assembled meal of cheese, crabsticks, salad and rice, they drank beer and eyed each other with cautious acceptance.

Mal glanced towards the sleeping woman, "I can see why you think she should be in hospital."

"Yeah, she's way too sick to be on the run…but she won't go back there, and I'm going to jail if I take her back. She's made out you're the Oracle, man. Get to you, and all our questions are answered. Is she right?"

Mal took his time, answering cagily, "Maybe…? What's she told you?"

"Very little, because she's struggling to remember things. What kicked all this off – got the hoodlums knocking at our door, started her climbing out of windows – was your article. It implied you knew a lot."

"I might. I might know a great deal…but you might not be the guy to tell it to."

"You *can* tell it to me! I think I'm in deep shit because of what's going on, and I have no understanding of why!"

"I've only got your word for that. I could be putting myself at risk by telling you – "

"You're *already* at risk! The suspicious guys from the hospital? They're watching your office!"

"One big and fat, one little and thin, in a black Chrysler?"

"Well, I've only seen the car in the dark at a distance but, yep, they're the ones."

"They've been outside the house too."

"Kennedy had seen them before, but she couldn't remember where. She only knew she was petrified of them...*so* petrified she climbed out a window when she could barely stand up!"

"What bothers me about all this is that you reportedly discovered her in the middle of nowhere. I mean, what were you doing there? Had you been instructed to find her?"

"*Instructed?* Are you for real? By whom?"

"You're a fearsome-looking gentleman, and you just appeared on the scene in the nick of time to rescue her?"

"A 'fearsome-looking gentleman'...that's one I haven't heard before. Look, Mal – is it all right if I call you Mal?"

"Sure."

"I'm Gage, by the way. Gage Rutter. Nice to meet you."

The two men shook hands cursorily over the table, an air of awkwardness surrounding the formality of the gesture.

Gage muttered, "Thanks, you know, for the food and the shower and everything. For providing Kennedy her first decent rest in days."

"You're welcome."

"The reason I look and sound like this – so 'fearsome' – is that I was in a wildfire back home a couple of years ago. My wife and son were killed. I struggled to process my grief... It was so sudden, I had no way of preparing for it. Our house pretty much exploded. One minute they were there, and the next I was all alone."

Mal observed the waves of pain traversing the younger man's damaged features, and felt a rush of fellow-feeling for him, "I understand. I do. I don't think it matters if it's fast or slow, it still rips your guts out. I lost my wife – my Sally – to cancer five years ago. It was a long and torturous process, as if she was steadily shrinking…just getting smaller and smaller until she disappeared altogether. There was nothing I could do. It hurt, Gage Rutter, and it still does."

"You got any kids?"

"We never had any. Careers and vacations and adventures…we just thought we'd have a family a little older, and then it didn't happen. By the time we realised it wasn't going to, we were too old to adopt. I'd never really planned for kids – too immature myself, I guess. I've got nieces and nephews, I had Sal, I didn't think about the future like I should have done, and then she was gone. I look upon Kennedy a little like a daughter, but I'm not sure she'd be that delighted if she knew."

"She sure puts a lot of faith in you, sir…"

"I only hope I'm worthy of it. Maybe losing Sal would have been easier if I'd had kids to fill the void. I don't know. How old was your boy?"

"Only a week. They were just home from hospital. He arrived early. I'd barely met him, and he was snatched away."

"I'm sorry…"

"Yeah, I'm sorry too…"

Gage sighed, sniffed, and deliberately didn't look directly at the older man as he caught sight of him wiping his eyes with suntanned fingers, instead glancing towards Kennedy, "Look at us, snivelling about past problems we can't change, when the one in genuine trouble right now is sleeping like a baby over there."

Mal smiled mournfully, "Typical guys, huh? Self-obsessed."

"That was one of the reasons I wound up in Florida. I knew if I didn't do something I'd just walk out onto the prairie with my shotgun and blow my own face off. I decided to go somewhere I'd never been before. I discovered how nice the beach is! It's become a place of peace for me, somewhere I can just tune out and watch the waves roll in. That's how I found Kennedy. I pulled off the highway to take a leak, saw the ocean the other side of the hedge from where I was, crawled through onto what I guess was a private beach, and spotted all these footprints. The beach belonged to a fancy house that was all closed-up for the hottest part of the year, and it bothered me where the prints had come from, so I went to look and I found her, more dead than alive. I carried her to my truck, took her to hospital, and stayed with her because I remembered how it felt to lie alone in pain…and nobody knew who she was or where she'd come from until the nurses saw the newspaper. One of them called the cops but they never showed. Instead, our two hoodlum buddies appeared – I'm pretty sure not by chance – and scared Kennedy so bad she climbed out the bathroom window to get away from them! I went after her to bring her back inside, but she was so freaked out I suggested just sitting in my truck. We could see Rocky and Bullwinkle in her room – "

"Rocky and Bullwinkle?"

"An old cartoon on tv…a huge moose and a little squirrel. Makes me think of it every time I see 'em. It'd be funny if they weren't so threatening. I locked the hospital room door, but they busted it within about two minutes, and we could see them in the bathroom, craning out of the window trying to spot where we'd gone. I proposed going to the beach for a little while until they went away. I knew it made me feel better, so I thought it might help her too. By the time we got in the truck to come back an hour or two later, I was Public Enemy Number One. We've been running scared since, with no idea who we can trust and whether this threat is real or a figment of our imaginations! We've been through a lot to get to you, sir."

"Right…and I truly don't know how much help I can be."

"What do you mean?"

"Well, I know plenty, but nothing to get the cops off your back, because I have *no evidence*. Kennedy has that, and it's hidden somewhere."

"So, you *do* know the story, but you can't print it because she's got all the proof and probably can't remember where she's put it?"

"That's about the shape and size of it, yeah."

"Can you at least explain to me why my 'recuperation vacation' has turned into a living nightmare?"

"Yeah, I think I can. I think you're all right, Gage Rutter."

Gage inclined his beer bottle in silent salute, and Mal cleared his throat, "Kennedy was doing a series of articles on women's issues, including a piece on domestic violence. She visited a refuge as part of her research. There, one of the women she interviewed claimed she'd escaped from the basement of a house where she'd been imprisoned, after the place got quite badly damaged during hurricane *Irma*. She said a bunch of girls were in that house. They'd all been fed much the same story. They'd gone for interviews with an agency at home for domestic service jobs in the US, but they didn't materialise, of course. Instead, they trustingly surrendered their passports, were shoved in trucks and in the holds of fishing boats, and brought up from South and Central America into the Keys via the Caribbean. Apparently, they got moved around pretty frequently, house to house, different girls came and went all the time, and there were these parties with gangs of men they were forced to have sex with. The girl didn't know where any of the houses were…apart from the hurricane-damaged one some of them had escaped from. She knew the number, the street name, where it was in relation to other buildings, and Kennedy checked it out. There was evidence of people having been in the basement, but the place was empty. It was a high-end seasonal rental. A luxury villa on a quiet, respectable development…and it belonged to the Governor of Florida."

"Shit!" Gage gaped, astounded.

"My sentiments exactly. On discovering this, Kennedy being Kennedy, she didn't elect to leave well alone, which would have been the sensible thing to do. Instead, she got a reasonably comprehensive list of the more secluded and luxurious properties in his portfolio, and started working her way through it."

"Oh my God…"

"I didn't know. If I'd found out earlier, I would have tried to stop her."

"She's hard to stop though, huh?"

"You have no idea! She's hidden outside houses where these parties were going on. At least, that's what she told me. She's apparently got photographs, video… She became obsessed with it, taking bigger and bigger risks, trying to check the basements of all the houses on her list…and someone obviously found her doing it, because she went off to follow up a lead one night after work, and never came back in the next morning."

"Jeez…no wonder everything keeps falling into place for the bad guys. Potentially, the most powerful man in the whole *state* is pulling the strings!"

"If what she says is true, and he's involved, he has influence on the cops, power over the news media, control of the release of information. It's very natural he'd want you out of the way to get to her. Labelling you a criminal removes you very efficiently…and you *do* look the part, if you don't mind me saying. Hence why the local media are being encouraged to push the hospital kidnap story."

"So, if we can find Kennedy's evidence…?"

"I could potentially print her full exposé, and then the shit'll really hit the fan for our whiter-than-white State Governor. It all depends on the integrity of her information. We might even have enough to take straight to the cops."

"If the cops aren't all crooked."

"All I'm repeating is what she told me. I've seen nothing."

"Are you suggesting it won't stand up to scrutiny?"

"No idea…but I got good reason to believe it's as hot as she says it is. Not only is she very good at her job, but the moment I printed the first article about Kennedy's disappearance – the one you saw – I had a *very* bullish guy in my office trying to intimidate information out of me. He said he was a cop, but we can't find any evidence of that. I've got a photograph of him standing with the Governor at an upstate rally a year ago, but we also can't find conclusive evidence he's on the Governor's staff either. He was very anxious to discover what we knew. I didn't tell him a thing. I don't know if he's on our side or not. He might well be legit, but I thought it best to check him out before I shared information with him. Unfortunately, I can neither track him down nor identify him."

"But he's mixed up in it?"

"Without a doubt. He wouldn't have shown up at the paper throwing his weight around otherwise. I just don't know whether he's on the side of good or evil. What I *do* know is that Kennedy's digging is touching a raw nerve, somewhere close."

A soft sound behind them made both turn to see Kennedy struggling to sit and extricate herself from Gage's overzealous blanket-wrap. She yawned, blinked, and looked about her in confusion, until focusing on Gage and Mal and smiling in visible relief.

Gage grinned, "Okay? Know where you are?"

"Mal's."

"Yep. You slept for ages. Feel better?"

"Yeah."

"Good. You hungry?"

"Yeah."

"Come and eat."

Gage stood to help her over to the table, but she pushed his hands away, determined to walk unaided, only beginning to sway halfway across the large room. The ever-watchful Gage was there to catch her, easing her down onto a battered La-Z-Boy by the French doors, "Just sit there. Rest your head back. Stop *pushing* all the goddam time! I'll get you some food. It's good."

She smiled faintly. Mal fidgeted, embarrassed, "Don't sit her on that awful old chair!"

The upholstery was ripped and the internal foam padding bulged out like a paunch above a waistband.

Gage chuckled, "It doesn't matter, man! You should see what we've been sitting on for the last few days!"

Gage spooned food onto a plate, rested it on Kennedy's lap, and passed her a fork, squatting by the chair, "I know why the whole world wants to kill you, Kennedy McKendrick."

She squinted quizzically at him as he explained, "Because you found out our Governor is a very naughty boy."

Her eyes and mouth formed three perfect circles of wonder and surprise, as the light of recognition dawned, "Yeah!"

"You met a trafficked girl in a refuge, and she told you she'd been kept in the Governor's big, fancy rental properties, and used in sex parties?"

"Yeah!"

"And you got evidence."

"Yeah…"

"Where is it, Kennedy?"

"Oh…Mal…?"

"Mal doesn't know. Only you know. You've hidden it, and no one knows where but you."

"Hmmmm…."

"Can you remember where?"

"No…" Her bottom lip wobbled, and Gage squeezed her wrist gently, "Never mind. Don't get het-up about it. Eat that plate of food, drink all that glass of water, and then drink another. We're dehydrated, we're hungry, we're strung-out…it's no wonder we can't think straight. Oh, and Rocky & Bullwinkle have been watching the house. They might be outside right now. I daren't open the blinds to look."

She indicated her wish for pen and paper. Never far from a notebook in the house of a career journalist, Mal provided them at speed, and she scribbled: **Life's still shit, huh?**

"Totally," Gage winked, eyes never leaving hers.

I asked you to bring me here, and you did. Our bargain's complete. Now you're free to do what you want, go where you will.

Gage eased forward and reached to brush her hair aside so he could whisper in her ear. The trailing touch of his fingertips made her skin tingle. In his lazy, gravelly drawl, he growled the words she'd secretly longed to hear, "Sugar, we both know I ain't going nowhere."

She reached up and tenderly caressed his damaged face, murmuring, "Gage…"

The first time she had truly spoken his name.

Gage's throat closed over with the surge of welling emotion. His eyes filled with hot tears, so he clamped them tightly shut and fought hard not to break down in front of her. At length, he croaked, "Eat your food. I need some sleep."

He turned to Mal, "Okay if I crash on your couch, sir?"

"Be my guest."

"Thanks."

Gage loafed to the other end of the long room, subsided wearily onto the couch, covered himself with the blanket discarded by Kennedy, and was soon snoring steadily, exhaustion overwhelming distress and fear.

Mal moved his dining chair close to Kennedy, and whispered, "Is he to be trusted?"

Kennedy scowled reproachfully at Mal, and rejoined, "Yes!"

"You sure? It feels right, in your gut?"

"*Yes*," she insisted vehemently.

"I hope so, because I've revealed damn near everything you said the other night. Did you leave the office and go straight up to that place like I told you not to?"

"Think so."

"Oh, *Kennedy*! And what happened?"

She shook her head, patted her temple. *Can't remember.*

"Do you know the name Quantick?"

"No…?"

"I'll find you a picture later. He paid me a little visit at work. He *really* wanted to know all about you…not where you were, but what you knew and who you'd talked to. That rang alarm bells for me, like he didn't need to discover your whereabouts because he already knew. He was just filling in the blanks."

"Looks?"

"Tall, suave, dark hair, well-dressed…confrontational manner, to say the least."

"Dunno…"

"Can you *really* not remember a thing, or is that a precaution for his benefit?" Mal inclined his head towards Gage, and Kennedy frowned at his insensitivity, reaching again for the pad, and writing:

Comes and goes. Fleeting recollections in the back of my mind. When I try to focus on them, they disappear. Clear thinking's not a given any more. I'd have been completely screwed without Gage taking care of me.

"What's between the two of you?"

What are you Mal, my Dad? Let it go, will you?

"I'm concerned for your welfare. Very sweet, very charming, very humble…he could be a plant designed to win your trust and find out exactly what you know before he disposes of you – "

"*No!*" The dull chink of metal on china as Kennedy tossed her fork onto her plate and snatched up the pen again:

Gage is a kind, trustworthy, gentle man! I'm screwing up the life he's trying to rebuild, and he's still on my side! He's stuck with me despite everything I've put him through! He's a good man, Mal. I trust him implicitly. He's lost his wife too, and his baby!

"He told me."

So, you must be able to sympathise?

"I can!"

Then don't be an asshole! I'd have died ten times over by now if not for Gage. Be nice to him!

"Whose food has he just eaten? Whose couch is he asleep on?"

"Okay…"

"I have your best interests at heart, honey."

"Oh-*kay*!"

"I'm going to have a coffee. Want one?"

"Yes."

Mal stood, wincing at the warning from his back, and hobbled to the kitchen to put on the pot.

A couple of minutes industrious bustle before he became aware of Kennedy's feeble call from the other room, "Mal! Mal!"

He shuffled into the lounge as fast as his sciatica would allow, "What?"

She was poking frantically into the exposed foam bursting from the arms of the ancient chair he really should dispose of, except it was so comfortable to sit in and read the weekend papers…

"Mal! Foam!"

"Yes…?"

"Foam!"

"Honey, I don't get what you're saying – "

She snatched at the pad, fumbling with the pen: **My evidence, Mal! I know where it is! It's at the office!**

"No, it isn't. I've looked. So has Glen. So have the Police. There's nothing there…"

Oh yes there is! It's a great hiding place, Mal. You'll never guess in a million years…

EVIDENCE

"No way!"

"It's what she said."

"You're telling me I've been scratching around for breadcrumbs of information for days and all the answers were three feet away from me the whole time?"

"Apparently."

"Well, let's see if she's full of it or not!"

Glen stalked furiously across to Kennedy's bare desk, tugged out her shabby chair, and probed long digits into the exposed foam padding on the side of the threadbare seat, starting in genuine surprise as his fingertips felt the alien object concealed within the upholstery.

"Oh my God..."

"There's something there?"

"Yeah...I can't..." Glen fumbled and stretched, "I guess you need little fingers...if I can just hook it...yes!"

He withdrew the hidden treasure and held it up triumphantly.

A memory stick.

Mal could have kissed him. Instead, he grabbed Glen's shoulders and joggled him around in pure delight, "Well done, Glen!"

The office was starting to fill up with staff arriving to begin their working day. Mal folded his hand cautiously over the memory stick and Glen took the hint, pushing it into his pocket as Mal muttered, "My office."

Once safely inside, Mal shut the door and turned sheepishly to Glen, "I've been holding out on you a little."

Glen feigned amazement, and crowed, "No shit, Boss!"

Mal reddened, "You knew, huh?"

Glen's look was kindly, but reproachful, "Boss, I may be inexperienced, but I'm not stupid."

"No, Glen, you're definitely not."

Contrite, Mal was quick to apologise, "I'm very sorry, son. I should have trusted you with all I knew. I've expected you to investigate with one hand tied behind your back. If what I believe is on that memory stick is actually there, then you'll see why I was so reluctant to involve you. I thought a level of ignorance would keep you safe. This is serious. Huge, political, and dangerous."

"Right. Concerning the Governor?"

"For sure."

Mal went to his desk, flipped open his briefcase, and drew out an old laptop, unravelling a power cable across the office and plugging it in, "Battery's shot, this thing's so old. Don't look at this memory stick on any of the work computers, okay? Don't leave a trail someone could follow."

"Okay…?"

Mal beckoned him round the desk, indicating Glen should sit before the laptop, "Plug it in. Let's see what we've got."

"What are you expecting?"

Glen plonked into Mal's chair with alacrity, easing open the laptop and shoving the precious stick into the USB port. Mal took another memory stick from his desk drawer, "Wipe whatever's on this and make another copy of everything on Kennedy's stick. Then put it back where we found it, just in case."

"Good idea. Mal, what do you think is on here?"

"The reason Kennedy's life's in danger." Mal glanced at his watch, "It's ten to nine already. I have to do Daily Briefing."

"What do you want me to do?"

"Start at the beginning and read every word she's written. Look at every video, every photograph, okay?"

"What am I looking for?"

"I think that will become clear. A watertight story, Glen! Something I can print without winding up in court…and maybe enough to give to the cops."

"You're kidding!"

"I wish I was," Mal paused with his hand on the doorhandle, "Glen, promise me – if anyone asks you, you know nothing about this stuff. You've never seen it, right?"

"Why?"

"For your own safety, son. Someone's already tried to kill Kennedy for what's on that memory stick, I'm certain of it. I really don't want to have to write to your mother telling her you've perished in the line of duty. Somehow, I don't think she'll understand. She's under the impression you've got a nice, safe office job."

Glen chuckled quietly, and nodded, "Okay, Boss, I get it."

"Good. Never leave that stuff unattended, not even to pee."

"What if I really need to go?"

"Then tell me, and I'll babysit it 'til you get back."

"But surely no one here...?"

"I truly have no idea who to trust any more..."

"You can trust me, Boss!"

"I know, Glen. I know. I have to go to Briefing. Get reading. Don't stop."

****

"I got you a Spicy Meatball Footlong. If you don't like that, you'll have to trade with someone else in the office."

"No, that's great. Thanks, Boss, I'm starving!"

"Coke, or 7Up?"

"7Up please."

"Here," Mal handed him an ice-cold, condensation-covered can.

"Thanks."

"Well?"

"I can't believe the stuff that's on here. It'd make a porn star blush! What did she do, hide in the goddam bushes or something?"

"I think that's exactly what she did."

"I can kinda see why you didn't want to tell me."

"I didn't want to involve you in something that could be incredibly dangerous."

"This is sex-trafficking, right?"

"According to Kennedy."

"That's what all this evidence suggests. Bringing in girls through the Keys, and...well..."

"Yeah."

"So, what now?"

"The evidence…is there enough for some kind of legal case? Enough to go to the cops with?"

"I'm not sure yet. I'm still going through it. There's a bucketload of stuff on here."

"I think she's been working on this for months."

"And never breathed a word…"

"Classic Kennedy, wouldn't you say?"

"And someone finally caught up with her, and tried to make her permanently disappear."

"But they didn't succeed, because of this Gage Rutter guy. Whether I'm suspicious of his motives or not, his quick-thinking did get her to hospital before it was too late. Regardless of his ultimate motive, there's no question he saved her life."

"I checked him out like you asked me to."

"Any dirt?"

"Not a speck. There's a local newspaper article about the wildfire he said killed his wife and son. He didn't make it up. If he's one of the Governor's hoods masquerading as a Wyoming rancher called Gage Rutter, he's done his homework thoroughly."

"Those burns would certainly be hard to fake…"

"Right. Well, I haven't seen him. The article talks about the effect of a wildfire going through this small rural community, that there was extensive damage on a couple of local farms, and at one the wife and son were killed, and the husband hospitalised when the fire destroyed their house…and it gives their names. Besides that, there isn't a whisper of him anywhere, and therefore no obvious link between him, the Governor, Florida…nothing…"

"I guess I should be glad. He does come over as a decent guy…I just…" Mal sighed, and tried to be reasonable, "He really does look after Kennedy. They seem very close…"

"Jealous of him, Boss?"

Mal's head jerked up. He barked defensively, "Why would you say a thing like that? Glen, this isn't a competition! All I want is for life to return to normal. I want to lift this threatening shadow from *all* of us, okay?"

"Sure, Boss…sure…"

A couple of moments of awkward silence followed, during which Glen made determined inroads into his immense sandwich, and Mal brooded over the accuracy of the perceptive young man's analysis. He *was* jealous of Gage Rutter: strong, vital, and able to keep pace with the headstrong Kennedy, something he could never have done, not even in his youth. This must be how it felt to walk your daughter down the aisle, place her trembling hand in the powerful palm of her new husband, meekly take your seat and placidly accept the usurpation of your position by your little girl's new hero.

Glen mumbled through his mouthful, "You know, Boss, I always found Kennedy real annoying. She had this superior attitude like she was better than the rest of us…and I just thought it was because she was the editor's little pet. No offence."

Mal grinned, wondering where this was going, and murmured, "None taken."

"I never thought it was because she was better at her job than the rest of us…but…looking through this stuff, it's just so well put-together! You can follow the evidence trail without her having to write a single word of copy explaining what she's done. The maps, dates, addresses, videos…it tells its own story, and at considerable personal risk. I'll admit…it sticks in my throat to say it, but she really *is* that good, isn't she?"

"She's the best, Glen. Not to take away from the sterling work you've been doing these last few days, but she's always just been a cut above the rest of you, prepared to go the extra mile. She's wasted here! She should be working for a major national newspaper or doing tv…but I'm not sure she's got the self-confidence. She's waiting for the scoop that'll catapult her to the big-time. I don't think she believes she's good enough without it."

"This body of work says otherwise."

"I agree, Glen…but you know the stubborn little madam listens to no one but herself…and, just recently, maybe Gage Rutter too, but I'm not sure either of them particularly care who's bossin' whom right now. I think staying alive and off Mr Governor's radar is paramount."

"You know, about the Governor –"

"What?"

"There's one thing standing out from Kennedy's research that strikes me as odd."

"Which is?"

"You can find out where the Governor's been – where he's made speeches, held rallies, done public appearances, all that kind of stuff – and Kennedy's got lists and lists going back months."

"And?"

"And unless I'm reading it all wrong – and I honestly don't think I am – every time there's one of these 'bunga-bunga' parties, Mr Governor is somewhere else."

"*What?*"

"Yeah. Somewhere in the state giving a speech, or travelling, or up in DC – "

"Hold on, Glen…you're saying the Governor is *out* of the Keys every time one of these parties takes place?"

"According to Kennedy's records…and I can double-check them easily enough."

"I thought he was using them as a political tool! I assumed that was what had enabled him to rise so quickly!"

"Blackmail, you mean?"

"Right! Get your rivals into an awkward situation, make it quite clear you'll release the pictures if they stand in your way, and walk over the compromised competition right to the top. It won't be the first time that's happened in DC, and it won't be the last, either."

"Sure, makes sense…but perhaps he's simply turning a financial profit out of it, and being absent helps keep his hands clean."

"You'd need a pretty trusted lieutenant to manage affairs of that delicate nature on your behalf…"

It took but a moment for the penny to drop, and for the two to crow in unison, "*Quantick!*"

"That would explain why I can't find him on the Governor's staff! He's a hoodlum-for-hire!"

"Or they're in it together? He provides the girls and the Governor provides the property?"

"Could be…"

"Right, Glen, *now* we're getting somewhere! Go back through all those pictures and videos. Forget spotting the Governor, because we know he's not there. You're looking for Quantick."

"Sure thing, Mal!"

"Did you copy the stick?"

"Yeah, and I put it back in the chair while you were all in Briefing. No one saw me."

"Good man, Glen. If the journalism dries up, a CIA career beckons, huh?"

Glen laughed and chomped his sandwich with an air of self-satisfaction.

Mal held out his hand, pushing his glasses on hurriedly, "Show me that map of all his places. Which was the last one she visited, according to her list?"

Glen pointed with a sauce-coated finger, "That one."

"Right. I'm going there."

"*Now?*"

"Yes. Chances are it's empty…and if it was the last place she visited, it's where they snatched her. There might be something that's been overlooked."

"Want me to come with you?"

"No, Glen. I want you to stay here, guard this information with your life, and trawl those photographs for the merest glimpse of that slimy bastard. I want evidence that places him at the scene."

"Okay, Mal…just…be careful. You're not twenty-five any more!"

****

Luxurious mansions nestled amongst landscaped tropical gardens, surrounding lush mangroves making the location both secluded and exclusive. It didn't look as if any of the houses were yet occupied. The couple closest to the highway still appeared to be under construction. It was the ideal place to host a risqué party and not upset the neighbours. It also explained why Kennedy had been discovered in a wetsuit. She'd obviously left her car down by the Marina where the cops had found it, and paddled her kayak the relatively short distance, cutting through narrow channels to shorten the journey time and permit her unobserved access to the canal at the rear of the development. Kayaking in was the perfect covert approach under cover of darkness. Secret, virtually silent, and it had obviously stood her in good stead at all the other locations. For some reason, this one had been different…or perhaps she'd simply got careless, become blasé after so many weeks snooping undetected, and paid a dangerous price. Mal knew he was making a lot of assumptions, but this was the last location Kennedy had listed in her detailed records, and Gage had found her in a wetsuit and rash vest. There was a map of this spit of land and the surrounding mangrove channels on the memory stick. She'd clearly scoped out a waterside way in. Mal was convinced she'd reached this house, been discovered on the grounds, and punished for her audacity. He therefore needed to get into the backyard of the place somehow. There was a slim chance some evidence of her presence might remain.

He parked outside the correct villa, prudently pushed the sheaf of Kennedy's papers into the glove box, got out of the car, and tried the wrought-iron gate. It was so securely shut it didn't even rattle when he gripped and shook it. The whole property was enclosed behind a high white-stucco wall. Mal jumped a couple of times, arms at full stretch, but couldn't even get a fingertip on top of it. Besides, he'd need to be a younger, stronger, fitter man to haul himself up and clamber over. Mal sighed dejectedly. It would doubtless be the sort of thing rippling Gage Rutter could do without batting an eyelid. Mal shook his head impatiently. What he lacked in brawn and stature, he could more than make up for in intelligence and guile. "If at first you don't succeed…"

Mal turned and meandered back the way he'd come up the sunny sidewalk, as if he might be in the market for a new and exclusive villa once the Realtor's board went up.

The unfinished houses didn't yet have gates. The wiring for lights and mechanism poked out through wonky holes in the otherwise-seamless render. Mal strolled up a partially laid drive with exaggerated nonchalance, preparing a plausible excuse for his presence. He needn't have bothered. The site was deserted. Access to the backyard was also ungated. Mal walked straight down the side of the building and out onto a sandy expanse littered with the detritus of the ongoing project, which would presently be cleared, raked, turfed, landscaped, planted and primped to multi-million-dollar perfection. Mal glanced up at the rear elevation of the mansion. He couldn't see any figures moving around inside the house. He decided to act as if he had every right to be here and keep ploughing on until somebody stopped him. He followed a shallow service trench snaking through the dirt, intended for canalside fresh water and boat-lift electricity supply. Mal smiled with satisfaction as he trod the path of the trench right up to the concrete retaining wall of the rear-access canal, and saw that, unlike the boat lift, the wooden jetty had already been completed. It was a similar set-up to where he lived. All the jetties joined together, making one unbroken line of moorings along the rear of all the properties. It was possible to walk from one end of the canal to the other straight along the linked decks.

He descended the nearest access-ladder and advanced cautiously towards his objective of the final house at the very end of the canal. Upon reaching it, he took some time checking the last jetty for evidence of Kennedy, but of course there was nothing. If she'd paddled up here, all she would have done was tied up her craft and crept up the steps to the lawn. She wouldn't have left any other trace of her presence, and even the dumbest of the Governor's associates could hide an unwanted kayak if they needed to. They'd probably holed and sunk it right where they'd found it.

Mal stared fruitlessly down into the opaque green water for any sign of the craft, then abandoned that pointless search, climbed the first few rungs of the wooden ladder, and popped his head up above the wall. He looked straight across the lawn at the house, and movement away to the far left caught his eye. A big, dark-haired man in a well-cut suit. It could only be Quantick! What was he doing?

Without considering the wisdom of proceeding, Mal edged soundlessly up the final few steps and scuttled speedily across the lawn into the cover of the shrubbery. Quantick was absorbed in pushing aside branches and rooting around in the undergrowth near the house. He wasn't listening out for any danger because he assumed he was quite alone. Mal waited until the younger man bent forward again before daring to edge closer, sinking back into cover the moment Quantick straightened up, moved a couple of feet and resumed his fingertip search. Mal gave it a count of five in his head, then repeated the process: watch, tiptoe, conceal, wait...

He was no more than six feet from Quantick when he suddenly saw him start, dart forward, and retrieve an object from the loamy topsoil.

Now.

Mal stepped confidently out of the bushes, and barked, "What are *you* doing here?"

THE INEVITABLE TRUTH

His unexpected appearance shocked Quantick so much Mal was sure his shiny shoes left the ground completely for a second or two. As he whirled around in horrified alarm, his find leapt from his grasp and landed with a soft 'pat' on the grass between the two men.

A small, clear, waterproof pouch containing a cellphone, screen-side-down on the clipped lawn. Mal recognised the case design immediately. It was a reproduction of an old and cherished photograph: a tall man and a petite, blonde woman held the hands of a very little girl with sun-bleached pigtails. All three grinned cheesily at the camera beside the sign for the Kennedy Space Center. Mal wondered whether he should just grab the cellphone and make a break for it…but, realistically, what were the chances of him bending down and being able to straighten up again at speed, or successfully outrunning the young, athletic Quantick?

He hesitated just a beat too long. Quantick dived down, fumbling unsuccessfully to tuck the pouch out of sight, and Mal saw the reason for his hamfistedness.

Both Quantick's hands were heavily taped and bandaged, with extra-bulky dressings across the palms, making him look as if he was wearing a pair of bright white boxing gloves.

Not thinking, Mal blurted, "What happened to your hands?"

Quantick stood up quickly, clumsily shoving the pouch into his jacket pocket, snapping, "Do you have permission from the owner to be on this property?"

Mal, knowing he was on shaky ground, countered, "Do *you*?"

Quantick rolled his eyes in exasperation, and growled, "Of course I do! Where did you come from?"

Mal gestured vaguely behind him, out towards the miles of mangroves, "There...?"

Quantick's face twisted involuntarily and he stalked around Mal as if he was a roundabout, marching to the edge of the canal and peering along the waterway, expecting to see the boat Mal had arrived on. There being no vessel visible, and manifestly discomfited by Mal having materialised from nowhere, Quantick radiated uncharacteristic tension. Unwilling to let it go as it seemed to upset Quantick's equilibrium so effectively, Mal again nodded towards his hands, "Did you have an accident?"

Quantick rounded on him with barely-controlled fury, "Jesus! Don't you *ever* stop asking goddam questions?"

Mal shrugged, "Once a reporter, always a reporter. You should know all about asking questions in your line of work...oh, no, wait, my mistake...because you're not a cop at all, are you?"

Quantick displayed enviable composure, calmly raising one eyebrow and asking, "Aren't I?"

"No...well, not a local Vice cop anyway."

Quantick folded his arms, lofted his chin, and smirked, "What am I then?"

Because he had absolutely no idea, Mal simply smiled enigmatically.

Quantick snorted contemptuously, "Nice try, Mr Lawrence. You're trespassing. Time to go. Don't you have a 'Who's Got The Biggest Lobster' competition to cover for your little newspaper?"

Irrationally stung, Mal retorted recklessly, "My little newspaper, as you so condescendingly put it, can punch well above its weight when it chooses! Stories have to break somewhere. Scandal doesn't only surface in Washington DC, as I'm sure you're well aware."

Quantick ran his tongue over his even teeth as rubbing off something unpleasant, "What scandal are you referring to, exactly?"

Mal smiled mildly, and replied breezily, "I'm just trying to make the point that a local newspaper can break a significant story as effectively as a national can. Are *you* aware of something brewing? I can keep you off-the-record, you know…"

Quantick sighed lengthily and rubbed his forehead gingerly with the back of one bandaged hand, as if he felt unwell, "Oh, Mr Lawrence, you *are* a pain in the ass…"

Mal grinned, pleased with himself. He gestured, "You found something then, in the bushes, there?"

Quantick's hard eyes settled on him, but they looked red-rimmed and bloodshot, as if the guy wasn't sleeping. Mal didn't know whether it was the bulky dressings, the oppressive heat, or the mystery of his own unexplained presence, but Quantick seemed a great deal less polished and self-assured than during their first encounter.

"Mr Lawrence, *I* am conducting a missing persons enquiry. What are *you* doing?"

"I might be in the market for a new-build. I heard about this nice development. Thought I'd check it out. Get the jump on everybody else."

Quantick mocked, "In the market for a new-build? However hard your little paper punches, Mr Lawrence, it'll be a cold day in hell before *you* buy one of *these* – "

"Just because I live here now and do the job I do doesn't mean I've *always* done it. You don't know what I can and can't afford. I had a successful career for a long, long time before I opted out of the rat race. I took this job in the Keys as an early-retirement project. My wife wasn't very well."

"Spare me the memoir, Mr Lawrence."

"What brought *you* to this particular property? Did you know Kennedy had been here?"

Quantick's eyes narrowed, "I could ask you the exact same question, Mr Lawrence…but you'd only answer it with one of your own. You're so good at the verbal swerve, you should go into politics."

"Know a bit about politics, do you?"

"There you go again. You just can't help yourself."

"What do you know, Quantick? Do you know where she is?"

"The one factor common to all missing persons investigations is *no one* knows where the subject's gone."

"*Someone* knows."

"And would that someone be *you*, by any chance?"

Mal's heart thudded forcefully in his suddenly-tight chest, "What makes you say that?"

"As you've been stonewalling all the way through this, I conclude you know more than you're letting on, because of everything from your suspicious behaviour to your increasingly inflammatory articles…not to mention your oh-so-coincidental house-hunting."

"You've got a vivid imagination."

"So, put me straight, Mr Lawrence! Steer me down the correct course."

"Ah, now, 'Detective' Quantick, our interpretations of right and wrong could be poles apart."

"I think my moral compass is aligned, Mr Lawrence. Can the same be said for a career sensationalist whose job is fundamentally based upon spin and hearsay?"

"You've clearly never taken the time to properly read my little newspaper. We don't allege, we *prove*. We uncover truths and facts that we report to our readers. They make up their own minds what they think about them. For example, the *fact* you're not a Vice cop."

"What am I then, Mr Lawrence? Come on, I can't wait to hear!"

Reluctant to admit it, Mal eventually had to confess, "That, I don't know…*yet*…but I'll find out, you can depend on it."

"I'll look forward to the headline."

"You could just tell me and save yourself a lot of embarrassment in the long run, when I finally go to print with my thoroughly researched and proven exposé. Are you working undercover?"

"For whom? To what end?"

Mal didn't reply. He couldn't, not without revealing the extent of his knowledge.

"*I'm* conducting an enquiry…and I maintain *you're* obstructing it for your own purposes. You wouldn't want me to start looking into your background, would you?"

"I couldn't give a damn what you do! I've nothing to hide. I've never so much as fished without a licence, avoided a speeding ticket, cheated on my taxes, had an affair, screwed a hooker or anything else remotely exciting. I get my kicks digging through the dirt of other people's lives. I don't have the leisure to build up a muck-pile of my own. You fit me up any which way you want. It won't stick to me for long, and it won't stop the truth coming out. Call it what you will – justice, karma – but there's an inevitability about truth. It always surfaces eventually, however heavy you might weight it down. Time and tide do their work in the end."

"How achingly poetic, Mr Lawrence. What did you study at college, 'advanced bullshit'?"

"You're punchy when you're rattled, aren't you?"

"You're leaving now."

"So soon? No tour? I've only seen the backyard!"

"Out."

Quantick pointed towards the front of the house, and stayed close behind him as Mal walked up the lawn towards the building. He tried to absorb everything he could about its layout. As Quantick directed him to the left, Mal noticed a small, square window at ground level, surely designed to admit some natural light into a basement. Mindful of what Kennedy had told him, he slowed imperceptibly, in case there was something to see, and Quantick nearly walked into him.

"Come along, Mr Lawrence, this isn't the Botanical Gardens. No dawdling."

Quantick pointed him through a side gate and out onto the sun-drenched driveway, noting the expensive Mercedes parked in the road, "Yours?"

"Yes."

"*Very* nice, Mr Lawrence. Perhaps you *are* in the market for a new-build after all."

Quantick pushed a fob button on his large bunch of keys, and the main gate swung inward as they approached it. Out of the pleasant shade of the tree-lined rear garden, Mal's cotton shirt was already sticking to his back. He wondered how Quantick could stand being in a suit and tie and not seeming to feel the heavy Florida heat.

"So, what *did* happen to your hands? It looks serious."

Quantick glanced down as if the bandages didn't belong to him, and demurred, "They're not that bad. The nurse went a little nuts with the dressings."

"What did you do?"

Quantick shook his head dismissively, "I got them…caught on some wire. No big deal."

"Ouch…bet that was painful! You doing some remodelling at home or something?"

Quantick's usually commanding voice was noticeably fainter and more distant, "Actually, no… I went to visit an old acquaintance. In the desert. Ventured somewhere I shouldn't have done. Paid the price."

"They sore?"

Quantick snorted mirthlessly, avoided eye-contact, and admitted, "Hurt like fuck, truth be told…but it was my own stupid fault, so…" It was only once Mal was on the sidewalk that he realised Quantick wasn't beside him. He looked back to see the younger man standing motionless on the driveway, still gazing down at the balls of bandaging as if they were someone else's hands. The massive gate was advancing rapidly towards his stationary figure.

Mal shouted, "Watch yourself, there!"

Quantick jolted, looked around in alarm, and danced away just in time. The heavy iron clanged shut right behind him like a dog snapping at the mailman's heels.

Quantick cleared his throat, straightened his jacket, recovered his composure and gestured to Mal's smart car, "Off you go."

Mal unlocked it, got in, started the engine…then had a brainwave, leant across, and lowered the passenger window.

Quantick inclined his head so he could see in, "Yes?"

"I don't suppose you've got a card on you, in case I remember anything useful to your investigation? I could call your office."

"Oh…" Quantick made a spectacularly sarcastic show of patting down his jacket pockets like a non-smoker who's just been asked for a match, "Seems I'm all out."

Mal treated him to an equally acerbic reply. "What a *shame*. Well, I *tried* to help you."

"Don't visit this address again, Mr Lawrence."

Mal feigned confusion, and queried, "Not even with the realtor?"

To his credit, Quantick threw back his glossy head and laughed richly, "Get the fuck out of here, and if you know what's good for you, never come back."

"Is that a threat, *'Detective'*?"

Quantick's smile was as wide and photogenic as a toothpaste commercial, "Think of it as a Public Safety Advisory Notice, *sir*."

"I hope your hands stop hurting."

"Good afternoon, Mr Lawrence."

Mal's agile brain contorted like a gymnast on the drive back to the office. Had Kennedy's cell been a fortuitous find for the opportunist Quantick, or had he known it would be there? Had the guy simply been tidying up?

JUST THE MAN FOR THE JOB

"Glen! He was there! Quantick was there! And, what's more, I think he found Kennedy's cell!"

"Where?"

"Out in the backyard. He was there when I arrived, rooting through the bushes. I hid and watched him. He bent down, picked something up, so I jumped out and scared him – "

"Boss, that could've been real bad!"

"Well, I got overexcited. I wasn't thinking about self-preservation; I was thinking I wanted to see what he'd just picked up. He jumped about a foot in the air, dropped it on the ground, and it looked for all the world like Kennedy's cell, with that old picture of her Mom and Dad on the back cover. If I'd gotten there ten minutes earlier…!"

"There might not be anything revealing on it, and if it's fingerprint or passcode protected, it'll take him a while to get into. I don't think it's that useful – "

"Except it places her at the scene, Glen! It's proof she was there!"

"Oh…yeah…I guess… Was there anything else?"

"Nothing I could see, but my freedom to hunt for clues was curtailed by him watching my every move. I just can't work out if he was doing the same as I was, or if he was cleaning up a crime scene." Glen's smile was broad, proud, and incredibly encouraging to Mal's flagging spirits, "I'm pretty sure it was the second one, Boss."

Glen placed five colour copies of Kennedy's grainy photographs onto the table with the flourish of a blackjack dealer.

Quantick – unmistakeably him – right in the thick of the action, as involved as anyone else.

Mal deflated into the spare chair like a punctured tyre. He wasn't sure whether it was a relief to finally see what he'd suspected all along, or whether it made life a million times more complicated.

"Well done, Glen. Great work."

"Thanks."

"There's every chance he could be running this whole illegal operation on behalf of the State Governor of Florida!"

"There is another possibility, Boss."

"Which is?"

"The Governor doesn't know about it."

"Glen, are you *crazy*? How can he *not* know, it's happening in his houses!"

"Well, he's a busy guy, right?"

"I'd like to think so, otherwise why did we all vote for him to represent us?"

"Exactly…so he can't be across everything, he's got too much to do."

"I'm not with you."

"You know your little place up in Colorado that you rent out for the ski season?"

"Yes...?"

"You got someone managing that for you?"

"Yeah, it's easier – "

"You see! You just pay the management fee, they worry about it, and you take the rent money. You don't know what's happening up there, do you? They could be organising sex parties in your apartment every night of the week! 'Après ski'…?"

"Why would you put a thought like that in my head?"

"I'm not saying it's actually going on! I'm saying it *could* happen, and you'd be none-the-wiser."

"I suppose not."

"And the Governor's realty company owns hundreds, maybe thousands of properties. How can he possibly know what's going on in all of them? He probably has someone to manage them for him. Someone reliable, someone security-vetted, someone on his staff, maybe?"

"Shit, Quantick's the *facilities* guy?"

"I don't know…but he could be, right? After all, Kennedy's records show the Governor's never around when there's a party going on. That might not be to ensure he remains above suspicion. It might be so he *never finds out*!"

"Good Lord, Glen, you've got a brain that goes around corners, son! I just assumed he was in on it…"

"Yeah, but that's a past career of Washington reporting, Boss. It's negatively clouded your judgement."

"In my experience, Glen, most politicians are dirty, rotten scoundrels to a greater or lesser extent."

"Okay, granted, and maybe our Governor is too…or perhaps he simply doesn't have a clue…?"

****

"I think that's the place they snatched you, and where you lost your cellphone."

Kennedy scowled, befuddled and uncertain, struggling to recall her visit to the house Mal had described. Suddenly, she grasped the sheaves of paper lying in her lap, shaking them in her agitation and crying out, "Worms! *Worms!*"

"Worms?"

Kennedy waggled her index finger in front of his face, but she could tell Mal didn't understand. She couldn't think clearly enough to describe the indistinct image that had fleetingly surfaced in her disjointed memory. Obviously frustrated at what he perceived was her lack of focus, Mal directed her back to the photograph uppermost on the pile clutched in her trembling fist, the original shot of Quantick at the political rally, "You've *never* seen him? You're *sure*?"

Kennedy shook her head helplessly and Mal impatiently whipped that picture from her fingers, exposing the next one down, one of the graphic images of Quantick participating with gusto at a secret party, "See? Same guy! *Sure* you've never seen him?"

Something stirred within Kennedy, a troubling sensation she couldn't explain. Dark eyes, cold and menacing, inches from her own. She opened her mouth to speak but the recollection instantly faded, leaving her unsure it had ever really been there. She pinched at the sharp headache forming across the bridge of her nose. She needed to sleep. She looked plaintively up at Mal, who growled with impatience. Kennedy comprehended his exasperation with her, but wasn't prepared to assent to something she couldn't remember just to satisfy Mal's evident personal vendetta against this unfamiliar man, whoever he might be.

She reached for the pad, and wrote shakily: **There are a million guys, Mal! You expect me to remember one of them in a room full of people, with everything else that was going on? With everything that's happened since?**

"Only because he was the guy who found your cell in the bushes…and I think he knew it would be there. It got me wondering if *he* made that dent in the side of your head!"

Gage, sitting at the table pretending to read the contents of the laptop but really observing the increasingly terse exchange, seized his opportunity to change the subject, and piped up, "You might not recognise that guy, but we know these two, don't we?"

He rotated the computer, pushing it across the table to Mal and Kennedy.

One big and fat. The other small and wiry. A black car parked outside one of the addresses on Kennedy's list, the men snapped in animated discussion on the driveway. The smaller of the two was nearest Kennedy's camera, hands on hips, jacket pushed aside to reveal not only the butt of a gun in a holster tight against his ribcage, but, clearly visible on his belt, a large and ornate buckle with a swooping eagle motif. Kennedy extended a finger towards the screen and pressed it on the buckle, as if touching the bird might bring it to life.

Mal looked from Gage to Kennedy, and queried, "Laurel and Hardy?"

Together, they chorused, "Rocky and Bullwinkle!"

Mal waved a dismissive hand, feeling like a dinosaur, "Whoever! Is that them? Sure looks like the guys who've been snooping around here."

"That's them, sir…and if you're searching for skull-cracking culprits, I'd put those badass dudes top of the list!"

Kennedy frowned intently at the image and again pressed her finger to the distinctive buckle, seemingly lost in thought.

Pleased his timely interjection had stopped the pointless bickering, Gage persisted, "There's something more interesting than that on here."

He walked around the table, squatted next to Kennedy's La-Z-Boy, balanced the laptop on the arm of the chair so all three of them could see, and clicked back through to Kennedy's map, "If you're looking for somewhere there might be more evidence of Kennedy's presence, you've gotta consider this place. Big house on its own on that spit of land. Nice and private."

Mal tapped the screen, "I agree it's on the list as belonging to the Governor's company, but it isn't marked up as one she's visited. There won't be evidence of her at a place she's never been, Gage." It was petty, but he quite enjoyed putting Rutter right in front of Kennedy.

Gage absorbed the dig placidly, and countered, "Never been, huh? See those woods there between the beach and the highway?" His earnest gaze settled on Kennedy's wide-eyed face as he explained softly, "That's where I found you."

****

Bobby Levine lay naked on the lumpy bed in the shabby condominium he called home. To someone who'd a basically itinerant life, keeping still always felt weird, dangerously vulnerable. Close observation of Uncle Harry had taught him that if you weren't the hunter, you'd better get used to being the prey. Beads of perspiration glistened on Bobby's olive skin, but he kept the door locked, the security chain fastened, the windows shut, the drapes pulled. The air was so heavy he didn't think he could get up even if he wanted to. His bandaged hands throbbed and itched agonisingly with the oppressive heat. They were taking an eternity to mend. It was as if his body was waiting to see what else would happen to it before expending energy on unnecessary healing, as if it knew this wasn't over.

Bobby turned his head to one side. The closet door was open. Robert Logan's expensive suits hung close together like a gaggle of nervous politicians in the ghetto, as out of place in the vile surroundings as a nugget of gold in a pan of silt. Logan was a triumph of invention, even by Bobby's standards. He supposed he should be proud, but it turned out he'd made this racket too fruitful. It ran so smoothly, Bobby Levine had become a victim of his own stratospheric success. Stop this now, and his life was forfeit. Continue, and the tenacious Malcolm Lawrence would persist in digging, and needling, and pushing, and undermining, until something gave.

Harry Grafton had been right about one thing; Momma *had* taught him well. Take a little, here and there, but not enough to matter to the big boys. They'll know, and don't ever get cocky enough to think they won't. That knowledge'll make them believe they have power over you…but use your brain. Make yourself so useful their hands are tied. Lose you and all the valuable work you do, and it'll cost them more than you're stealing. They have to let it continue. They haven't a choice.

He'd devised the parties because it was the perfect way of taking money from Uncle Harry without the avaricious old bastard ever being able to work out exactly *how* Bobby profited from their arrangement. He wore Rolex watches and designer suits yet took no more from Harry's coffers than the agreed fee for moving the villain's merchandise from the impoverished South to the wealthy North of the American continent. Harry didn't really care what happened to the product on the journey, providing his contacts in Vegas and LA weren't whining too loud about the state of what they were sent by the time it reached them. Bobby didn't see any point in good pussy literally sitting idle in the meantime, when it could be earning a thrusting young entrepreneur a little flash money on the side.

He was indifferent to the unfortunate women who passed through his hands. If they weren't prepared to lift themselves out of the shit, that wasn't his fault. He'd also come from nothing. His childhood bedroom had been the back seat of a battered old car. He'd learned his math at the racetrack and his ABCs from Sesame Street on flickering Motel tv sets. He'd used his brain to get where he was today. Just thirty, with more than a million dollars in a Panamanian bank account.

That was why he so regretted his one significant lapse of judgement. He could chalk all this recent chaos down to one event, one decision, the firing of a single synapse responsible for the ruination of all his meticulously laid plans. The night he'd squatted in the old boathouse and stared intently at the barely conscious female flopped in the green ooze before him, then turned around and left it to Tyler and Floyd to fix. At that point, he hadn't understood the portent of Kennedy McKendrick's unexplained presence. He'd considered it a minor issue, an interfering bitch who'd got what she deserved. The biggest mistake of his life.

As he'd crouched over her, he could have – should have! – slit her goddam throat, but he'd believed his position unassailable. Momma had warned him all those years ago not to get complacent, but he'd disregarded the prophetic wisdom of her words. The power had gone to his head. He'd fallen for his own elaborately constructed illusion, believing he *was* Robert Logan, with his brilliant qualifications, excellent prospects and glittering future. He'd forgotten he was a piece of shit just trying to turn a buck before the axe fell.

What Bobby Levine needed was to take a long, crisp gulp of refreshing reality. The world was an auspicious place for a young man with wealth and imagination. Preppy fusspot Robert Logan had been very, very good to him. It was a shame to hang him up like his fancy suits in the closet, but his promising political career was about to grind to an enforced and permanent halt. Trapped between Uncle Harry's certain death and Malcolm Lawrence's terrifying truth, the estimable Robert Logan was going to have to retire well before he'd fulfilled his true potential. Bobby Levine allowed himself a rare moment of uncharacteristic regret. Poor old Robert. He genuinely would miss him.

****

"I agree someone's got to check it out, but I just don't think it can be me this time. There've been too many coincidences. If I get there and Quantick's there too, there's no telling what might happen! Crooked cop, corrupt official, hoodlum-for-hire – whatever he is, he's a dangerous guy, and he's already warned me off twice. I can't pretend I'm not intimidated by him – "

"*I'll* go," Gage's gravelly voice insisted with quiet determination, "After all, I know the place. I've already been there once."

"No!" Kennedy's cry of alarm touched Mal as much as it wounded him. He watched her clutch desperately at Gage's arm, as if that would prevent him leaving. He absorbed the hurt that she'd made no similar protest on his account, and had a quiet word with himself about acting his age. Mal didn't begrudge the sweet simplicity of their subconscious need for one another, but witnessing their unfolding union at such close proximity only served to highlight the considerable loneliness of his own existence. Mal swallowed down the futile longing to be able to glance towards the kitchen and see Sally's familiar outline through the frosted glass door, and did the decent thing, "No, Gage, you can't go either. Quantick certainly knows my face, but he'll know yours too. Your ugly mug's still all over the local news! Besides, you need to stay here and look after Kennedy."

Wallowing in his martyrdom, Mal noted the flush of pleasure on Kennedy's pale features, the slump of relief through her body, and the thankful expression she upturned to her gratified self-styled surrogate father. He leant across from his dining chair to the La-Z-Boy, patted her little hand gently, smiled reassuringly at them both, and confided smugly, "No need to worry. I've got just the man for this job."

****

"Okay, I'm off the highway, outside the gates. They're open."

"So, go in."

"*What?* What if there's someone there? What do I say? 'Oh, hi, you don't happen to have any hookers in your basement, do ya?'"

"Glen – lead reporter? The whole 'cut above' conversation? Remember it?"

"Yes," said Glen, tersely.

"Right. Leave all evidence of your identity in the car and get in there! It could be empty – "

"Or there could be a whole bunch of crooks waiting for me!"

"How? They don't know you're coming."

Glen sighed heavily and Mal relented, "You don't have to do this, son. Not if you don't want to. This isn't your battle to fight – "

"Yes, I do."

"You don't – "

"I *do*! If I don't go in there, I'll always know I'm not up to being lead reporter, that I'm just a gopher and a features writer, but not a credible investigative journalist! My pride can't handle accepting my career's over before it's even properly started."

"Glen – "

"No, Mal, you don't understand. I've never done anything like this.
I have to test myself or I won't know if I *can*."

"Your decision, son."

"I'll call you back in a bit."

"Be careful."

"Sure thing."

Glen cut the call, pushed his cellphone, wallet and notebook into the
glove box, locked the car, buried the keys in a pile of dust behind the
rear wheel, and strolled as casually as he was able down the wide
and shady drive, doing his t'ai chi breathing exercises and resisting
the temptation to turn and run.

The land sloped gently down from highway to house. At first, all
Glen could see were recently mowed lawns, with stands of self-
seeded palms dotted across the wide expanse. As he turned a corner,
the full panorama opened before him. He paused to absorb the
majesty of the view. Beneath him, nestled against the shore, the
turquoise roof of a huge property. To one side, sunlight sparkled on
an uncovered pool surrounded by a large deck. To the other, grass
terraces formed wide natural steps down onto a half-moon of white
sand, the whole property framed by a horseshoe of woodland
shielding it from the noise and notice of the highway behind. To one
extremity of the curved bay, a rock and sand promontory, covered by
an attractive grove of swaying palm trees, shielded the house from
the worst of any wind and weather. At the farthest end of the large
private beach, Glen could just see another spit of rock jutting out
into the ocean, forming a second natural boundary. And this was but

one address within the Governor's extensive portfolio! No wonder Mal was convinced the guy had designs on the White House. He was every bit rich enough to finance his bid all the way.

The place looked deserted. Although the pool was uncovered, Glen couldn't see any figures moving about on the terrace or beach, and no parked cars were visible.

He crunched onward down the stone-chipped drive. The rustling canopy of palm leaves protected him from the worst of the sun's intensity, dappling the ground with attractive geometric patterns. Bougainvillea provided vibrant bursts of scarlet and pink amongst the watery palette of blues and greens.

As the drive levelled out, Glen took in the imposing plantation-style property. White weatherboarding and turquoise shutters. French doors opening to verandas. Terraces overlooking garden, beach and pool. Balconies encircling second and third floors. All the windows at the front of the house were firmly closed and there was no obvious evidence of occupation. He would attempt a circuit of the whole building. If unchallenged, he'd begin a thorough search for a basement access.

Glen walked cautiously around the side of the house, stepping lightly, trying not to allow his sneakers to crunch on the gravel path. If he spotted anyone, he'd just creep away again, disappearing up the driveway as fast as he was able.

As he tiptoed down the side of the house and prepared to turn onto the flagstones ringing the pool, a huge man in a suit and tie rounded the corner at speed and bowled straight into him, bulldozing him to the ground!

Horrified, Glen saw the big guy's fist dive across his body and beneath his jacket, like cops did when they were reaching for a shoulder-holstered pistol in a movie shoot-out. On his backside in the dirt, Glen instinctively held up his hands, and squawked, "Is this the place for the marquee?"

The guy stopped short of pulling his gun and blowing Glen's brains out, instead squinting in puzzlement, cocking his head to one side, and asking, "The *what*?"

Glen scrambled to his feet – no easy task while holding your hands up by your ears – and repeated, "The marquee. For the lawn? You ain't expectin' a marquee?"

The guy simply stared for a moment as if Glen was speaking a foreign language, then shrugged, grunted, "Hold on," turned back towards the house, and roared, "Mr Logan? You having a marquee for this thing?"

Glen experimented with lowering his hands. No one seemed to care. The clip of an efficient footfall sounded around the side of the house, followed by an impatient voice Glen had definitely heard before, "*What*, Floyd? A *what*?"

"A marquee, Mr Logan. For the lawn."

Glen edged subtly to the left, trying to get over far enough to catch a glimpse of the other speaker, "This ain't the Feller Wedding? They ordered a marquee."

The figure rounded the side of the house and it was all Glen could do not to leap up and down with glee as he beheld him, narrow eyes assessing the unwelcome interloper with unsettling suspicion. Glen pulled his cap down further over his eyes, relieved he hadn't bothered shaving for a few days, hoping the guy wouldn't recall their one thankfully-brief encounter at the newspaper office.

"If you're delivering a marquee, where is it?"

A good question, and one Glen really should have anticipated. He thought fast, tried to look as hopeless as possible, and admitted, "Well, I ain't had my licence long, and it's a big rig… I got stuck last week and wrecked somebody's rose garden. I mean, I *flattened* it! My boss gave me hell, so now I scope the place out first before I drive the thing anywhere remotely tight or expensive. It's parked back up the highway, there."

Glen gestured vaguely, grinning like the idiot he was pretending to be, "So, this ain't the Feller Wedding? F-E-L-L – "

"No, it's not. You have the wrong place. We're not expecting a marquee."

"No weddings here, then?"

"None whatsoever."

"Ah…my bad. I sure am sorry to have bothered you two gentlemen. Bet you're glad I didn't drive it in now!"

"*Ecstatic.*" Pure ice dripped from every syllable of the flatly intoned word. The black eyes glittered menacingly.

Unnerved, Glen immediately tried to leave, "Well, have a nice day, now."

"Wait."

Shit. Glen swallowed, turned, fixed the same idiot grin to his sweating face, "Yessir?"

"Your company. What's it called?"

Glen was privately proud of what he came up with under such extreme pressure, "InTents Events…you get it? Like Intense, but In Tents…because we do marquees. Good, huh?"

"Genius."

"Yeah…okay, well, bye-bye, now!"

Glen trotted off up the driveway as if returning to his truck like a conscientious employee. He glanced back a couple of times. Both men stood exactly where he'd left them, silently watching his departure.

As soon as he rounded the bend in the drive and was out of sight of the house, he sprinted the remaining distance to his car like Olympic Gold awaited him back on the highway, frantically digging his keys out of the dust with the heel of his shoe and speeding off before Quantick managed to place him.

By the time the obese, hot and unenthusiastic Floyd had shuffled unwillingly up the long driveway in response to Logan's paranoid instruction, Glen's scruffy old Corvette was already back in the anonymous flow of highway traffic.

In a parking space outside a roadside liquor store several miles of safe distance down the road, Glen took his cellphone back out of the glove box and called Mal.

"Glen? Are you all right?"

"Yeah, I'm fine."

"Have you been in?"

"Oh yeah, I've been in." Glen surprised himself with how much swagger he injected into those few words.

"That was quick! What did you find?"

"You called it right."

"Huh?"

"Quantick was there."

"Somehow, I *knew* it! He didn't recognise you, did he?"

"If he did, he kept it to himself."

What happened?"

"I pretended I needed to deliver a marquee for a wedding, and I wasn't sure I had the right address…"

"You're such a clever boy, Glen! What did you see there? Evidence of anything suspicious?"

"You mean, apart from Quantick and his goons? I don't know how relevant this is, but when I said I was delivering a marquee, the guy who stopped me on the drive shouted round the side of the house to Quantick, 'You having a marquee for this thing'."

"This thing?"

"Yeah, like there was something planned and he thought it was perfectly plausible Quantick might have ordered a marquee for it."

"An event of some kind…"

"Seems that way."

"A legit political soirée on behalf of our esteemed Governor, or another dirty party?"

"Who knows? Best way to find out is to check the Governor's diary with his office. Ask for an interview or something. If he's out of the Keys, it's a dirty party."

"Good point, Glen. You're *on fire* today!"

Glen chuckled at the gentle teasing, but lapped up the praise all the same.

"Oh, Boss, careful who you speak to if you do call the Governor's office. I found out Quantick's name."

"Well done, Glen!"

"It's Logan."

"Logan? L-O-G-A-N?"

"That's what it sounded like. The big guy called him 'Mr Logan'."

"Great work, Glen! Fantastic progress!"

"Thanks, Boss."

"Now, get out of there, fast, before they have a chance to follow you or get your licence plate."

"Already done. I got safely away before I called you. They didn't see my car, which way I went, nothing."

"Glen, I have no idea why you worry, son. Carry on like this, and I have absolutely no doubt you'll be one of the very best lead reporters our newspaper has *ever* had."

"Hey…thanks, Boss…really…thanks…"

"Now, get your butt in here double-quick! We've got serious work to do!"

****

By the time Glen arrived back at the newspaper office less than thirty minutes later, it seemed Mal's plans were well-advanced. He met Glen at the door, fizzing with excitement, gabbling frantically as he took the stairs two at a time. Despite his much longer legs, Glen had to jog to keep up.

"I checked with the Governor's office like you suggested, and – whaddya know – he's scheduled to fly from Miami tomorrow afternoon to give a speech at a party fundraiser up in Maine the following day! Unavailable for comment or interview until the end of the week."

"So, it's a dirty party."

"It's got all the classic signs, doesn't it?"

Already at the top of the stairs, hand on the door leading to the newsroom, Glen tugged at his sleeve to slow him down, and demanded, "What do you really think, Mal. Does the Governor know or not?"

"Only one way to find out."

Glen felt unease twist in his belly, "And that is?"

"Ask him, Glen! I'm going to go and ask him."

MR GOVERNOR

"How on earth are you going to ask the Governor anything? He's flying to Maine tomorrow – "

"Yes, and I'll be waiting in the first-class lounge at MIA when he arrives."

"Mal, get real! How are you going to get in the lounge? You need a ticket, a boarding pass!"

"Well, I'll just have to buy one."

"For a flight you'll never take?"

"Speculate to accumulate, Glen."

"You won't get within ten feet of him. He'll have minders – "

"An airport lounge is a public place, only safer, because we've all been through Security to get in! I'll have more chance of approaching him there than I ever would at his house or office."

"You can't guarantee him being in the lounge at MIA. Won't he charter a jet?"

"Glen, have you not read his sickeningly virtuous campaign promises about not wasting public money? The overpaid slimeball flies first class all right, but at least he has sufficient decency to take a seat on an existing flight, rather than chartering his own at twenty times the cost. He'll be there."

"But you won't get close to him – "

"I don't have to get *close*. When I start bellowing all the juicy details across the lounge, he'll pretty swiftly decide a discreet tête-à-tête is preferable to letting me rattle on unchecked."

"He'll have you arrested."

"And deliver our detailed dossier directly to the cops? He definitely won't do that if he's in on it, will he? Even if he isn't, all politicians are paranoid about the slightest whiff of scandal! A whispering campaign can destroy a career. He'll let me talk, I'm confident of it. I just need to be in that lounge at the right time."

"It's dangerous – "

"It's more dangerous to do nothing. Logan is out for Kennedy's blood. Gage's too, by the look of it. I'm *also* really starting to annoy him, so I bet I'm next on the list...and rest assured, he'll have checked out your sweet little story by now, discovered it's a steaming pile of horseshit, and be homing in on you too."

"Oh..."

"If this is people-trafficking on an industrial scale, can you *imagine* the money they're making? You think they're going to let three local-rag reporters and a cowboy stop their party, literally?"

"I guess not."

"The only reason Logan hasn't taken us out before now is he doesn't know how much evidence we'll leave behind for the Feds to pick through. Our articles are unnerving him, Glen! And we haven't even started getting into the meat of Kennedy's evidence yet. I think the threat of exposure in the press is about the only thing keeping us safe from him at the moment."

"And yet you're just going to show our hand and tell the Governor what we know!"

"Not *all* we know…but I'm going to tell him enough. For the first time since this thing started, we know where a party's going to take place and we know when. Before now, Kennedy's just shown up randomly at properties and it's been pot-luck whether something was going on or not. Now, thanks to your excellent work earlier today, we've got the jump on 'em! I'm going to tell the Governor most of what we know, that I'm about to print the bits I can prove, and that we'll just let the voters fill in the blanks. Then we settle in, watch the house, document everything that happens, and call the cops when they're all way too committed to do anything about it. We can catch that asshole Logan red-handed."

"Red-dicked!"

"Exactly! If I speak to the Governor and he's in on it, we'll know."

"How?"

"Because the minute I leave him, he'll call Logan, and we'll be able to observe them running scared, leaving the house, clearing those poor girls out and moving them somewhere else…and we can call the cops, this time with knowledge and proof of Mr Governor's involvement!"

"That *is* a good plan."

"Thank you, Glen. I still have my moments."

Mal took his credit card from his wallet and placed it on the desk in front of his lead reporter, "I need to be in that first-class lounge at MIA the same time as the Governor. Look and see which Maine flights have an executive cabin, check the times, and get me on a plausible flight that fits with the most likely one he's taking. It doesn't matter if I have to sit there half the day to catch him. Then get on with preparing the evidence dossier. Make it sharp and shocking. I'm hoping it'll be Mr Governor's bedtime reading for the next few nights at least."

Mal pushed back his chair, stood, and reached for his car keys.

"Where are you going?"

"Home, to see if my decent suit still fits."

****

The elevator was empty. He was glad of the extra seconds to compose himself. He had one shot at this, and there was every chance his maverick stunt might put him in a jail cell for the night. He'd acted cool in front of Glen, but Malcolm Lawrence was sincerely afraid of what he was about to do.

As the doors slid open and Mal stepped out into the lobby, a glamorous receptionist looked up from her monitor, "Good afternoon, sir. Welcome to the American Airlines lounge. Your passport and boarding card, please."

Mal handed them over wordlessly. Two thousand bucks on an air ticket he wasn't going to use. It had better be worth it.

"That's all in order, Mr Lawrence. Have you used our lounge before?"

"I have, but many years ago."

The receptionist pointed like a stewardess conducting an in-flight safety briefing, "Function Rooms are right behind you, there. To the left is lunch service, the open-plan lounge and the cocktail bar. To the right for workstations, private seating, showers, coffees and pastries. This card has the password for our WiFi."

"Super," Mal still smiled with robotic politeness, but inside his guts were sinking through the floor. It had only just occurred to him that if he was on the Governor's staff and faced with the difficult task of keeping the state's most prominent politician safe whilst honouring his ridiculous campaign promise to remain a man-of-the-people, where better to ensconce your precious charge to await his flight than a pre-booked Function Room, with door safely closed and blinds prudently drawn? He'd told Glen he'd stand in the middle of the lounge and shout if that's what it took…but Mal could scream himself hoarse. Mr Governor would never hear from within a private room down the other end of that long corridor. All he'd get was filled in by airport security for causing a scene. Two thousand dollars ventured, nothing gained. Goddam it! What should he do now?

"Is everything all right, Mr Lawrence?"

The receptionist was standing, holding out his passport and boarding card, concern across her attractive features.

"Sorry!" Mal grinned, embarrassed, "Miles away…"

He clamped the evidence folder more tightly under his arm, took back his travel documents with a grateful smile, and decisively chose the left-hand archway toward a coffee and some space to think.

He was here now. It had cost enough. He might as well eat the most expensive danish he'd ever buy and thoroughly double-check the entire floor. He might get lucky and spot a security-guy getting a coffee, or a political aide in the men's room. At least then he'd know for sure the Governor was here. He just needed to find a seat with an uninterrupted view of the foyer, and wait it out. He'd have fifteen feet of polished floor between Function Rooms and elevator to accost the Governor and, most importantly, pass over the dossier. The guy'd have to be nice to him because everyone would be watching. All was not yet lost.

Calmer now he had a sketchy plan of action, Mal strolled past the wood-partitioned office cubicles, for those who were simply too indispensable to pause what they did even to travel or, heaven forbid, relax for an hour. Mal smiled sorrowfully. Had that once been him, too fired-up by the possibilities around the next corner to ever stop and savour what was right beside him? Now it was too late. He had all the time in the world to appreciate everything, and nothing left to truly value. He shrugged at the bitter irony, suppressed the visions of his beloved Sally that were never far from his mind, and continued past the deliberately darkened work area, making for the central lounge, its huge windows looking out onto the confusing sprawl of a modern, international airport.

He stood at the coffee machine, made himself a latte, sprinkled a generous layer of powdered chocolate across its bubbling top, and wondered how best to structure his search. It seemed such an eminently sensible notion that Mal was now utterly convinced the Governor was in a Function Room. The efficient scoping-out of every nook and cranny in the warren of little snugs, observation areas, shower and rest rooms comprising the quieter side of the lounge was therefore merely a formality to ensure he was leaving no stone unturned, before heading back to the open-plan seating surrounding the bar to commence his stakeout of the foyer. Carefully slurping just the pleasing layer of chocolatey foam from the top of his too-hot drink, Mal turned from the coffee machine and found himself gazing into a semi-private seating area ringed with slatted wooden dividing screens, and overfilled with side tables, velour armchairs and large reading lamps in the manner of a fashionable hotel. The dark shades muted the harsh electric light to create a more restful atmosphere in the secluded corner.

Sitting calmly beneath an angled reading lamp marking up a document which might well be his speech for the following day, Mal was flabbergasted to behold the State Governor of Florida himself! Before he had time to overthink his approach, Mal abandoned his coffee next to the machine and strode assertively across the thick carpet, proffering his passport to the imposing man who instantly rose to block his way. Mal raised his voice a decibel or two above normal range, and called insistently, "Mr Governor, my name is Malcolm Lawrence. I'm editor of *The Key*. This is my passport, sir." He waved it in front of him like a flag of truce on a battlefield, pushing it into the outstretched hands of the sentry, who was actually reaching out to physically restrain him.

Mal stopped, as if the partially screened seating area was a completely private room into which he was awaiting a formal invitation, and held up the folder, "I need to speak to you urgently, Mr Governor, in connection with serious evidence contained within this dossier."

By now, the Governor, all the aides surrounding him, and everyone in the lounge within earshot, was gawping at Mal with unconcealed fascination.

The security guy shoved a firm hand against Mal's breastbone and tossed the passport backwards without even looking at it. It rapidly went through the hands of three minions, who glanced at the photograph, compared it to Mal's flushed face, and passed the decision up the chain of command like a hot potato in a children's party game until the music stopped with the Governor himself, who held the passport aloft in front of him, bright eyes flicking between digital reproduction and perspiring reality.

Eventually, he nodded with surprising willingness, and Mal found himself efficiently patted down by the sentry, who relieved him of cellphone, wallet and keys as speedily as any subway pickpocket. The guy whizzed a small detector of some sort over his keys, and took his cellphone apart, removing the battery and scanning this too. He then dumped Mal's pile of deconstructed possessions unceremoniously onto the table and jerked his thumb to signal permission to proceed.

The Governor stood slowly, and Mal sympathised silently. It looked as if he suffered back trouble too.

The older man extended a tanned and leathery hand, "Mr Lawrence. Good afternoon. Excuse the paranoia, but we live in uncertain times."

"Yes, sir, we do." Mal shook the Governor's dry and papery palm.

"Take a seat." The Governor indicated the armchair opposite his own.

"Thank you, sir."

Mal sat, and held the folder upright before him like a nervous kid about to read his essay to the rest of the class.

"Thank you for seeing me, Mr Governor. I understand my approach was somewhat unconventional."

The Governor smiled, but his intelligent eyes assessed Mal keenly, "I *like* unconventional, Mr Lawrence. If you never shake things up, how do you ever find out whether you can make them better?"

Mal grinned, the spontaneity of it surprising him. He'd intended to keep this exchange brisk and businesslike: neutral expression, serious tone, firm focus. He wasn't supposed to be allowing Mr Governor to gain the upper hand. The wily old dog was meant to be reeling from the shock of Mal's ambush, not already dictating the direction of this unscripted encounter. He was *good*. Mal would need to keep his wits about him.

He suddenly realised the aide to his left had a notebook in his hand, pen poised, and seemed about to minute their conversation.

Glancing up, he saw the remaining faces flanking the Governor in a crescent of naked curiosity.

Mal leant across the table, and murmured, "Sir, what I have to discuss with you is of a delicate nature. It concerns a gentleman I believe you employ…although I'm not certain whether that is in a *private* capacity. By that, I mean not at all connected with the political office of State Governor, but related to your other business interests."

The onlookers were now craned so far forward in their desperation to catch every sensational syllable, that the angle of their inclined bodies came close to defying the laws of physics.

Wary but intrigued, the Governor turned in his chair and formally requested some privacy. The unwilling staff mooched moodily to the opposite corner of the snug and huddled together, occasionally throwing a venomous glance in Mal's direction.

"Satisfied, Mr Lawrence? They'll be mad at me all afternoon now."

"Believe me, sir, you'll thank me when you hear what I have to say."

"I'm listening."

"I appreciate it."

Mal opened the folder on his lap and took out Kennedy's marked-up map and list of addresses.

"Mr Governor, could you confirm whether these addresses and locations are – to the best of your knowledge – owned by your realty company, and a part of your extensive rental property portfolio?"

The Governor retrieved his fashionable, rimless spectacles from the arm of his chair, slid them on, and took his time perusing the paper (from which Glen had been careful to omit the seaside mansion he'd visited most recently).

The Governor passed the paper back, "Mr Lawrence, I made my money from property, as you probably know. I've developed a lot, sold a lot, still own a lot – all over southern Florida, not just The Keys. If you expect me to recall every single address…a man of my age, with everything else I have to juggle…?"

A clever response – reasonable, plausible, personable – but not an answer. Undaunted, having never expected this to be easy, Mal withdrew the picture of the Governor on the rally podium.

"This picture appears under an internet search of your name, sir. The information says it's from a rally in Tallahassee last year. I assume on the campaign trail."

Mal passed it across to the Governor, who smiled, and muttered self-deprecatingly, "I almost look as if I know what I'm doing, eh?"

Mal mirrored the indulgent smirk, "Every bit the consummate politician."

"What's the issue with this picture?"

"You see the gentleman in the background of the shot?"

The Governor looked, glanced back up at Mal, nodded, and raised his eyebrows questioningly.

"Please could you confirm his name, Mr Governor?"

"Well, yes…it's Robert."

"His full name?"

"Robert Logan. Robert Christopher Logan Jnr."

"Thank you, Governor."

"Mr Lawrence, where is this going?"

The first shadow of unease darkened the Governor's previously relaxed features, and Mal noticed his left eye twitch minutely behind the designer lenses.

Investigative senses sharpening by the second, Mal steadied his wavering breathing and delivered what he hoped would be the first destabilising blow in a potentially arduous contest, "Do you have confidence in Mr Logan, sir? Do you consider him a good employee? I'm assuming he *is* a member of your staff?"

"Yes…he is… Mr Lawrence, I'm not sure – "

"Please, sir, indulge me. I will explain myself fully and in great detail, but I cannot prejudice your responses by attempting to influence your replies in any way. That's not responsible journalism."

The Governor raised one sardonic eyebrow, "Is there such a thing?"

"Well, I would obviously say yes, sir."

"Naturally. Perhaps we'll agree to disagree on that point, given the slating I've had in the press over the years. So, Mr Lawrence, you want my opinion of Robert Logan…"

"Yes please, sir."

"Okay. He's an intense young man, almost maniacally devoted to duty. Ask him to get something done, and he'll deliver. He's highly intelligent, razor-sharp, resourceful, reliable, thorough to the point of obsessive. He has a superb political and tactical brain. He's a lone wolf. He doesn't need anyone's approval; he just needs to achieve. He isn't part of the silver-spoon brigade. He put himself through his law degree at night school so he could care for his sick mother. There's no father on the scene, as far as I know. He hasn't relied upon nepotism to get where he is. He's done it with hard work, determination, utter focus and shining ability. He should be a top-flight corporate lawyer billing thousands of bucks an hour. With his exam scores, he could so easily have followed that path with one hand tied behind his back, but he put his mother first. A *dutiful* young man. An *accountable* young man. A young man who could very well get all the way to a senior political office himself...but..."

"But...?"

"He's...*different*, Mr Lawrence, I can't deny it. A quirky character, no question, but one of my very best people, for all his social oddities. I think it's being the donkey in a stable of thoroughbreds, if you see what I mean. The guy's got a chip on his shoulder about position. He despises privilege, but that's hardly surprising. In my office, where you come from doesn't matter half as much as where you're going. Make sense? We promote based upon performance. That's why Robert has risen fast. Does that answer your question?"

"Most comprehensively, Mr Governor. Could I possibly ask you one more thing about Robert Logan?"

"If you must, Mr Lawrence. I do have a speech to prepare, and I can't really see where this is going –"

"All will become clear, sir. As I mentioned, it would be irresponsible of me to steer you."

"So...?"

"Would you be happy with him dating your daughter?"

The Governor squinted at Mal over the top of his glasses, "What sort of a question is that?"

"A highly relevant one."

Mal withdrew five pictures Glen had printed from Kennedy's X-rated photo collection, and placed them in a row across the coffee table, "An intense young man, you said? Utterly focused? I'd say he's *intensely* focused in these pictures, wouldn't you, sir? You'll notice the date and time stamps on these photographs match occasions you were out of the The Keys on political business, and the locations they were taken correspond exactly to the map I showed you a moment ago. They *are* all your properties, Governor. We checked. There's a lot more. This is simply a sample of what our dossier contains."

Mal watched, grimly fascinated, as the healthy colour drained from the Governor's richly tanned face like dirt down a plughole. He moistened his lips, removed his glasses, and rubbed his eyes as if that would dispel what he'd seen. Replacing them, his face twisted with revulsion when he discovered the hideous images had failed to vanish like he'd wanted them to. He managed to growl, "Who put you up to this? I've seen what can be done. Fake news, Mr Lawrence! I've watched that body-swap mock-up of Obama giving one of Bush's speeches. I know what they can do now. The fact you're using Robert – a young man with serious prospects, a threat to your side in the very near future – as a tool to get to me is cheap and underhand. You Establishment assholes just can't handle the fact that a kid from the wrong side of the tracks is making some serious waves for our side – and our *kind*, come to that! He's smashing every barrier you people erect to keep us out! I know. I rose the same way. I've fought every day to be accepted, to be recognised for my achievements, not pigeonholed and penalised by my past. Now Robert's doing the same…and he's doing it younger, faster, and more effectively, and all of you are shitting yourselves! As a consequence of the impact Robert's already having, you're trying every cheap trick in the book to discredit him, and by association me, my department, my office! You won't succeed, Mr

Lawrence, neither you nor your party paymasters! Superimposing Robert's face onto someone else's body in that…situation…proves nothing except the press is as corruptible as it's always been – "

"No, Mr Governor! With the greatest respect, sir, you're wrong! These pictures have not been doctored in any way. I'm very content to have independent corroboration of their authenticity if it comes to that. They were taken at considerable personal risk by one of my investigative reporters. She literally hid in the bushes and filmed through the windows! She subsequently went missing. Don't you think that's rather too coincidental?"

Mal withdrew a copy of the paper containing his first article about Kennedy's disappearance. He placed it over the photographs on the table and watched the Governor's brows knit in troubled confusion. "She's thirty-four, Governor…about the age of your youngest daughter, I believe…?"

The Governor swallowed like he had a golf ball stuck in his throat. Mal continued in an insistent tone, "I can't wait any longer, sir. That young lady's life is in danger, as are the lives of every one of the girls in these photographs of your golden boy, here. They're not willing participants, Governor, as I think it's clear to see. My newspaper is going to press with this, and a dossier of evidence is going to the authorities. I don't have all the answers, not by any means, but I'm printing what I've got and letting public opinion do the rest. Your property = Fact. Your employee = Fact. My missing reporter = Fact. Whether you are up to your neck in this or not, it doesn't look good for you, sir, because you were the one who recruited and promoted him. He's your creature, so you'll be held responsible for his actions, regardless of whether you actually *are*." Mal passed the folder across, "Yours, Governor. Needless to say, it's not the only copy."

Struck dumb, the Governor meekly accepted the proffered papers. "Sir, I appreciate you don't want to hear any of this, but Robert Logan is abusing his position to traffic women from South and Central America. He's holding them in your extensive collection of large, secluded and frequently empty properties, cultivating a profitable sideline in exclusive sex-parties for Florida's bored playboy generation, and then moving the poor girls on, I know not where. Either he's doing that with your willing collusion or utterly without your knowledge. I've yet to conclusively prove which, but I'm not sure it'll matter once my latest and most sensational exclusive starts to hit newsstands right across The Keys. Irrespective of your involvement, your reputation'll be destroyed. I understand coercion isn't the most honourable way to get things done, but you're a politician; you should recognise its effectiveness well enough. *Someone* needs to stop him, and they need to do it *now*. It's gone on quite long enough. *You* might not have the guts to do it, sir, but luckily, *I* do. If you want to stop me going to press, I'll be at my office, preparing the biggest political exposé my paper's ever run. I'd be inclined to shelve your speech for the time being. I think you have something more pressing to deal with, like your long-term future in high-level politics. Thank you for your valuable time. Good afternoon to you, Governor."

Mal stood, scooped up his pile of vetted possessions, nodded to the security guy as he passed him, and made for the elevator, expecting with every step to feel the weight of authority's heavy hand upon his shoulder.

****

It had been a long time since he recalled feeling such exhilaration! Jogging across the parking lot to his Mercedes, Mal tugged off his wool suit-jacket. He'd sweated so much in there that his shirt was stuck to his back, his arms, his paunch. He loosened and slid off his tie, unfastening his collar buttons. He untucked his shirttails, flapping them frantically to cool and dry the soaked cotton and his clammy skin. His heart thudded. His body trembled. He'd done it and made it out of there alive! Okay, two thousand bucks lighter, but he'd have paid double to replay the look on the Governor's face as he'd laid out the shots of Logan getting his rocks off. Safely inside the car – doors locked, engine running, climate control whooshing on the coldest setting – Mal swiftly reassembled his cellphone and dialled Glen via the hands-free kit as he reversed speedily from the parking space. Glen answered so fast he must have been camping out by the 'phone, "Boss, you okay?"

"I've done it, Glen! Package delivered!"

"Wow! What happened?"

"To cut a long story short, he was already in the lounge when I got there. I asked to speak to him, he was curious enough to agree…and I hit him with it! I told him what we knew, up to a point. I showed him the pictures. I told him we were definitely going to press with *facts* and letting the voters make up their own minds."

"Okay, now you've looked right into his eyes, do you think he's in on it or not?"

"I'm even more unsure than I was before I met him. He comes over as a personable old guy…which could mean that's exactly what he is, or that he's an adroit politician and I was almost taken in. I asked him what he thought of Logan and, predictably, he sang his praises…so I pushed a little harder and asked if he'd be happy with the guy dating his daughter – "

"No way!"

"And while he was huffing in confusion, trying to decide whether I was disrespecting him or not, I whipped out the shots of Logan in full effect. He nearly passed out!"

"But that could have been with shock at what was going on, or – "

"Shock that we'd found out, exactly…and I truly cannot tell which it is. Well, I've planted the seed. Now we just have to wait for it to bear fruit. If we watch the house and they clear the girls out, Mr Governor is definitely in-the-know. If the party goes ahead tonight, he has no idea. Is everybody ready to go, all the kit packed up, Gage and Kennedy suitably disguised?"

"As far as I know, Boss. I'm picking them up on my way through."

"Okay, I'll drive straight home, get changed, and meet you all there. We'll get set up in shifts and settle in for the night watch."

"Where are you now?"

"Just driving out of MIA…hold on, Glen, there's some idiot trying to squeeze up the inside of me here. What is he *doing*? WHOA!"

"Boss, what's happening?"

"*Jesus*! Some *loser* who got his licence out a pack of Cheerios! *Hey*! Why don't you hold your lane, pal? *AAAGGH*! What the –?"

"Boss! What's going on?"

"I just got fucking *shunted*, Glen! What is *wrong* with you, man? Yeah, I'm talking to *you*!"

Suddenly, the tone of Mal's voice altered completely.

"Shit…this isn't an accident. Something's going down here, Glen."

"What?"

"Can you record on your cell?"

"Yes, I can…what's –?"

"Don't say another word. Just press 'record' and stay on the line."

"Boss, what –?"

"*Shut up*, Glen! Shut *up* and stay on the line!"

TRESPASSER

Glen fumbled to the correct screen, activated the record function, and pressed his ear so tight to the receiver he could feel it getting hot, pen at the ready to write down everything he heard in case the recording didn't work. Mal's voice had been husky and tight. Not much ever rattled the worldly Malcolm Lawrence, but Glen could hear the older man's heavy breathing on the sensitive in-car microphones. He was terrified.

What Glen couldn't see was that two dark cars boxed Mal's Mercedes tight against the barrier on the concrete flyover exiting the airport. The car behind – the one that had shunted him in the rear – had two burly men inside. One remained behind the wheel. The other got out and officiously started directing traffic around the attention-grabbing roadblock. The other car – the one that had edged into his lane and squeezed him over – was parked diagonally across his front fender. Mal had been inches from t-boning it. Again, the driver remained in-situ and the passenger got out, approaching Mal's car with right hand tucked inside his coat and left hand reaching for the door. Not wanting to antagonise the clearly armed man, Mal deactivated the locks and edged his still connected cellphone beneath his jacket on the passenger seat. The monitor on his dash showed the map screen. Only a small telephone icon in the bottom corner indicated a connected call. Mal hoped the guy wouldn't notice that.

The door opened. The man withdrew his hand. Mal held his breath, anticipated the appearance of the gun that would surely kill him, and instead found himself staring at an official ID.

"FBI. Take your hands slowly off the wheel, release your safety belt and step out of the car, please."

Mal, palms already aloft, gestured to the dash, "You want me to cut the engine?"

"No need. Out of the car please, sir. Hands where I can see them."

Mal stepped out swiftly and was patted down for the second time in as many hours. The FBI agent took hold of his elbow in a vice-like grip that made Mal wince. A large limousine with darkened windows drew to a smooth halt alongside Mal's stranded car. The FBI agent reached down, opened the door, and pushed Mal forward, "In you get, Mr Lawrence."

"But – "

"*In.*"

Mal's stomach turned over. He belched into his dry mouth and tasted harsh bile. He hoped to God Glen was getting the gist of this. Unable to delay further, he ducked his head and slid into the limousine's chilly interior. The FBI agent closed the door, and Mal glanced fearfully over his shoulder as the auto-locking mechanism clunked into place. He watched the FBI guy step lithely into his still-running Mercedes and prepare to drive it away. He prayed Glen wouldn't assume it was him and betray his presence on the other end of the telephone line.

He turned back into the car and looked across the wide seat at the stony features of the unsmiling Governor. Silhouetted against bright afternoon sunshine, the gaunt face was hollow-cheeked, sunken-eyed, more ghoulish corpse than living man.

The Governor lifted the dossier in one desiccated claw, "A fine performance back there, Mr Lawrence, but you left too much unsaid. Did you expect to be able to threaten me and simply walk away? Did you think a man in my position would allow the press to hold me to ransom in such a fashion? Oh no, Mr Lawrence, we have a great deal more to discuss before I'm through with you."

****

Blobs of carelessly applied dye spattered every previously pristine surface, and Gage anxiously worried at them with an old towel, imagining what Mal would say when he saw the state of his bathroom. Kennedy stood before the mirror and pulled long tresses down either side of her face like a hippy, frowning, "Look ill…"

While her long, blonde hair was now an unnatural and unflattering black, Gage's unkempt, sandy mop was bleached almost white.

"It doesn't matter. It ain't a fashion statement, it's a disguise." Kennedy pushed her ruined locks impatiently off her face, grinned across at Gage's reflection – his still-damp hair sticking straight up from his head – and sniggered, "You…look like…a paintbrush!"

Gage paused in his energetic efforts to clean the apparently indelible black stains off the sink, and said, "A paintbrush?"

Kennedy turned from the mirror, rubbed his deeply tanned, weather-beaten face affectionately with dye-stained fingers, and explained, "Varnished handle," before skimming her hand across the top of the cursorily towel-dried spikes, and giggling, "New bristles."

"Oh *yeah*?" Gage tossed the towel aside, picked her up, plonked her onto the granite counter surrounding the basin, hooked the front of her bra with his finger, and pulled her forward until their noses touched. He pretended to glower. Kennedy beamed throughout, delighted by the banter, as Gage growled, "I think I liked it better when you *couldn't* talk."

Kennedy stuck out her tongue and tried to lick the end of his nose, but he dodged away, digging strong fingertips into her ribcage to tickle her. She jumped, squirmed, and he darted forward to blow a raspberry on the golden skin just above her collarbone. She jerked up in surprise and their faces bumped together. Each abruptly aware of the proximity of the other, the unintended intimacy immediately stopped their playfighting.

Until then, Gage hadn't noticed Kennedy's legs wrapped tight around his hips, or her hands gripping his bare shoulders to keep him close. Kennedy hadn't realised how comfortably Gage cradled her buttocks in his big palms.

She clasped her arms around his neck, soft, plump cheek pressed to his rough, disfigured one. Gage's hands slid up her back and folded her body firmly against his chest. She could feel a rapid, strong heartbeat, but wasn't sure whether it was his or her own.

She tipped her head back to whisper in his ear, "Hey, Billy Idol."

A shudder ran through Gage. Her breath was warm, and the brush of her moist lips tickled his ear, "What, Morticia?"

She smiled, and stuttered out, "I'm sorry…for…all this mess. Spoilt vacation…sadness inside you…"

Many months pressure of unspent tears built across the bridge of Gage's nose and behind his tightly closed eyes. He vividly remembered resolving to leave. He'd agonised for days over how to broach the subject of an indefinite absence, knowing his mother would view it as cowardice, well-aware his little sister would jump to the immediate conclusion he'd need to sell his share of the farm, thereby threatening the security of the whole family. He hadn't wanted to cause a scene or be made to feel any more of a failure, so he'd taken the easy way out and told Vern instead, mostly because he knew his brother-in-law would absorb the bombshell in the same way he processed every piece of news from celebration to crisis, with predictably-comforting equanimity.

"I can't stay here, Vern."

Vernon had nodded in his ruminative way, and tossed the crust of his sandwich to Lacey, who'd caught it expertly in snapping jaws, chomping with enthusiasm on the remains of butter and cheese. Lunch break over, they'd got on with the fencing repairs, working in their usual companionable, efficient rhythm for such a long time he'd wondered whether Vernon had been nodding in response to a private thought of his own and hadn't actually heard him at all.

They were two hundred yards further on before Vern muttered, "Do you mean in the house with all of us, or on the farm?"

"I mean here, on the farm."

"But it's your family's land – "

"It's *our* family's land, Vern. Your wife is my sister. Your daughters are my nieces. It's *our family*."

Vernon had blushed with shy pleasure, and fixed his earnest, brown-eyed gaze on the fence post supported in his big hands. Gage recalled smirking at Vernon's glowing cheeks and swinging the sledgehammer powerfully, driving the new post into the pliable soil, "That's it."

Vernon had effortlessly stretched the uncooperative snake of barbed wire across the top of the post, hammering down two metal cleats to hold it in position, "Are you saying you want out? We can't buy your share, Gage. We haven't the money."

"Did I ask you to? I don't want to give up my share in the farm, Vern...I just can't be here right now. Momma keeps saying I should move on. I don't see how I can do that unless I move *out* for a while."

"And go where?"

Gage had rubbed a dusty wrist across his perspiring forehead, leaving a muddy stripe between eyebrows and hat band, "I dunno, just away from here. I've got the insurance to live on. I don't need to take anything out of the farm."

Troubled by Gage's implication he was only concerned about the money, Vern had blurted, "But you have every right – "

"But I don't have a *need*. I only need...distance, I guess. How can I begin to get over what happened when every day I'm staring at that cleared patch of land where my house used to be?"

Vernon had begun shifting distractedly from foot to foot, unable to look at him, "There's just a big, flat, featureless expanse of nothing where those hopes and dreams used to be. If I don't have to look at that constantly, I figure it won't be so raw inside of me. How can a wound heal if you allow it to reopen every day?"

Pained, Vernon had stuttered, "This is your home, Gage. You were born here. It's been your family's land for generations – "

"It still *will* be my home. You guys aren't leaving, are you? I'm not saying I need to go forever, just for the time being."

"Right." Clearly relieved the disruption would be minimal, Vernon had flicked at the taut wire with one gloved finger, making it rattle and hum, "You told anyone else?"

"Not yet. Thought you might need a heads-up…scratch around for some hired help while I'm gone."

"Yeah, I guess. How long you think you'll be away?"

Gage recalled twisting the long-handled hammer into his gloved grip, anxious to resume work, recollecting how unwilling he'd been to discuss that part of his plan, "I dunno…does it matter?"

"Course it matters! But you gotta do what's right for you. I can see that."

"Am I letting you down, Vern?"

"Nah, forget about it. There's always guys looking for work. Reckon I could get somebody within a couple of weeks if I need 'em. Where will you go?"

Gage had hooked the heavy end of the hammer over his shoulder, glad Vern hadn't pressed him to say when he might come home, shrugging, "Wherever."

Vernon had taken off his baseball cap and scratched his sweating head, "*When* will you go?"

Another shrug, "Whenever."

Gage recalled Vernon's bemused chuckle, "You don't seem to care all that much."

He'd tried to be honest, "I just need to get away from here. Don't much matter where or when."

Vernon had spent an inordinately long time scrutinising Gage's exhausted countenance, before cautioning sagely, "What if you're just transporting the problem? What if the baggage travels with you, wherever you decide to go?"

For once grateful his voice was always husky, Gage hugged Kennedy closer, savouring the sensation of a soft, female form squashed tightly against him after so many months of self-inflicted isolation, and whispered, "I wasn't on vacation. I haven't told anybody this. I was running away. I had to leave home. The guilt of staying became insurmountable. I swore it was about grief, but truthfully, I just couldn't stand the evidence of my mistakes staring me in the face every day. The night the fire hit our farm, I made a stupid decision. We'd been watching the weather channel for days, praying the dry spell would break. We'd discussed as a family what we'd do if the fires got real close. I was pretty relaxed about it. Probably too relaxed, but wildfires are a way of life out West. Some years are worse than others. Vern and I cut firebreaks on the farm every season, just to be on the safe side, but all my careful planning went down the shitter when Jo's blood pressure suddenly shot up. She had to have an operation to get the baby out. The two of 'em were okay, but they had to stay in hospital for a while. I was going back and forth, trying to spend as much time as I could with them and still do the chores I was responsible for. They let them home the day before the fire. She wasn't supposed to be lifting the baby. She couldn't manage the stairs. We were asleep. It wasn't that late, but we were shattered by everything that'd gone on. Ryan was in the bassinet on Jo's side of the bed. My sister called and told me to put my boots on and get outside. Vern, my brother-in-law, was already running down towards our house, yelling and pointing behind him. I turned around and the smoke was the closest I remembered it getting since I was a teenager. You could see the brightness of the flames just over the horizon, no more'n about three miles away…but the wind was blowing away from our land. The forecasters said the fire would pass right along the valley and peter out in the mountains to the North…and it sure looked as if it was going to do just that. I ran up the track to meet Vern, discussed what we should do, decided we'd turn the stock loose and get the families out, but both of us were viewing it as a precaution. We thought we'd get away with it. I went back inside and woke Jo. I told her to get the baby ready, that I'd be back and we'd go to town until the fire blew through…and then I went down to the stables to turn the horses loose. That was the wrong thing to do. What I *should* have done was put the two of them in the truck *first*, drive it up to the stables, release the horses, and get the hell off the farm until the fire passed on…" Gage could feel the pressure inside his pounding head, and this time he couldn't stop the tears. He tried to keep talking, desperate not to give in, "In the time it took for me to get to the stables, the fire turned and came straight for my house before I knew what was happening. I hadn't even factored in the chance the wind might change… I *tried* to get to them – I ran faster than I ever had in my whole life – but you can't outrun a wildfire when the wind's pushing it along. I learnt that as a little kid, yet I didn't even *think* of it at the time…! Even over the roar of the wind and the flames, I could hear my baby boy crying, my wife screaming. I failed them. They died because of me…"

Gage finally succumbed to croaking, heaving sobs, violently convulsing his whole body.

"Shhh…not your fault…"

"If I'd used my goddam brain, I could've saved them…but instead I worried about how much money we'd lose if the stock died! Like it matters now. Like *any* of it fucking matters! I can't even stand to be within a hundred miles of the goddam place any more, and it's supposed to be my farm, my inheritance, my legacy…"

Horrified by the extremity of his anguish, she held him, pressing her body to his as if she could somehow absorb his suffering, stroking the nape of his neck with her cool fingers. Eventually, the ferocity of the shuddering sobs did ease, and Kennedy rubbed his broad back in a gentle, circular motion, like a mother soothing a fractious child. At length, face against her neck, Gage muttered thickly, "I've probably put snot in your hair...sorry…"

Kennedy patted his back, "Never mind – can't make it look any worse than it already does."

Gage sighed heavily, lifting his tear-stained face to look at her. Kennedy tugged at a length of toilet paper, bunching it in her fingers, padding at his eyes and nose. He was still talking even as she wiped at his upper lip and chin. The words tumbled over one another in his haste to tell it all, the backed-up dam of guilt breached and overflowing, "It became easier to go than man up and face what I'd done…and once I got on the road, life *was* simpler, believe it or not. No one knew who I was or why I was there. In my head, if I never stopped moving, I never had to address reality. I never had to look anyone in the eye ever again. I could just keep rolling on, putting off judgement day…but you can't do that forever. One way or another, you run out of road. *You* taught me that, not to turn and run but to stand and fight. I've thought more about my wife and son since running into you than I have in the two years since I lost them. You've shown me the only way to triumph is to face down the fear. I didn't have the guts to do it before. All this," Gage prodded his own scarred cheek roughly, "This is my punishment, my penance for not saving them. It's so when I look in the mirror, it's impossible to forget. The pain might lessen as time goes on, but it'll never leave me completely…and nor should it. I *deserve* to hurt."

Kennedy hated to hear the awful things he was saying about deserving the pain. It didn't seem right for him to suffer so, not after all he'd done for her. She stroked the pad of her thumb slowly across his slightly parted lips, as if this would stop the troubling confession tumbling out, and insisted, "You saved *me*, Gage."

His watery smile was so heart-rendingly melancholy, she thought she might cry too.

"Too little, too late, huh? Anyway, that's bullshit."

"What's bullshit?"

"I didn't save you. You saved me."

To Gage's amazement, Kennedy immediately reached up, cradled his face in her hands and drew him towards her, brushing her soft lips across his. Startled by her response, instantly energised by her touch, Gage thrust his hand into her hair, cupping her skull firmly, pulling her decisively to him and pressing his mouth hungrily to hers. Far from a mere demonstration of base desire, the intense kiss communicated limitless trust and boundless fondness. For two lost souls, until then utterly convinced they were condemned to walk life's path alone, it was a revelatory and joyous homecoming.

As Gage's lips travelled lusciously down her neck to the hollow of her throat, and his exploring tongue slid over her breastbone and tickled its way down her cleavage, Kennedy clutched his strong shoulders, leant back against the reassuring support of his arms, and sighed contentedly. The stirring sweep of his mouth across her bare skin and the soft caress of his moving hands over her still-bruised body were rapidly becoming the only sensations she wanted in her world. Eyes closed, head thrown back, she felt him unclasp her bra and slide it away. His hot mouth kissed its way down her stomach, making her stimulated skin tingle pleasurably. She giggled as his tongue flicked into her belly button, arching her back into his splayed palms, unreservedly open to him. His warm hands travelled down her body and around her hips, pushing urgently at her skirt until it bunched at her waist. Each featherlight touch of his lips up her inner thigh made nerve-endings explode like fireworks. His fingers probed, deftly drawing aside the gusset of her panties. Gripping fists in his hair, Kennedy shuddered uncontrollably, anticipating the imminent penetration of his gliding tongue, when suddenly…

Rattle…

Thump!

Gage lifted his head, reluctantly breaking the deliciously deepening connection to hiss, "Did you just hear something?"

Bodies still entwined, heads cocked, ears straining for the slightest sound, they waited…

Creeeaak…

Thump!

Rattle…

"There! Hear that?"

"Yeah."

"Outside. Out the front?"

Rattle…

"Shhh," Kennedy pressed her fingertips to his lips and listened again, "No… Bolt. Side gate?"

"Shit! Stay here." Gage slid his hands from her body and shot out of the bathroom, dashing across the guest room to peer between the partially closed blinds, "There's someone out there! I think it's just one guy…"

Kennedy edged down off the bathroom counter and wobbled to the doorway, struggling on her bra and wriggling hurriedly into her t-shirt.

Gage, pressed tight against the window and straining to see along the back of the house, whispered, "What time is that colleague of yours picking us up for our stakeout?"

"Seven."

Gage glanced across at the bedside clock, "It's not even four. Who the hell is that out there?"

Kennedy squeezed up beside him, noting with delight that his hands instantly curled around her waist, "Can't see…"

Gage ran through a list of possibilities, "It's not Mal. He's probably barely left Miami yet. The other guy's not coming 'til seven…"

Kennedy turned fearfully to him, "Rocky and Bullwinkle?"

Gage stroked her cheek comfortingly, craned around her, peeked again and exhaled in frustration, "I can't see either! Only someone's back…their shoulders… I'm sure it's a guy, but he's right round by the kitchen door. You think those assholes've got tired of sitting in that sweatbox car, eating *Wendy's* and waiting for us to open the drapes?"

"Who knows?"

Gage groaned, rubbing his face with his hands, eventually stating decisively, "I'm sick of hiding in here waiting for Mal to tell us what to do all the goddam time! I think there's only one guy out there. Where's that baseball bat?"

Kennedy pointed behind them, "Front door."

"Right," Gage checked outside again, then gingerly unlocked the bedroom's French doors as quietly as he could, "Go get it. I'm going out of here, along the back of the house, and I'm gonna jump him. You hide in the kitchen. As soon as you see me get a hold of him, swing that bat at his head like it's the World Series!"

"And if there's two?"

Gage gripped the door handle, squared his jaw grimly, and growled, "Then we just gotta fight harder, right?"

****

Trying to suppress the burgeoning panic and work methodically through the display of pots by the back door, looking for the concealed spare key he was sure would be there, suddenly a huge arm like a tree trunk wrapped itself around his neck and wrenched his unprepared body backwards, as if seeking to detach his head completely. Airway constricting, he gurgled and spluttered, clawing at the arm until a swinging punch like a wrecking-ball to the right kidney buckled his legs and momentarily prevented him struggling at all. His assailant dragged him mercilessly towards the house. His frantic, digging heels left parallel tracks in the dust as he unsuccessfully endeavoured to hold his ground. He gripped around the powerful forearm as best he could, trying with all his might to wrench it away, but lack of oxygen made his limbs weak and vision blur. He was on the verge of unconsciousness when the kitchen door swung open before him and a wild-eyed woman leapt out, black hair flying behind her, wielding a baseball bat above her head like a medieval battle sword.

****

Baring her teeth, charging out onto the stoop with bat raised, Kennedy swiftly absorbed the scene, stopped dead in astonishment, and let the weapon droop in her trembling grip.

Gage, fired up and ferocious, ready to tear the intruder's head off with his bare hands, reacted furiously to the unnecessary delay, demanding, "*What?*"

She pointed, "Don't kill him!"

Gage shook the barely conscious interloper roughly, "Why the fuck not?"

"Because it's *Glen*!"

BACKS TO THE WALL

"Glen from your office?"

"Yes."

"*Shit!*" Gage released him immediately, but it was too late. Glen dropped heavily to the deck, faint and groaning.

Kennedy anxiously surveyed the garden, and muttered, "Inside, quick!"

Contrite, Gage hefted Glen back to his feet and bundled him hurriedly into the house, apologising profusely as he helped him onto a dining chair, "I'm so sorry, buddy. I thought you were a bad guy! Why didn't you just knock on the door?"

Dazed, and quite considerably intimidated both by Gage's shocking appearance and the brutality of his attack, Glen simply stared open-mouthed at this unlikely ally until Kennedy reappeared with an inch-deep measure of dark rum in a tumbler, standing over Glen and forcing it into his shaking hand, echoing Gage, "Why not just knock, Glen?"

"I was looking for a key. I thought the house was empty! I thought you were *hiding* somewhere!"

"We are. Here."

"Well, I didn't know that, did I? I thought I'd need to get inside to find a clue to where you were. I didn't expect you to be waiting for me!"

"Why not?"

"Do you mean to say Mal's been keeping you here the whole time, since the postcard thing? He never said a word!"

Gage grinned, "The postcard. You know about that, huh?"

Furious at Mal for keeping yet another vital secret from him, Glen angrily knocked back the spirit in one gulp and trumpeted self-importantly, "I know everything. I've been working this alongside Mal the whole way through!"

Given what he'd just admitted, Kennedy looked understandably suspicious, but Gage shook his hand affably, "Well, I sure am sorry I tried to rip your head off. We weren't expecting you 'til seven…and I thought we were gonna meet you in the woods, in case anyone's watching the place…?"

Kennedy interrupted, and Glen resented the implication behind her sceptical tone, "You're *three hours* early, Glen. Got a good reason for screwing with the plan?"

Glen glared at Kennedy and turned back to Gage, deciding he was definitely the more amenable of the two, blurting, "I couldn't wait until seven!"

Again, it was Kennedy who spoke, "Why not? What's changed?"

"Something real bad's happened. The FBI has Mal!"

"*What?*"

"Yeah…he saw the Governor, delivered the dossier…it was going better than we could've hoped. He called me when he was leaving Miami, said he'd meet us up at the house – everything as we'd arranged – and then suddenly it all went crazy! It sounded like he got forced off the road – "

"Where?"

"MIA somewhere. I don't think he was even out of the airport. First of all, he was shouting like it was some bonehead driving dangerously, and then his voice just...*changed*... He said something was going down and I should shut up, stay on the line and record it all."

Glen fumbled his cellphone from his pocket and pushed it into Kennedy's hands, "It's on there. You gotta listen... I don't know what to do now."

Troubled by Glen's disquiet and feeling guilty for hurting him, Gage put a supportive arm around the younger man's trembling shoulders and met Kennedy's eyes over the top of Glen's bowed head, "Real Feds, do you think?"

Kennedy queried impatiently, "Glen?"

"Huh?"

Gage spoke gently, "Real FBI, or someone pretending to be FBI, so Mal didn't resist?"

"I don't know! I only know what I heard."

Kennedy wordlessly passed back the handset. Glen unlocked it and played the recording. They all listened in silence until it finished. Kennedy signalled, "Again."

Gage asked, "Who gets back in the car? Mal?"

"It can't be. He knew I was there. He would have said something. Whoever it was either took the precaution of switching everything off because that's procedure, or they saw there was a connected call and they just cut it so it couldn't be traced."

Calm and measured, Kennedy concluded in her almost-recovered voice, "So, they have Mal's cell. They'll know who he's talked to, and where he's been."

Once again, it was galling for Glen to witness how good she was when it mattered. She reasoned things out, established the facts, and didn't panic.

"Yeah. He had to have left it in the car somewhere or the bluetooth would have lost the signal when he got out."

Gage sighed heavily, "Where's that rum?"

"Kitchen."

He returned with another two glasses, and poured generous measures for all three of them, swigging his down in one gulp. Glen slugged his second, but already his head was swimming with fear, near-strangulation, and strong alcohol on an empty stomach. Kennedy pulled a face and pushed her glass away, so Gage downed that too, drawling, "They force him off the road, open the door, say 'FBI', get him out, you hear another car pull up – so you've gotta assume they put him in that – then someone else gets in his car, cuts his call, and presumably drives it away. To dump it? To hide it? To ensure he gets it back?"

"I don't fucking know, do I?"

"I don't expect you to…I'm just throwing questions out there!"

"Sorry…" Glen glanced up fearfully.

"Forget it." Gage looked across at Kennedy, "Look, we can't just sit here. I told you, I'm sick of it! We have to *do* something."

Glen sank his head into his hands and moaned despairingly, "But *what*?"

****

Glen read it all, shook his head dismissively, passed the pad to Gage, and rounded upon Kennedy, "There's something wrong with you, you know that? I go to the cops, what's to stop them arresting me on the spot as soon as I open my mouth? Then you two are on your own, in the lion's den – no backup!"

"It's your job to convince them, Glen."

"Fine! Sure! No problem!"

"What are you so afraid of? We've done nothing wrong."

"Bullshit! How about the million and one rules we've all broken?"

"What 'rules'?"

"I've read all your evidence, Kennedy. I've seen every picture you took, every video you made. You've committed so many acts of trespass, it's impossible to count them all. Mal's trespassed too, looking for evidence of where you'd been! Also, he's knowingly withheld the whereabouts of a fugitive. The cops still want to talk to Gage about abducting you from hospital! It's on local news every day. Yet Mal's let him stay here and hasn't breathed a word. He flat-out *lied* to the cops about you! Everyone thinks you're still missing, not sitting in his house drinking him dry! Mal let me in on most of the secrets, and I never went to the cops either! We've knowingly hidden information the whole way along! That dossier I prepared for the Governor was a very carefully edited version of the truth. We're all in seriously hot water for what we've done!"

"No, Glen…investigative journalism…"

"Argue that in court, Kennedy. I'm not sure you'll get very far. It's a fine line, I agree, but I'm pretty sure we've all crossed it."

Witheringly judgemental, Kennedy spat, "No balls, Glen!"

Glen retorted furiously, "You know, I don't actually *care* what you think of me. You've never wanted to be a part of our team. You've always thought you were better than the rest of us, but who poked her nose where it didn't belong and nearly got herself killed in the process? You could have told me about your tip, we could have worked it *together* and I might have been able to help you nail your story months ago. Instead, you wanted to keep every piece of glory for yourself, and look where it got you, dumped in a ditch and left for dead. If Gage hadn't shown up when he did, you'd be nothing but a bug buffet, all because you couldn't share! The only reason I'm here now is Mal's in trouble...and I'm not too proud to ask for help, unlike *some* people I could mention. I just wish I wasn't assisting you at the same time, because the way you treat everybody, I'm not sure you deserve it."

Kennedy curled her lip and snarled contemptuously, "Weiner – "

"Hey!" Gage slapped his huge palm down hard on the table, making them jump, "Cut it out, both of you! We have enough enemies without fighting each other! Bickering will not help Mal, and it won't dig the three of us out of the shit...so just quit it, or I'll knock your fucking heads together! You wanna test whether I'm kidding or not?"

Kennedy pouted and glowered into her lap. Glen shook his head frantically, eyes wide with fright. He'd already had a taste of how it felt to tangle with Gage Rutter when his blood was up.

"Good. Just shut up arguing and let's get this plan straight."

"I'm not comfortable with it."

"You got a better one, Glen? Come on, let's hear it!"

Glen chewed his lip nervously, and stuttered, "I don't…"

"Right. Nor do I. So Kennedy's plan is the one we're sticking with. Our backs are to the wall here! Those assholes tried to kill her. They're trying to frame me for kidnapping. Potentially, they now have Mal too. You just gonna sit quiet and wait for them to come get you as well? We gotta *fight* this thing! No more creeping around, running scared, hiding in the dark! No sitting up there in those woods tonight waiting for something to happen. We gotta *make* it happen, Glen! We gotta *force* the issue! Are you in or not?"

"I'm…well, I'm…"

"No half-hearted maybes, Glen! Imagine if it was your sister, your cousin, your girlfriend trapped up there wondering if that misery is the rest of their lives! You'd want someone to at least *try* to bust 'em out, wouldn't you?"

"I guess…"

Gage flapped the notepad in his big hand, "Glen, we need your help. Your role in this plan is key. Right, Kennedy?"

"Right. Can't do this without you, Glen."

"I'm frightened."

He expected the guy to ridicule his admission, but to Glen's surprise, Gage nodded readily, "So am I, but I'd rather go down fighting than cowering."

Amazed, Glen gasped, "I wasn't expecting you to say that!"

Gage snorted, tossed the pad into the centre of the table, and quipped, "Yeah, 'cos I bust defenceless women out of sex-dungeons all the time!"

Glen grinned. He couldn't help it. Irritated by the delay, Kennedy tapped the pad with impatient fingers, "Glen?"

He turned to her, "Okay, I'll do it. I'm on board with this crackpot scheme that's probably doomed to fail."

Kennedy simpered sarcastically, and drawled, "Hey, *thanks*, Glen."

"I'll do it, okay? Even though it's dumb, and dangerous…"

Gage grinned across the table at Kennedy, "I'm dumb. You're dangerous."

She giggled. Observing the carefree flirtation with increasing incredulity, Glen couldn't prevent his exasperation with her from bursting forth, "Aren't you even *remotely* worried about this?"

Kennedy crossed her eyes and pulled a face in reply, further incensing the disquieted Glen.

Seeking to dispel the growing tension, Gage placidly explained, "If Kennedy's plan works, by tomorrow breakfast all this'll be over. We can eat pancakes and stare at the ocean. If it doesn't, we'll be dead. Either way, what's the point in worrying? All that'll do is stack the odds more heavily against us. We've gotta just believe we *can* and go for it. Right, honey?"

"Right!"

"You make a great couple, you know? You're both as nuts as one another!"

"Awww, Glen, you say the sweetest things."

Stuffing potato chips, Kennedy squawked with laughter at Gage's teasing, and nearly choked. Glen reached over, thumped her vigorously on the back to clear the blockage, and grudgingly confirmed, "I'll do it. I'll go to the Sherriff's office, I'll present all the evidence, and I won't leave until they agree to send in the cavalry."

"You'd better, Glen!"

"I'll do my very best! If they don't believe me…?"

"*Make* them believe you, Glen!"

"I'll *try*, Kennedy! I'll do everything I possibly can. I *promise*."

"We can't do this without you, buddy!" Gage punched Glen's arm in hearty gratitude, numbing the limb from shoulder to wrist. "Make it abundantly clear if they don't get their butts to that mansion tonight and dish out some long-overdue justice, my twelve-bore and I are gonna do it for 'em."

GATECRASHERS

"I don't want you to go."

Kennedy sighed, rolled her eyes, began, "Gage – "

He held up his hand, "No, it's okay, I ain't gonna stop you. I've realised wild horses can't stop you once your mind's made up. I just wanted you to know that if I *could* stop you, I *would*.

Placated, she smiled, "Okay, heard and understood."

"Here, take this."

His hunting knife. Even in the half-light beneath the trees, the unsheathed blade glinted menacingly, before disappearing into the leather sleeve again. Gage crouched and slid the knife down the side of the long boot she wore, borrowed from Mal's dead wife. It was as if Sally Lawrence had passed only the week before. Mal hadn't thrown anything away. Five years after her untimely death, the closets were still packed, the dressing table littered with half-empty perfume bottles and jars of lotion. The task of cobbling together a suitable disguise had certainly been simplified, but it had felt weird to riffle with disrespectful haste through Sally's possessions, preserved like a shrine to her memory.

Sally had been an imposing woman, and her boots were far too big for Kennedy. She'd had to pad them out with a pair of Gage's thick socks, useful now to hold in place a weapon she didn't want to possess.

"Okay like that?"

"I guess…"

"Let's hope you won't need it."

Feebly, Kennedy muttered, "I was thinking exactly that…"

"You *sure* you're okay to do this?"

Irritably, she snapped, "*Yes!*" and instantly regretted it. Ashamed of being unnecessarily short with Gage, she stared fixedly at the house, cheeks burning. She could feel his eyes on her. After a while, he simply said, "Give me some time to bust in back before you break cover…in case they spot you quicker than you want them to."

"How long?"

"I don't know…a five-minute head start…?"

"Okay."

A momentary, pregnant pause and he resumed talking, as if repetition was preferable to a silence heavy with undeclared significance, "Remember, the basement door is the one closest to the kitchen."

Quietly, but firmly, she stated, "I know."

"Don't mix the doors up, because the second one along is the cloakroom – "

"I *know.*"

"You've gotta do all you can to manoeuvre Logan and his buddies up close to that door without standing in front of it yourself –"

"I *know*, Gage! It's *my* plan!"

"I know you know…it's just…*God*! There's so much that can go wrong, Kennedy!"

"I thought you wanted to 'do something'?"

"Yes – "

"Well, this is the only something we've got."

"I'm well-aware of that."

"You want a better something, you've got to think of it!"

"I can't. You're the brains of the operation."

"You have to bait a line to catch a fish, Gage. You're a country boy; you should know that."

"Oh, I know that. I'm just uncomfortable with the fact *you're* the bait in this scenario."

She smiled shyly, took his hand, squeezed it gently in her little fingers, and whispered, "But I'm the one they want. Stand and fight, right?"

Gage acknowledged her words with a resigned nod, brought her hand to his lips, kissed her knuckles, and repeated, "Stand and fight."

"Okay. You go. I'll give it five minutes, then I'll go. Five minutes after that, it's showtime."

"All right. Just a second…" Gage tapped his pockets, bulging with spare cartridges, gave the gun a swift check over, and turned back to Kennedy as if he'd just remembered, "One more thing…" He slid the slim band off his little finger and held it out to her, "I want you to have this."

Confused, unsure of the etiquette – she was already wearing one dead woman's clothing; must she now wear another's jewellery – she hesitated over taking it, not certain he'd fully-considered the momentousness of the gesture, convinced he might later regret bestowing it so lightly. It was all very well to borrow an old pair of shoes from the back of someone's closet. It was quite another to misappropriate a wedding ring.

"No…Gage…I can't…"

"Please. I want you to have it. Joelle doesn't need it any more, does she?"

"That doesn't mean – "

"I honestly think it's kept me safe. If she's watched over me while I was wearing it…maybe if you wear it, she'll watch over you too?"

Kennedy looked down at the ring, sitting benignly in the centre of Gage's calloused palm. Whether or not there was a Heaven, she very much doubted any residual essence of Gage's dead wife would be inclined to look favourably upon another woman wearing her ring.

She stepped forward, floundering for a respectful way to let him down gently, tripped in her ill-fitting borrowed boots on the uneven ground, and stumbled against him. Gage smiled indulgently, as if he thought she'd done it deliberately, curling an arm about her waist, easing her tenderly to him and gazing into her eyes. Kennedy blushed, concerned he was misinterpreting her discomfort for delight. She didn't know how to refuse the ring without seeming to disrespect Joelle Rutter's memory in some way. They stood face to face for an awkward heartbeat before he drew her close, wrapping his arms tightly around her and murmuring into her hair, "If all this turns to shit, I want you to know I don't regret a single moment. Being with you has brought me back to life. I will never forget your admirable strength, your infuriating stubbornness! I will always relish how brave and how beautiful you are. My time with you has been an adventure, in every way."

Affected more than she could explain by the disarmingly candid utterance, Kennedy thought it better not to look directly at him lest she embarrass herself further by crying. Instead, she stroked the back of his neck with gentle fingertips, and stood on tiptoe to whisper in his ear, "Gage Rutter…you're my motherfucking hero."

His deep chuckle made her feel warm inside despite her perturbation. It washed over her that maybe the pain of the past and uncertainty of the future weren't so important after all. In ten minutes, they might both be dead, and what would it then matter if she felt slightly uncomfortable sporting Joelle Rutter's wedding ring? If it reassured Gage to have her wear it, what real harm could it do? Joelle was well beyond hurt of any kind, and if they got out of this alive, she would have a chance to return the precious object to him the instant he regretted giving it away.

She took the ring, pushing it onto her left index finger, "If you ever want it back, you just ask me…"

He kissed her forehead, released her, took a firmer grip of the gun, winked, and croaked, "See you later, right?"

"For *sure*," replied Kennedy, secretly unsure about everything.

He crept to the very edge of the treeline, turned back, and mouthed, "Be. Careful."

She signalled: *You too*.

His damaged face crinkled into a boyish grin. He checked the time, and with one last, lingering look at her, was gone, out onto the moon-dappled lawn, sprinting swiftly towards the dense shadow at the back of the house.

Kennedy glanced at Sally's borrowed watch, tilting its face to the weak moonlight, and waited behind a tree, distractedly spinning Joelle's wedding ring around her index finger, as if the fidgety revolutions of precious metal against grubby skin could speed up time.

****

Gage dropped to his knees before the ground-level window identified on the plans obtained by the resourceful Glen. He checked the immediate vicinity, concluded he was alone, laid the gun across his lap, cupped his hands around his face to block out any light, and peered inside. It was completely black. Did that mean the room was empty, or the girls were kept in the dark?

The heavy thump of the bass from the loud music playing inside the house would doubtless mask any noise he might make, but he had one chance to pull this off. Kennedy was relying on him. He decided on a precautionary measure. He tugged off his t-shirt and wrapped it around the butt of the gun. Its sound-deadening properties impeded its glass breaking effectiveness, but Gage was able to counter that with a sufficiently full-bodied rain of blows to swiftly shatter the flimsy, single-glazed unit. To his bewilderment, the broken pieces didn't fall into the black basement like he'd expected them to. Some shards dropped from the frame and slid behind others, but all remained in the window opening as if held there by magic. Mystified, Gage prodded the barrel of the gun at the hole, expecting no resistance. When it instead struck an unyielding surface, Gage recoiled as if it was indeed sorcery. He extended tentative fingers into the blackness. Wood. Planks of wood affixed across the inside of the window. Gage got his ear down as close to the opening as he could without being cut to ribbons, and listened intently. He could hear nothing but the distant splash of ocean on shore, the constant thud of the bass, and the rustle of wind through the palm leaves.

He couldn't delay here. Whilst watching in the woods, ten minutes had seemed ample. Now, it felt like an impossibly short time to get into position. He looked at the smart diving watch he'd taken from Mal's nightstand. Less than seven minutes available to get through this window.

Gage squared his shoulders, lofted the gun once again, and drove it forcefully into the wood, powering inexorably until his shoulder muscles screamed the way they'd used to after a morning of chopping logs back home. The planks bowed encouragingly beneath the onslaught, cracking and splintering so Gage could see faint chinks of light through the gaps he was making. Regardless of what awaited him on the other side, he had to keep going. Shoulders almost spent, he span onto his buttocks, supported himself with hands thrust into the dirt, and kicked aggressively at the weakening wood with all his might, delighted to feel huge sections bursting loose and falling away beneath his thrusting heels. The shattered glass tumbled through the large hole he'd made, but the music masked the sound of it hitting the basement floor several feet below. Springing back onto his knees, Gage peered inside. The dim light was coming from the other side of the room, away from the window, and no tell-tale human shadows were visible on the only small square of wall and floor he could see. He used the t-shirt covered stock to chip the remaining upstanding spikes of glass from the frame, before gingerly easing the ruined garment loose and tossing it clear, pushing it under a nearby bush with the barrel of the gun. He didn't want anyone wandering past and discovering it, and it was too coated with slivers of glass to contemplate ever wearing again. He rolled onto his stomach and backed cautiously through the narrow window, glad he'd lost so much weight over the preceding couple of miserable years. He tried to grip onto the rough concrete wall with the toes of his sneakers, to halt the speed of his downward progress until he felt himself balanced and ready. Leaping, pulling the gun in after him, he span sharply on his heel, holding the weapon out like a lance.

Stubs of candles wedged inside old pickle jars guttered in the fresh sea breeze he'd introduced to the stuffy prison. The inadequate light flickered eerily across an empty, dusty floor to the opposite corner, littered with grimy mattresses, discarded clothing, food wrappers, and plastic water bottles.

He'd thought he was quite alone down here until sudden shuffling shadows closing around him made him whirl in alarm, gun jabbing defensively. As they stepped one by one into the inadequate light, he realised he'd dropped directly into a small group of silent young women. Some cowered in fright. Others gaped in frank astonishment. A few were heavily bruised. All were grubby, wide-eyed, and prematurely haggard.

Gage looked slowly around the circle of dumbfounded, distrustful faces. Some expressions reflected only incomprehension. In others, however, he detected an encouraging flicker of hope. He lowered the gun and brought a hushing finger to his lips as his face broke into a broad smile.

****

Maddened by impatience, Kennedy only managed to wait three minutes before leaving the safety of the tree cover and pelting across the lawn to the huge house. Her objective was simple. Get inside, create as many escape routes as she was able, and only then make herself known to the men who mattered, luring them towards Gage's gun. Needing to look plausibly similar to any of the poor women trapped in this house, she wore underwear with one of Sally's short satin and lace nightdresses over the top. A thin, crocheted bolero cardigan and Sally's long wedge-heeled boots completed the look Kennedy imagined a South American sex-trafficker might force his unfortunate victims to assume.

The hidden knife pressing against her leg made walking awkward. Every time she stepped forward, the handle poked her shin bone sharply, causing her to limp. The presence of the knife didn't make her feel any safer, especially pitted against men she knew carried guns…but at least it might be a useful tool to smash windows or force locks. As for using the knife for the defensive purpose Gage had intended when he gifted it…she couldn't imagine slipping the blade from her boot and plunging it into another living thing but, like the borrowed talisman of dubious luck around her finger, Gage had given it in good faith, for her protection, and she adored him for it.

He was a good man, simple as that, and she unquestionably owed him her life.

At the French doors opening onto the swimming pool terrace, she pressed herself against the wall and peeked cautiously in. Stretching all the way along the back of the house to the promontory of rock and swaying palms in the far distance, this was not the room to break into. Kennedy observed that it was the sickening same as always, whatever property they occupied. Strategically placed disco lights flashed and pulsed in the otherwise-dark house, as if the whole hideous spectacle was a fashionable party rather than a revolting mass rape. She felt the familiar disgust rise in her throat as she observed what still had the power to shock and repulse, despite all the occasions she'd witnessed it. Kennedy McKendrick was no prude. She'd seen sexual excitement on the faces of past boyfriends, and experienced their urgent, demanding arousal, but the mania radiating from the faces of all these men was different and chilling. Attendance at these gatherings evidently granted tacit permission to abandon all normal conventions of behaviour with apparent ease and few misgivings. What she observed time and again were supposedly 'respectable' men committing appalling acts of animal aggression, unfettered depravity and loathsome violence.

She tried never to look as intently at the faces of the women, for doing so left her hopeless, sickened, petrified and, right now, she needed to retain what little bravery and self-belief she still possessed, otherwise this venture would founder before it had even begun. Close to her current hiding place, feet away on the other side of the glass, one poor girl was in the hands of two men, forced to perform fellatio on one whilst simultaneously enduring violent vaginal penetration from the other. They turned the music up loud to drown the vocal cries of pain and screams of terror. Kennedy couldn't look any more. She swung back against the wall, focusing on the lights shimmering across the uncovered surface of the dark pool. She tried to channel the revulsion and horror into indignation and fury, and glanced again at her watch. With only nine minutes until Gage came through the basement door, Kennedy took a chance and sprinted along the entire beach-side of the house, past a whole bank of uncovered windows. Unnoticed and unchallenged, she popped breathless onto the front veranda, thinking she'd use the hilt of Gage's knife to smash one of the large windows next to the front door and wriggle through. On the off chance, she gripped and turned the knob, expecting the front door to be locked. To her amazement it opened soundlessly, and the stiff breeze immediately caught the large door and swung it inward. She grabbed at the handle with both hands and skidded across the silvered wood of the porch in her oversized boots like a novice waterskier. Steadying the door before it struck the internal wall and attracted attention, she inched around it into the main hallway and closed it quickly behind her, comforted by the knowledge she could rush straight up here and open it again once their choreographed chaos took hold. Way down at the other end of the huge space, a grand staircase curved upward. Beneath it, an archway opened into a large kitchen. Next to that were two doors. The one closest to the kitchen was her target. She wondered whether Gage was already on the other side of it, gun at the ready, counting the minutes.

The living room lights swirled from the doorway and span like kaleidoscopes on the hall's high ceiling. The thought of Gage just metres away emboldened her, and she slipped along the dark wall, edging ever closer to the basement door.

****

A red-faced, sweating man, his erect penis protruding from underneath a considerable expanse of overhanging belly, hauling a petite black girl after him by the wrists, trundled up to Tyler Dann with all the indignation of a restaurant customer making a complaint about a meal to a disinterested waiter.

"Hey! You one of them?"

Tyler's eyes narrowed, "Why?"

"Because this isn't what I paid for. This bitch won't stop wailing…and, well, she scratched me – look!"

The guy turned and held up his fleshy elbow, displaying a line of bloody fingernail gouges across his armpit. Tyler, who was uncomfortably hot in his suit in the locked-down house and couldn't have given less of a shit about either the product or the customer, smirked rudely, gripped the girl by the hair, yanked her roughly towards him, and drawled over his shoulder, "Relaax, man! Go have a beer. I'll find you another one."

The man pouted like a teenager, and whined, "Hurry up, I took a Viagra!"

Tyler got away from him fast, before he laughed right into his sweaty, fat face. He decided to toss the useless, near-hysterical broad in the basement, and was dragging her out of the living room, extracting the bunch of keys from his pocket, when a movement caught his eye, a shadow slipping along the hallway wall, a place no girl was supposed to be. Tyler stopped dead for a moment and simply stared…before swearing aloud, shoving his distressed captive aside, and sprinting up the grand staircase as fast as his skinny legs could carry him. At the top, Floyd sat in a chair at the head of the landing, yawning and picking his teeth. Logan instituted a two-tier policy at these parties. For the lower-paying attendees, a chance in the downstairs bear pit with everybody else. For those prepared to put their hands sufficiently deep into their capacious pockets to guarantee exclusivity, a private room and, crucially, no witnesses. Tyler and Floyd tossed a coin for who got which job on each occasion. Tonight, Floyd had won.

He looked up hopefully as Tyler appeared, "Something kicking off downstairs?"

"Bored?" spat Tyler, sarcastically.

Floyd smirked, "What's going on?"

"Remember the old boat house, that reporter-bitch who just wouldn't die?"

Floyd nodded warily, knowing Logan still blamed him for that whole humiliating mess, "What about her?"

"She's downstairs."

GAGE MAKES HIS ENTRANCE

"*What?*" Floyd nearly fell off his designer armchair.

"Where's Logan?"

Floyd pointed behind him, "Far end. Right hand side. He won't want to be disturbed, man!"

"Tough shit. Get down there and keep an eye on her. *Do nothing*. I'll be back in a minute."

Tyler ran down the landing, didn't bother knocking, and opened the door Floyd had indicated. The room was empty, the smart bedcovers undisturbed. Tyler blinked in puzzlement, then saw a strip of light shining underneath the closed bathroom door. He strode purposefully across the tiled floor, bursting into the en-suite. Fully dressed, tie still knotted, Logan was standing, easing aside a condom and tossing it into the trash basket beside the toilet. Fastening his fly, he checked the perfection of his slick hair in the bathroom mirror and completely ignored the whimpering, terrified girl bent across the bathroom counter before him, naked but for a short, grubby satin kimono, pushed up to reveal her bare buttocks, which bore some prominent, already-darkening bruises closely resembling the indentation marks of gripping fingers. Only once completely satisfied with his appearance did Logan turn from the mirror to his panting, fidgeting visitor, and state with icy calm, "You *know* I don't like to be disturbed, Tyler. Where is Floyd?"

"Taking over from me. There's something downstairs right now you're gonna want to see."

****

In the basement, Gage explained fast. There were enough girls who spoke and understood English to relay Kennedy's plan to those who didn't. He was amazed both by their resilience and their willingness to trust him. They immediately got to work, moving the mattresses into a pile beneath the smashed window, creating a makeshift ladder up which they could scramble as soon as Gage fired his first shot. Gage checked his watch. Two minutes. He gave an encouraging smile and double thumbs-up to the cluster of girls, some of whom responded hearteningly by mimicking the gesture. The others just stared, still in the same unresponsive fog of uncomprehending bewilderment as when he'd dropped from the sky into their dungeon mere moments before. At least enough of the group were reenergised by his unexpected arrival to assist those whose fight had already left them. They promised to remain in the woods, collect all the fleeing girls together if they could for safety-in-numbers, and stay hidden until the cops arrived. Gage didn't see any point articulating his private fear that if the cops never showed, he had no idea what any of them would do.

He tiptoed up the basement's concrete staircase, braced himself against the wall, aimed down towards the lock at close range, and stared fixedly at his watch, counting the revolutions of the luminous hands, waiting for the exact moment.

****

Alone in a bare police interview room before a table spread with the comprehensive contents of the evidence folder, Glen looked at his own watch, sighed, sank his elbows onto the piles of paper and his head into his hands. He'd failed. Two minutes from now, Gage Rutter would blast his way out of the basement into a huge house packed with people knowingly breaking the law, some of whom meant him deadly harm. Kennedy's plan hinged upon most of the participants instantly grabbing their pants and making for the nearest door at a gallop, desperate to avoid any stain of scandal. The ensuing confusion was intended to provide Kennedy with a chance to lead as many imprisoned women as possible to freedom, thus leaving behind only the individuals with a vested interest in being there, and gung-ho Gage, with his shotgun and a limited supply of ammunition to keep them pinned down in the house until the cops arrived.

It sounded plausibly simple, but it wasn't, because they all knew Robert Logan's associates carried guns, Gage was but one man, and Kennedy was a small, slight woman still recovering from serious injury. Glen understood it was up to him to get there as fast as possible – while confusion still reigned – and instead he was sitting here, getting nowhere. Glen had sensed the cops believed him and were prepared to hear him out. He even knew a few of them from reporting on crimes and traffic incidents all over the Keys, which had certainly helped get him through the door in the first place. It had been progressing encouragingly until he'd said the G-word. That was when he'd started to lose them. There was absolutely no doubt they believed in justice and respected the law they were employed to uphold…but it was crystal clear they valued their jobs more. Diligently listening to the report of a crime-in-progress was one thing. Digging through the dirt of the guy with whom the buck stopped was quite another. That caused them to cough, stutter, prevaricate, need to refer the decision higher, get authorisation, apply for warrants and other such delaying tactics Glen didn't have time for – not if he didn't want the imminent deaths of Gage Rutter and Kennedy McKendrick on his conscience for the rest of his life. Glen glanced behind him, through the open door and out into the corridor beyond. It was happening now – *right now* – and every cop in this place was too gutless to make a decision that could prevent needless loss of innocent life, in case they got their knuckles rapped by the boss of the boss of the boss.

A profound sense of foreboding sparking urgency within him, Glen stood abruptly, the metal chair scraping harshly on the tiled floor. He didn't know what he was going to say or do that would make a bit of difference, but he couldn't just sit here…

A sudden commotion in the corridor captured his attention – thudding doors, urgent voices, rapid footsteps, barked instructions – perhaps something was happening after all? Glen ran to the door, smack into Mal, who was pelting in no less hurriedly than Glen was rushing out.

Mal yelled, "Glen!" and hauled the younger man into a clammy embrace against his damp shirt.

"Mal! Are you okay?"

"Yes, yes, I'm okay."

"What happened to you at the airport?"

Mal coloured, uncharacteristically embarrassed, and muttered, "The Governor didn't…um…appreciate my…er…direct approach. He thought it was a smear campaign! His people…erm…grilled me pretty thoroughly, if I'm honest."

Mal certainly looked sufficiently crumpled, sweat-stained and drained to corroborate his stuttering explanation. Glen opened his mouth to probe further, but Mal beat him to it, "Anyway, what are you doing *here*? You're supposed to be at the house! Have you been arrested?"

"No… Have you?"

"No!"

The indignation with which Mal greeted the question was such a relief to Glen that his legs buckled slightly, and he grabbed at his editor's arm, "Oh, Mal, I really need your help!"

"Are you in trouble? What have you done?"

"I can't get anyone to listen to me properly! They've taken all the evidence, they've looked at it, but – "

"What's going on, Glen?"

"Kennedy and Gage aren't in the woods watching the house. They've gone to bust up that party!"

"*What?*"

"We thought the bad guys had you! We didn't know what else to do except take the fight to them!"

"So, let me get this straight, Gage and Kennedy have gone up there *not* to watch and wait and call the cops at the right moment, but to *go inside*?"

"Yeah…"

"Glen, *Kennedy* is going inside?"

"Yeah."

"Oh my God…"

"It's her plan!"

"Oh, Jesus…"

"Gage is shooting his way out of the basement in a bid to create mass panic," Glen glanced down at his watch, "*Right now*…and no one here will touch this with a ten-foot pole because I mentioned the Governor – "

"Ah." A regiment of ringing footfalls behind them made Glen whirl around. Mal stepped swiftly in front of him, "Sir, I think we might need your help rather sooner than I suspected."

He gestured behind him to the flabbergasted Glen, "This is my lead reporter, Glen Brown. Glen, you'll recognise our State Governor." Mal's gaze was steady, communicating nothing, so Glen dusted down his manners, closed his gaping mouth, and extended a hand with alacrity. Whether or not the guy was culpable, at least he could tell his mother he'd shaken hands with the State Governor of Florida, *before* he fell from grace, "Yes. Yessir. Good evening, Mr Governor, sir."

"Mr Brown."

The Governor was a small, white-haired, elderly man who looked considerably discomfited, but nevertheless exuded a powerful aura that Glen found surprisingly reassuring under the circumstances. At last, here was someone who could make some decisions and move some mountains! He was flanked by four severe-looking men in crisp suits. A gaggle of ashen-faced local cops also straggled into the now-overcrowded room like chastened schoolboys attending detention. Behind them, stuck in the corridor, Glen could see further individuals in smart suits, some on cellphones, some in animated discussion with other cops.

Mal, who seemed to Glen supremely confident, even rude, in his brusque treatment of the silent Governor, pulled out a chair and said, "Please sit down, sir." The Governor complied, Glen thought rather meekly.

Mal gestured to the suits, who all looked to Glen like carbon copies of the inscrutable Robert Logan. They made him nervous.

"Glen, these gentleman are from the FBI."

Glen looked around sharply. Again, Mal's expression betrayed nothing until he registered the alarm on his lead reporter's face, and explained soothingly, "It's okay to talk. These are the good guys. They'll need fully briefing."

One of the FBI agents sat at the table opposite the Governor, took a notebook and pen from his inside jacket pocket, and drawled laconically, "Urgently, by the sound of it."

Mal sat quickly, all sharp and sparky like he got in editorial meetings when they had a newspaper to print and absolutely nothing remotely interesting to put in it. He pointed bossily to the only vacant chair, right beside the Governor. Glen sank down into it, head whirling, trying to get his thoughts in order so he didn't sound like a lunatic when he eventually opened his mouth. He instinctively looked to Mal for direction. Mal thumped his elbows onto the desk, steepled his fingers under his chin, and barked like he was the lynchpin hero in an apocalyptic disaster-movie, "Give it to us straight, Glen. What the hell is she up to?"

****

Kennedy had caught sight of Rocky sprinting up the stairs as she'd tiptoed cautiously along the dark hallway. She'd rapidly taken cover.

Now, concealed in the shadow behind a providentially large sculpture halfway to the basement door, she awaited developments with an anxious eye on her watch.

When Bullwinkle bundled down the stairs seconds later, stood feet away from her hiding place and began scanning the faces in the crowd with concerted effort, she understood her cover was already blown.

****

At the foot of the grand staircase, Logan tugged at Floyd's jacket sleeve, "Well?"

Floyd shrugged, "I dunno, Mr Logan. I can't see her anywhere."

Logan sighed heavily and turned to Tyler, "Flush her out. *Now.*"

Grim-faced, Tyler nodded, "Yessir."

Floyd's massive frame lumbered off towards the kitchen as instructed. Tyler peeled off confidently, back towards the hot, noisy, crowded living room, hand already sliding beneath his jacket, reaching for his gun.

Logan remained motionless at the foot of the stairs, nothing moving but his eyeballs. He'd spot that troublesome bitch. Whatever it took, she wouldn't slip through his fingers again…and this time, he'd deal with her personally.

****

Oh Lord, thirty seconds! The swirling disco lights suddenly switched to strobe setting. Kennedy's eyes swam with the sensory dislocation. Her recuperating brain struggled to make sense of the stop-time images pulsating on her retina. Encouragingly, if she couldn't see properly, then hopefully neither could anyone else. There was no time for further delay. It had to be now.

She edged out from behind the sculpture and flitted across the hall, running in a swerving zigzag, too muddled by the intermittent flashes to navigate a straight line.

Glancing to her left, she saw Logan stiffen like a hunter scenting prey, leaping up several stairs and hanging over the ornate bannister in an attempt to keep her in sight.

Behind her, Rocky spotted her running figure, executed a smart about-turn and charged back out of the living room in pursuit. Bumping the wall and tottering sideways, Kennedy wobbled as close to the basement door as she dared, hoping he was still following, desperately making for the dubious safety of the kitchen, knowing she had only seconds to get out of the way. Suddenly, Bullwinkle's massive frame filled the doorway, an immense, immovable wall of aggression. Adrenaline surging, Kennedy feinted left, darted right, and ducked under his grabbing arms, flinging herself headlong into the kitchen as the boom and splintering crack of the discharging shotgun blasted into the hallway behind her.

A DIRTY PARTY

Bullwinkle squealed like a snared rabbit. Kennedy skidded across the floor on her satin-clad belly, thudding hard into a kitchen cabinet and yelping in pain. Groping clumsily to her feet, she slipped and nearly fell again, gripping the counter to steady her shuddering legs. Rapidly collecting her wits, she ran back to the kitchen doorway. Bullwinkle writhed on the floor in agony, a pool of blood spreading from where half his foot had been a moment before. Lumps that might once have been toes sat like little islands amongst a widening sea lit first red, then green, then black in the spinning party lights. Good old Gage. One down, with one shot. His unexpected appearance – shirtless, making her wonder distractedly where it had gone – brought Rocky up short, only for a fraction of a second, but it was enough for Gage to recognise his face and fire the second barrel straight at him.

Rocky's reactions were lightning-fast. He somehow anticipated it and dropped instinctively to the floor, the shot blasting a hole in the wall a couple of feet above him as he rolled away, crawling for cover as Gage broke the gun, ejected the spent cartridges, reloaded and pursued him.

In the living room, Gage fired again. She heard shattering glass, and then the screaming started. *Boom!* – the other barrel. Kennedy's anxious eyes flitted towards the staircase. Logan had vanished.

Boom! Another splintering crack of wood and glass. Gage was certainly doing his best to create as many escape routes as possible. She needed to do her bit. Scampering back across the kitchen, she hefted up the stainless-steel trashcan and launched it with all her might at the picture window opening onto the garden. The safety-glass instantly shattered into a million pieces but remained solidly within the frame. Kennedy swore, weak arms fumbling with the slippery can to try again when, to her amazement, she found it wordlessly wrested from her grasp by a whey-faced, half-dressed man who thundered towards the fragmented glass using it as a battering ram. The damaged pane ballooned outwards, then surrendered to the relentless pressure, giving way and curling downward in one intact sheet like marbled paper, creating a perfect hole some eight feet square through which a stampede of fleeing humanity instantly poured. Kennedy was shoved unceremoniously aside, her shoulder blades thudding painfully against the refrigerator door, trapped in the corner of the room as silhouettes both male and female dived out into the sultry night.

****

Shotgun at his shoulder, Gage whirled frantically in the emptying room. Where was that little bastard? Had he run with the rest, or was he still hiding in here somewhere? In the darkness, with only the sanity-shredding throb of the music and strobe of the lights, the guy could be standing directly opposite and Gage doubted he'd spot him. He was too vulnerable staying in one place. Besides, he needed to find Kennedy.

****

She needed to find Gage. She could roughly determine his location all the while he was firing, but he'd gone worryingly quiet in the last few moments. Fighting against the perceptibly thinning tide of escaping bodies, Kennedy shoved and elbowed her way back into the hall. Bullwinkle was…flat…

His once-solid body looked crushed and broken, his previously pristine white shirt coated with a million footprints made in his own blood. The tracks not only traversed his trampled bulk, but criss-crossed the hallway and trailed all the way up to the wide-open front door. The strong sea breeze funnelled down the corridor and ruffled her hair. She stood in Sally's tacky white boots in Bullwinkle's sticky blood, at a total loss where to look first, when strong hands grasped her roughly, one slapping across her mouth, the other closing powerfully around her throat. A voice she recognised but couldn't immediately place, growled, "At fucking last. Let's go, Kennedy McKendrick."

****

Inside the Governor's limousine, speeding along in the hastily assembled convoy of police, State Troopers, FBI and available ambulances, Glen tried hard not to surrender to the inappropriate excitement that bubbled around the edges of his brittle terror like caramel crystallising in a hot pan. If he allowed himself, he thought he might just burst with the exhilaration of this. Here he was, in the official car of the State Governor of Florida, flanked by FBI, cops and troopers, racing to a definite emergency…and all because of *him*, little ol' Glen Brown from Marathon! He permitted himself a nervous glance at his watch, even though he knew all it would do was make him feel sicker with dreadful anticipation than he already did. So far, they were seven minutes late, and still several miles away. Glen suspected seven minutes was an awfully long time when you were slugging for your life. On one side of him, Mal sat bolt upright, nose almost pressing the tinted window-glass, as if remaining on physical high alert could get them there faster. By contrast, the Governor slumped in the facing seat, a diminished, shrunken figure, especially when contrasted with the two massive, sober-suited security men on either side of him.

Out of nowhere, the Governor spoke – not directly at anyone, but out into the tense, tightly-packed vehicle, as if he simply needed to unload the one thought constantly circling his troubled brain, to be purged of the gnawing guilt, "How could I not *see*? I mean, truly, *how* did I not *SEE*?"

****

As far as Gage could tell, Rocky was no longer in the empty living room. Using the shotgun as a bayonet, he'd jabbed the swagged drapes framing the windows and checked behind every chair and couch. Back out in the now-deserted hallway, Gage scooted across to the motionless mess of Bullwinkle. The guy didn't look as if he'd ever make trouble again, but Gage dealt him a hefty boot to the guts to make sure. Bullwinkle's unnaturally positioned mass didn't even move. Gage winced, and turned smartly away from the corpse. He wasn't about to mourn the untimely passing of any of those assholes, but a dead body was still not something his gentle character could ever become accustomed to.

The grand staircase curled away to his right. Should he check up there? He'd expected more heavies with guns. So far, this was all suspiciously easy…but he'd only taken out one bad guy, and had completely managed to lose the only thing in this whole mess that mattered to him. As the disorientating lights strobed again, Gage thought he heard a sound away to his left, a distant, high-pitched cry breaking through above the pounding bass and discordant treble. For a moment, he was somewhere else, running back towards his farmhouse with the fire raging all around, hearing his helpless, already-doomed wife fruitlessly screaming his name.

Swinging left, heart thudding, Gage caught movement in his threat-heightened peripheral vision. Someone was dragging the unmistakeable silhouette of a struggling, kicking Kennedy up the hall and out of the wide-open front door.

He didn't hesitate, but pelted up the corridor after them from pulsing light into dangerous darkness, damaged voice straining to roar his fury.

****

Even outside, his ears still rang with the thump of the bass. The earlier oppressive cloud had lifted, the breeze stiffened, and wisps scudded across a moon now high and bright enough to illuminate the scene before him. To his left, indistinguishable figures ran into the woods bordering the highway. To the right, wide, grassy steps led down to the beach and the floating pontoon beyond, at which a small launch was moored.

Kennedy and her captor were the only figures on that side of the house. Gage could see her struggles already weakening, little legs flailing ineffectually. The man dragged her down the grass steps and into the fine, sinking sand, shining bright white in the moonlight. The guy was too tall to be Rocky. It must be Robert Logan himself. *Why* he was taking Kennedy, Gage couldn't fathom. It would surely be far easier for him to simply kill her, and make his escape unencumbered by a wriggling hostage. Gage ran forward, confident Logan was yet to notice him, stopping at the grass steps, trying to use the height advantage to get a shot off…but the guy was clever. He held Kennedy up in front of his head and chest. There was no way of shooting him without hitting her.

Hesitating, gun stock rammed against his shoulder, taking aim, popping his head up, re-sighting, trying again, Gage suddenly felt a sensation like a sharp slap to his back, as if someone had snapped a rubber band against his bare skin, taut and stinging. He jerked involuntarily and dropped the gun, right arm floppy, shoulder, back and chest burning. He reeled, limbs like jelly, unable to understand why he couldn't turn his head. There was that little weasel, way back on the drive, down on one knee, pistol extended.

The bastard had *shot* him!

IMPOSSIBLY FAR AWAY

Gage stood with his mouth open, breath impeded by the hot, needling agony in his back, self-preservation gradually permeating the fog of paralysing pain. He had to *move*.

He hobbled hopelessly sideways like he had marbles in his shoes. Rocky shifted position minutely to track his quarry's pathetic attempts at avoidance, and Gage understood he'd comprehensively failed: Joelle, Ryan, and now Kennedy too. Lord only knew what was happening to her behind him…and he was presenting no challenge whatsoever to a man who clearly had exceptional aim and, judging by his solid, expert stance, some serious firearms training. Gage wondered what you were supposed to do, think and say when you realised you were about to die. All that filled his mind was a profound sense of frustration. He'd never find out whether fulfilling happiness might actually be achievable for him without his sassy little wife and sweet baby son. In the last few weeks, he'd finally begun to believe he could relish life again, and somehow that conviction was bound up in the maddening, exciting complexity of the intriguing Kennedy McKendrick, and now he'd never know if there was a future in it. That made him furious with his own shortcomings, and impotently enraged at the nameless evil that had allowed all this to happen in the first place.

As Gage wobbled around ridiculously like a badly operated puppet, bracing for the impact of the second bullet, he suddenly saw dark shapes dash from the undergrowth to the far right of the driveway. He started in alarmed recognition. They were three of the women he'd discovered in the basement! Too far-gone to comprehend what was happening, Gage just gaped as they fell frenziedly on the weasel, catching him completely off-guard. The moonlight captured the glinting trajectory of his pistol as it was kicked from his helpless hand. He tumbled backwards under the onslaught of the three stamping, punching assailants. They stood on him, trapped his hands beneath their feet, and Gage saw something white, big and jagged swung high, perhaps a rock. Their restrained tormentor writhed and kicked wretchedly in the gravelly dust on beholding this weapon. Once the blows rained down onto his unprotected face, the desperate struggling instantly ceased.

Almost too stunned to take in what had just happened, one thought surfaced in Gage's stupefied brain. Kennedy.

Grunting, panting, body hunched, right arm swinging, Gage hauled himself around with considerable effort and stumbled forward, sheer determination driving him on. Logan was already dragging Kennedy's increasingly limp form along the wildly bobbing pontoon. He couldn't let him get her into the boat! Gage lurched onward, trying to run, but there was no ground beneath his faltering feet. Unable to stop himself, he pitched headfirst down the grass steps, so slippery with night-time humidity that he rolled and bounced violently to an abrupt landing flat on his back in the fine sand of the private beach he'd once coveted so enviously. The agony of the flailing fall and thudding halt made him yowl aloud, mouth wide, a tiny mew and rush of air all that escaped from his impaired larynx to betray his helpless position.

He couldn't get up. He couldn't move at all. His shotgun was…back there…somewhere…useless to him now. Eventually, he managed to turn his head to the right, but his eyes couldn't focus. His face was gritty with sand that stuck to the running sweat. He shivered uncontrollably despite the warm night air.

What was that? Sirens, or wishful thinking? Just the continual and worsening ringing in his ears.

"Kennedy…"

He couldn't see her. He couldn't see anything. His vision converged until all that remained in the blackness was a pinprick of light at the distant vanishing point. It might have been the moon…or it might just as easily have been Heaven. It didn't matter. Both were impossibly far away…

****

Thrown bodily into the boat, Kennedy's neck whipped painfully, and her fragile head smacked the damp deck hard, making her still-recovering senses swim. Groggy, she nevertheless strained to sit up, convinced she could hear sirens in the distance. Of course, it could just be the electronic thud and blare of the trance music still booming from the house.

Looking cautiously behind her, she saw her shadowy captor bent double, frantically unwinding the ropes that secured the launch to the pontoon. She seized her chance, pushing unsteadily to hands and knees and crawling clumsily across the deck towards the far side of the boat, intending to slip over unseen and swim the short distance back to shallow water before he realised she'd gone, but it didn't work. She was still more than an arm's length from the side when the boat rocked alarmingly as he leapt in behind her. She heard his heavy tread across the deck – stride, stride and he was on her, gripping her hair and hauling her bodily backwards. She squealed in pain, hands shooting up to clutch at her head, which enabled him to easily grasp one of her arms and drag her agonisingly the length of the deck to a metal ring affixed in the stern, from which a length of frayed and salty rope trailed. He wound the cord so tight around her wrist that it rubbed a red weal across her skin, burning and constricting the more she tried to twist free. She kicked out at him, aiming between his legs, but he sidestepped deftly, bent over her, and gripped her jaw tight in his strong fingers, pressing so hard into her cheeks she feared he might actually puncture the skin. She grunted and lashed out with her free hand, but he caught it easily in his fist, dropping to straddle her powerfully, knees pushing into both her biceps until she thought her arms would snap. She could see who it was now, the man they knew as Robert Logan, the guy Glen was so convinced directed all this wickedness.

He wore the same ravening expression on his suave features as all those other men when they violently dominated a woman, that identical leer of distaste and delight, as if it was possible to both despise and desire simultaneously. Logan eased down further, thrusting his groin towards her face. The pressure on her arms was unbearable. She screeched, trying to roll free, but he was strong and heavy. Completely at his mercy, she looked up fearfully, and started at the horrifying realisation. Until that moment, she hadn't understood she and Robert Logan were already acquainted. The implacable stare of her cruel captor was unmistakeably the same as the evil, dark eyes haunting her frequent nightmares! It was *him*! *He'd* been in her prison! She knew she'd recognised his voice, and now she knew why.

He smirked nastily, and snarled, "Nice try, but you're not going anywhere. I have something particularly special planned for you. Given how very obsessed you are with my business, I'm going to pass you on to somebody who'll personally ensure you experience *all* our network has to offer. VIP treatment, Ms McKendrick! You'll get a chance to do *everything*, don't you worry."

He was reaching for another length of rope, seeking to tie her other wrist to a nearby handrail, when suddenly his head snapped around to look over his shoulder. At first, Kennedy wasn't sure she'd heard correctly, but...yes, there it was! The definite whoop and whine of sirens, the roar of many speeding engines. Glen had done it!

Logan bared his teeth like a cornered animal, hissed, "Shit!" and levered himself off her. The immediate relief in her bruised arms was blissful. The cops were here! Rescue! She must get as far away from the lethal Robert Logan as was humanly possible. She needed to get off this boat and into the water. The end of the pontoon was only a few metres from shore. If she escaped now, she could swim to safety despite her increasing exhaustion.

She struggled to a sitting position, arms weak as wet string, tugging frantically at her one pinioned wrist as if effort alone could snap the rope. It was no good. The more she pulled, the deeper the nylon strands dug in. The knots were so tight it was impossible for the fumbling fingers of her free hand to unpick the loops.

On the pontoon, desperately unwinding the dockline in uncoordinated haste, Bobby Levine saw the first of the emergency vehicles swing through the huge gate and down the drive, followed by another, and another, and another. Illuminated clearly in the approaching headlights, Bobby saw Gage Rutter's unmistakeable form tumble headlong, rolling like a ragdoll down the grass steps onto the sand, and he saw why, a thick trail of blood ran from a wound at the top of his shoulder, down his bare back and around under his armpit.

Shot.

It had to be the handiwork of Tyler Dann. All those years as a military sniper in the Middle East hadn't been a waste of time. He was a dumb shit, but he was a well-drilled dumb shit, with morals loose enough to manipulate at the right price. Bobby was almost sorry to be leaving his useful little henchman behind. After a couple of hefty bounces, Rutter finally stopped rolling, hitting the beach with heavy finality. His long limbs twitched several times, and then he was still.

Bobby Levine chuckled in malevolent satisfaction and hurried to untie the painter. He'd get around this headland to his right and out into the mangroves. The stupid cops'd never find him there. He'd lie low until first light, then make for the Caribbean as fast as his fuel cache could carry him. He'd drop the McKendrick bitch off at one of his contacts, with instructions to transport her directly back to Uncle Harry. Delivery of such an interesting package might go some way towards mollifying the old man…or simply provide him something upon which to exact his terrible vengeance at Bobby's betrayal. Whatever happened to her would be justice enough for Bobby Levine, as long as she suffered. The clouds were returning, providentially covering the bright moon once more. He glanced down. Even in the fading light, the marks on his hands were still humiliatingly noticeable. Bobby wondered whether they'd ever completely fade.

The pervasive thud of the bass stopped. Someone had switched it off. Looking up, rope clutched in his fist, Bobby saw every window in the house was lit, bright squares of yellow like a chequerboard against the navy sky. Squad cars crowded the driveway, headlights splaying their blinding beams down the sand and across the first few feet of pontoon, flashlights raking the surface of the water in front of the house and lighting the extensive lawns and tall trees behind. It was only a matter of time before they obtained a searchlight powerful enough to pick out his little launch, at present only a dark shape on a shifting sea, too far out to distinguish with any clarity now the moon had gone in. He had to push the boat away from the pontoon without starting the engine, turn it 180 degrees, and only then fire it up to make his escape. He thought of the stories Tyler had told him, about how good the rifle 'scopes were, about how far away a well-trained marksman could be and still make the shot count. Tyler could hit a running iguana at impossible distance, seemingly without needing to aim. The last thing Bobby wanted was to draw attention to his undefended back too soon, before he was ready to gun it and go. He knew if he did this right, the cops jogging down to check the beach would have mere seconds to react once the boat's engine fired into life. Before they got their thumbs out of their butts, he'd be around the palm-covered promontory and safely beyond rifle range.

Leaping swiftly back into the boat, Bobby squatted down behind the dashboard and reached to pick up the long-handled fishing hook he kept on board, crouching between driver's seat and wheel and extending the pole to push the metal hook into the side of the pontoon, shoving hard, trying to get the launch moving. Frustratingly, the tide was coming in and the current flowing right to left across the beach, floating the boat back against the pontoon as relentlessly as Bobby tried to push it away. His chest and back ached with the effort of shoving against the force of the incoming water and the strengthening onshore breeze. Lightning flashed behind him, way out to sea, and Bobby feared he'd be silhouetted starkly against the threatening sky. Feeling the first stirrings of panic agitating his guts, he jabbed jerkily, having to risk standing upright as he deliberately made the boat rock, trying to lift the bow over a wave or two and use the direction of the current to swing the vessel. The rocking motion created some space between launch and pontoon, into which Bobby thrust the fishing pole and levered like a Gondolier. He strode swiftly to the rear of the boat, leaning out, pushing hard. Round swung the stern, further and further, the tide now assisting the vessel's rotation. Eyes flitting between the increasing onshore activity and the free-floating bow of the boat, lest it surge forward on a larger wave and strike the pontoon, Bobby looked around sharply at the girl, convinced he'd just seen her move, but she remained where he'd left her, tied tight, legs drawn up defensively in front of her body, free arm clutched protectively across her chest, eyes wide and fixed unblinkingly upon him.

SNIPER

Now in open water, too far from the pontoon to push but not rotated sufficiently seaward to risk firing the engine, the launch bobbed erratically, side-on to the beach, the current carrying it back into shore faster than it was swinging the stern. Bobby snatched up a plastic paddle and tried unsuccessfully to steer. Looking over his shoulder, he saw the cops seemed so obsessed with the house and grounds that no one had yet noticed him out here. He just had to be patient. The back was coming around. Another six feet and he was home free. He tossed the paddle aside and stood before the wheel, flicking the kill switch on, pumping the shift lever back and forth a couple of times to prime the engine, all the while watching the bow straighten minutely.

Come on, baby. Come on.

A low shot whined across the side of the boat, feet behind Bobby, the bullet embedding itself in the starboard side.

"Fuck!"

He dived beneath the dash panel, trying to crane out and see where the danger was coming from. High on the rocks now dead-ahead of the bow, Bobby could see intermittent faint light amongst the grove of swaying palms. Shit! He *had* been seen, and the Feds, or whoever was directing operations back there, had sent a shooter up onto the high ground either to hole his boat or put a hole in him.

Neither outcome seemed particularly palatable to Bobby Levine. Dammit! The precious seconds wasted on securing that McKendrick bitch were coming back to haunt him now. Perhaps he should have foregone the sweet taste of revenge for the expediency of a swift getaway, but the idea of leaving her behind without exacting any form of punishment for all she'd cost him seemed grossly unfair. She'd been worth the risk. He'd sleep well every night from now on imagining the hell she'd experience at the hands of Harry Grafton, and every guy who got his grimy paws on her thereafter, if there was anything left of her by the time Uncle Harry had finished. He only had a couple more feet to go and he could fire up the engine. Then the Feds, SWAT or whoever was up in that wood with their torches and their night-sights, could kiss his Arizona ass. He'd be gone, and there was nothing anyone could do about it.

He edged a tentative hand up across the plastic of the instrument panel, feeling blindly for the throttle, easing it into the idle position and groping along towards the ignition button, eventually identifying it, depressing it decisively and starting the engine on the first try. The bark and roar were music to his ears. Another shot skimmed down low across the dash in response to the movement of his arm, glancing off and shattering the triangular pane of glass on the starboard side of the windshield.

Bobby instantly snatched back his hand and hunkered down beneath the cockpit again. The engine burbled reassuringly, ready for action. He took a chance, poking his head up, seeing that the bow now pointed directly out to sea, and lunged for the throttle, shoving it forward hard. The deceptively powerful little boat surged aggressively, bow lifting and scything through the waves, craft bouncing off the surface of the wind-whipped water.

Another shot, this time thudding into the back of the driver's seat, causing him to dive for cover again. Another two shots peppered the seat back, the third whining in a couple of feet higher and shattering the windshield. There had to be more than one guy up there. Frantic now, his vision completely obscured, Bobby popped up recklessly, shoving at the ruined glass until it burst free and slid off the foredeck into the black ocean. He could see again, the horizon always lighter than the water, and currently the only way he had of navigating at full throttle in the practically pitch dark, with bullets ringing off the dashboard like a fairground shooting gallery. Flashes of distant lightning periodically confirmed his course. He was going too straight, too fast. He needed to slow and turn, or he would miss his opportunity to get around the promontory and into the mangrove swamps, escaping the shooters in the trees.

Another shot, ricocheting off the instrument panel inches from his body, way too close for comfort. Despite the dark and the moving target, they were really getting their eye in now. Bobby yelped and dived back beneath the cockpit, again using the driver's seat for cover. He needed to turn instantly, or he would miss the mouth of the mangrove channel and have to return, head on to the threat above. There was zero margin for error at this rash speed. He got his hand decisively on the wheel and, steering blind, swung it sharply to the right, sending the lightweight launch into an unbalanced arc. Sniper or no sniper, he needed to check this course correction. He darted his head and shoulders up above the dash panel to look through the space where the windshield had been, the powerful breeze and icy spray making his eyes sting and water. He was way too close to the jutting spit of rock. Another shot thudded home, this time embedding itself in the instrument panel three feet away. As he ducked again, the girl sprang from behind the driver's seat, the securing rope about her wrist severed and swinging. He didn't have time to wonder how she'd got herself loose as she lunged for the throttle, seeking to pull it back and stop the boat. He leapt and caught at her arm, twisting it hard around her back until she howled in agony and crumpled to her knees. They were still heading straight for the rock promontory at full throttle. Was this stupid bitch trying to make sure they hit it?

Bobby shouted his frustration aloud, shoving her roughly aside and diving for the wheel with both hands, grabbing and turning it onto opposite lock, the boat digging in and corkscrewing out of the turn, the trajectory now way too tight to make the opening of the narrow channel. He'd have to go around again, and he needed to make it fast. He could see the wavering lights of the torches as the marksmen sprinted to the end of the jutting spit of land to assume a better firing position. As he gripped the smooth plastic of the wheel, yanking the boat around, eyes bulging, breath whistling through gritted teeth, such agony cleaved between his neck and shoulder that he slumped forward helplessly over the instrument panel, head lolling, right arm hanging, left arm simultaneously losing its grip and sliding through the wheel, wedging against the dash and snapping his wrist. He tried to cry out at the intense pain, but something thick and hot was running into his open mouth, making him splutter and choke. His filling throat gurgled and bubbled as his body shook spasmodically.

Horrified, Kennedy staggered backwards, tripped over the discarded paddle and fell straight down onto her already-bruised coccyx, gasping and shuddering with extreme distress. Deciding not to look at the gushing, burbling, convulsing Robert Logan again, she turned tail and crawled to the stern of the speeding launch, pulling herself upright and staring fixedly down into the roiling wake, teeth chattering with terror. She couldn't jump here. The propeller would cut her to pieces. She tottered away, forcing herself to place a foot confidently on the side of the boat, drive down through her knee, and power her body up and out into the churning water like a long jumper stretching for a world record.

Completely submerged, surrounded by the deafening noise and rush, all was freezing, petrifying, bewildering blackness. She thrashed in the dark, unable to understand which way was up, chest tightening, dangerous panic gnawing at the edges of her consciousness, before buoyancy and instinct returned her powerfully and amazingly to the surface. Gulping huge mouthfuls of air, coughing and retching up swallowed seawater, she circled and kicked, trying to get her bearings, deliberately not thinking what might be swirling about her legs in the deep, cold ocean.

She could feel the push of a current at her back, the rolling waves propelling her steadily towards the distant lights she could see flashing across the surface of the water. She curled her knees up, reaching down and unzipping Sally's heavy boots, letting them tumble into the depths for the barracudas to fight over, then filled her lungs with life-giving breath, and kicked for shore with all the strength remaining in her resolute little body.

Behind her, Bobby Levine remained slumped across the dashboard of his damaged launch, his trapped left arm wedged firmly between the spokes of the wheel, ensuring the maintenance of his present bearing straight out into the vastness of the Atlantic Ocean at full throttle.

Blood soaked his right shirt-sleeve, dripped from his cuff onto the back of his hand, and ran from the ends of his drooping fingers into a slick lake on the floor at his motionless feet, the surface of which vibrated with every thump of the bow across the choppy waves, glutinous droplets splashing up the precisely-turned hems of his tailored trousers, soiling the expensive fabric. From the right-hand side of his neck protruded the weapon that had severed his carotid artery: Gage Rutter's hunting knife, gifted with love to Kennedy McKendrick on the off-chance it might save her life.

MANY THE MILES

Curled in a functional hospital armchair, a small woman sleeps soundly. She is wrapped in an Emergency Services blanket. The sandy soles of her bare feet poke out from beneath it. Her black hair is knotted, straggly and salt encrusted. There is a slim, gold band on the index finger of the hand clutching the blanket tight around her. The unconscious man in the bed two feet away is propped on his left side by a bank of pillows wedged from neck to knee.

Outside the half-open door sits a snoozing cop on a plastic chair. His radio emits a burst of chattering static that has him spluttering in surprise and fumbling for the volume control.

The man in the bed starts, grunts, and his eyes snap open, squinting and winking at the early morning sunlight streaming through the large window he faces. Disorientated, convinced he's falling, he instinctively reacts to his unnatural position by attempting to roll back the other way. The movement forces a violent croak of exhaled agony from his straining throat, and he grabs for the rail surrounding the bed, his wedding band striking the metal and causing it to ring.

At the sound, the woman lurches upright, gasping, the clasped blanket falling away to reveal a grubby, wrinkled nightdress. Residual trails of sand and salt have dried between her breasts, in the fine down on her forearms and across her shoulders, where the satin straps are rubbing against the tiny grains to create new soreness on a body already a patchwork of healing scars, and bruises both fresh and fading. She dives forward and grasps the fist that grips the rail in both her own, "I'm here! I'm here!"

Weak with relief, the man subsides gingerly onto the pillows, wincing. He entwines his fingers with hers and lifts her hand to brush his lips across her knuckles, murmuring, "Are you okay?"

She nods, suddenly tongue-tied with embarrassment, eventually stuttering, "I…I…lost your knife…"

He smiles, and drowsily shakes his head, "When that asshole shot me, I thought it was over. I don't care about the stupid knife. I'd rather lose everything I own than lose you."

She blushes, and radiates fidgety, self-conscious delight.

He hooks a stiff ringlet of her sticky hair, rubbing it between his fingers. Tumbling crystals of salt catch the dawn sunlight as they float onto the coverlet like microscopic raindrops, "Shouldn't you go get cleaned up?"

She eases over the bed to whisper in his ear. One small palm strokes up his bare chest, her little fingers sliding lightly across the padding of his heavily dressed right shoulder. He slips his left hand around her hip to squeeze her buttock, a lopsided, sedated grin on his face, hooded eyes gazing up at her in dreamy adoration. She beams enchantingly, mimics his Western accent, and drawls the way he once did to her, "Sugar, we both know I ain't goin' nowhere."

www.ingramcontent.com/pod-product-compliance
Lightning Source LLC
Chambersburg PA
CBHW030156200626
46812CB00017B/2118